D1304383

SANTIAGO RONCAGLIOLO

RED APRIL

Santiago Roncagliolo was born in Lima, Peru, in 1975. He is the author of two other novels; *Red April,* which has appeared in thirteen languages, marks his debut in English. He currently lives in Barcelona.

Edith Grossman is the award-winning translator of such masterworks as Cervantes's *Don Quixote* and Gabriel García Márquez's *Love in the Time of Cholera.*

VINTAGE

INTERNATIONAL

RED APRIL

To: my Marxian conservative friend, Anderson Storms, whose dark sense of humor, countless drunk stories, and matchless messiness I have come to appreciate during the past two months.

Merry Christmas.

from: Your Peruvian friend,

Rony Gonzales

Dec 2011

RED APPRIL

SANTIAGO RONCAGLIOLO

Translated from Spanish by
Edith Grossman

VINTAGE INTERNATIONAL
Vintage Books
A Division of Random House, Inc.
New York

FIRST VINTAGE INTERNATIONAL EDITION, AUGUST 2010

Translation copyright © 2009 by Edith Grossman

The Library of Congress has cataloged the Pantheon edition as follows:
Roncagliolo, Santiago.
[Abril rojo. English]
Red April / Santiago Roncagliolo ; translated from Spanish by Edith Grossman.
p. cm.
I. Grossman, Edith, 1936– II Title.
PQ8498.28.O4187A6313 2009
863'.7—dc22
2008036654

Vintage ISBN: 978-0-307-38838-4

Book design by M. Kristen Bearse

www.vintagebooks.com

Printed in the United States of America
10 9 8 7 6 5 4 3 2 1

To Rosa,
because I'm from
wherever you are

Contents

Thursday, March 9   1

Sunday, March 12 / Tuesday, March 21   23

Thursday, April 6 / Sunday, April 9   61

Monday, April 10 / Friday, April 14   103

Saturday, April 15 / Wednesday, April 19   151

Thursday, April 20   185

Friday, April 21   207

Saturday, April 22 / Sunday, April 23   243

Wednesday, May 3   267

Author's Note   273

Observe the orgy of corruption that is flooding the country;
the hunger that annihilates some, the excess that fills
others to bursting;
talk to the people on foot, observe those on horseback
. . . In this way the violence will be explained . . .
And if you don't want present-day explanations,
read the Gospel of Saint Matthew (21:12, 13) again
and you will find the millenarian explanation
of a rage that many in the world deem holy.

> —EFRAÍN MOROTE, Rector of the
> National University San Cristóbal de Huamanga

We are people with an abundance of faith . . .
In the Fourth Plenary Session we promised to confront the
bloodbath . . .
The children of the people have not died, they live in us and
vibrate in us.

> —ABIMAEL GUZMÁN, Leader of Sendero Luminoso

War is holy, its institution is divine
And one of the sacred laws of the world.
It maintains in men all the great emotions
Such as honor, magnanimity, virtue, and valor,
And in a word it keeps them from falling
Into the most repugnant materialism.

> —HELMUT VON MOLTKE, quoted in the Senderista
> pamphlet "On War: Proverbs and Citations"

THURSDAY, MARCH 9

———————————

On Wednesday, the eighth day of March, 2000, as he passed through the area surrounding his domicile in the locality of Quinua, Justino Mayta Carazo (31) discovered a body.

According to his testimony to the duly constituted authorities, the deponent had spent three days at the celebration of Carnival in the aforementioned district, where he had participated in the dancing of his village. As a result of this contingency, he affirms he does not remember where he was on the previous night or on the two preceding nights, at which time he reports having consumed large quantities of alcoholic beverages. This account could not be confirmed by any of the 1,576 residents of the municipality, who attest to having also been in the aforementioned alcoholic state for the past seventy-two hours on account of the aforementioned celebration.

During the early-morning hours of the eighth day of March, the abovementioned Justino Mayta Carazo (31) states that he was on the main square of the municipality with Manuelcha Pachas Ispijuy (28) and Deolindo Páucar Quispe (32), who have been unable to corroborate this. Then, according to the testimony of the deponent, he remembered his employment obligations at the Mi Perú grocery store, where he fulfills the duties of a sales clerk. He stood and began walking to the above referenced establishment, but when he was halfway there he experienced the inconvenience of being victimized by a sudden attack of exhaustion and decided to return to his domicile to enjoy a well-deserved rest.

Before he reached his door, the attack intensified, and the

abovementioned subject entered the domicile of his neighbor
Nemesio Limanta Huamán (41) to rest before resuming his tra-
versal of the remaining fifteen meters to the door of his own domicile. According to his testimony, upon entering the.property, he
noticed nothing suspicious and encountered no person, and he
went across the courtyard directly to the hayloft, where he lay
down. He states that he spent the next six hours there alone.
Nemesio Limanta Huamán (41) has refuted his version, affirming
that at twelve o'clock he surprised the young woman Teófila Cen-
teno de Páucar (23) leaving the hayloft, the aforesaid young
woman being the wife of Deolindo Páucar Quispe (32) and en-
dowed, according to witnesses, with sizable haunches and a lively
carnal appetite, which has to all intents and purposes been denied
not only by her spouse but by the above referenced deponent
Justino Mayta Carazo (31).

One hour later, at 1300 hours, as he stretched his arms upon
awakening, the deponent states that he touched a hard, rigid object partially obscured in the hay. In the belief that it might be a
strongbox belonging to the owner of the property, the deponent
decided to proceed to its exhumation. The Office of the Associate
District Prosecutor lost no time in reprimanding the deponent on
account of his manifestly evil intentions, to which Justino Mayta
Carazo (31) responded with demonstrations of genuine repentance, declaring that he would immediately confess to Father
Julián González Casquignán (65), pastor of the aforesaid municipality.

At approximately 1310 hours, the abovementioned deponent
decided that the object was too large to be a box and resembled
instead a burned, black, sticky tree trunk. He proceeded to move
away the last stalks of straw that concealed it, discovering an irregular surface perforated by various holes. He found, according
to his statement, that one of those holes constituted a mouth filled
with black teeth, and that on the length of the body there still re-

mained shreds of the cloth of a shirt, also calcinated and fused with the skin and ashes of a body deformed by fire.

At approximately 1315 hours the screams of terror of Justino Mayta Carazo (31) awoke the other 1,575 residents of the municipality.

In witness whereof, this document is signed, on the ninth day of March, 2000, in the province of Huamanga,

Félix Chacaltana Saldívar
Associate District Prosecutor

Prosecutor Chacaltana wrote the final period with a grimace of doubt on his lips. He read the page again, erased a tilde, and added a comma in black ink. Now it was fine. A good report. He had followed all the prescribed procedures, chosen his verbs with precision, and had not fallen into the unrestrained use of adjectives customary in legal texts. He avoided words with ñ—because his Olivetti 75 had lost its ñ—but he knew enough words so he did not need it. He had a large vocabulary and could replace one term with another. He repeated to himself with satisfaction that in his lawyer's heart, a poet struggled to emerge.

He removed the pages from the typewriter, kept the carbon paper for future documents, and placed each copy of the document in its respective envelope: one for the files, one for the criminal court, one for the case record, and one for the command of the military region. He still had to attach the forensic report. Before going to police headquarters, he wrote once again—as he did every morning—his supply requisition for a new typewriter, two pencils, and a ream of carbon paper. He had already submitted thirty-six requisitions and kept the signed receipts for all of them. He did not want to become aggressive, but if the supplies did not arrive soon, he could initiate an administrative procedure to demand them more forcefully.

After delivering his requisition personally and making sure the receipt was signed, he went out to the Plaza de Armas. The loudspeakers placed at the four corners of the square were broadcasting the life and works of eminent Ayacuchans as part of the campaign of the Ministry of the Presidency to breathe patriotic values into the province: Don Benigno Huaranga Céspedes, a distinguished Ayacuchan physician, had studied at the National University of San Marcos and dedicated his life to the science of medicine, a field in which he reaped diverse tributes and various honors. Don Pascual Espinoza Chamochumbi, an outstanding Huantan attorney, distinguished himself by his vocation for helping the province, to which he bequeathed a bust of the Liberator Bolívar. For Associate District Prosecutor Félix Chacaltana Saldívar, those lives solemnly declaimed on the Plaza de Armas were models to be followed, exemplars of the capacity of his people to move forward despite poverty. He wondered if someday, on the basis of his tireless labor in the cause of justice, his name would deserve to be repeated by those loudspeakers.

He approached the newspaper cart and asked for *El Comercio*. The vendor said that today's edition hadn't arrived in Ayacucho yet, but he did have yesterday's. Chacaltana bought it. Nothing can change much from one day to the next, he thought, all days are basically the same. Then he continued on his way to police headquarters.

As he walked, the corpse in Quinua produced a vague mixture of pride and disquiet in him. It was his first murder in the year he had been back in Ayacucho. It was a sign of progress. Until now, any death had gone directly to Military Justice, for reasons of security. The Office of the Prosecutor received only drunken fights or domestic abuse, at the most some rape, frequently of a wife by her husband.

Prosecutor Chacaltana saw in this a problem in the classification of crimes and, as a matter of fact, had forwarded to the criminal court in Huamanga a brief in that regard, to which he had not yet received a response. According to him, such practices within a legal marriage could not be called rapes. Husbands do not rape their wives: they fulfill conjugal duties. But Prosecutor Félix Chacaltana Saldívar, who understood human weakness, normally drew up a document of reconciliation to bring together the parties, and had the husband pledge to fulfill his virile duty without causing lesions of any kind. The prosecutor thought of his ex-wife Cecilia. She had never complained, at least not about that. The prosecutor had treated her with respect; he had barely touched her. She would have been astonished to see the importance of the case of the corpse. She would have admired him, for once.

In the reception area at police headquarters, a solitary sergeant was reading a sports paper. Associate District Prosecutor Félix Chacaltana Saldívar walked forward with resounding steps and cleared his throat.

"I am looking for Captain Pacheco."

The sergeant raised bored eyes. He was chewing on a matchstick.

"Captain Pacheco?"

"Affirmative. We have a proceeding of the greatest importance."

The prosecutor identified himself. The sergeant seemed uncomfortable. He looked to one side. The prosecutor thought he saw someone, the shadow of someone. Perhaps he was mistaken. The sergeant wrote down the prosecutor's name and left reception, carrying the paper. The prosecutor heard his voice and another in the room to the side, without being able to make out what they were saying. In any event, he tried not to hear. That would have constituted a violation of institutional communications. The sergeant returned eight minutes later.

"Well, the fact is . . . today's Thursday, Señor Prosecutor. On Thursdays the captain only comes in the afternoon . . . if he comes . . . because he has various proceedings to take care of too . . ."

"But procedure demands that we go together to pick up the report on the recent homicide . . . and we agreed that . . ."

". . . and tomorrow's complicated too, Señor Prosecutor, because they've called for a parade on Sunday and we have to prepare all the preparations."

The prosecutor tried to offer a conclusive argument:

". . . The fact is . . . the deceased cannot wait . . ."

"He's not waiting for anything anymore, Señor Prosecutor. But don't worry, I'm going to communicate to the captain that you appeared in person at our office with regard to the corresponding homicide."

Without knowing exactly how, the Associate District Prosecutor was allowing himself to be led to the door by the subordinate's words. He tried to respond, but it was too late to speak. He was on the street. He took a handkerchief from his pocket and wiped away perspiration. He did not know exactly what to do, if he should forget procedure or wait for the captain. But Monday was too long to wait. They were going to demand a punctual report from him. He would go alone. And submit a complaint to the General Administration of Police, with a copy to the Office of the Provincial Prosecutor.

He thought again of the corpse, and that reminded him of his mother. He had not gone to see her. He would have to stop by his house on the way back from the hospital, to see if she was all right. He crossed the city in fifteen minutes, went into the Military Hospital, and looked for the burn unit or the morgue. He felt disoriented among the crippled, the beaten, the suffering. He decided to ask a nurse who, with an attitude of competent authority, had just dispatched two old men.

"Dr. Faustino Posadas, please?"

The nurse looked at him with contempt. Associate District Prosecutor Félix Chacaltana Saldívar wondered if it would be necessary to show his official documents. The nurse entered an office and came out five minutes later.

"The doctor has gone out. Have a seat and wait for him."

"I . . . I just came for a paper. I need a forensic report."

"Generally I don't know anything about that. But have a seat, please."

"I am the Associate Dist . . ."

It was useless. The nurse had gone out to restrain a woman who was screaming in pain. She was not hurt. She was simply screaming in pain. The prosecutor sat down between an ancient woman weeping in Quechua and a policeman with a bleeding cut on his hand. He opened his paper. The headline announced the government's fraudulent scheme for the elections in April. He began to read with annoyance, thinking that these kinds of suspicions ought to be brought to the Ministry of Justice for the appropriate decision before being published in the press and causing unfortunate misunderstandings.

As he scanned the page, it seemed that the recruit at the entrance was observing him. No. Not now. He had looked away. Perhaps he had not even looked at him. He continued reading. Every six minutes, more or less, a nurse would emerge from a door and call one of the people in the waiting room, an armless man or a child with polio who would leave his place with groans of pain and sighs of relief. On the third page, the prosecutor felt that the police officer beside him was trying to read over his shoulder. When he turned, the policeman was absorbed in looking at his wound. Chacaltana closed the paper and put it in his lap, drumming with his fingers on the paper to while away the time.

Dr. Posadas did not come. The prosecutor wanted to say something to the nurse but did not know what to say. He looked up. Across from him a young woman was sobbing. Her face was bruised and red, and one eye was swollen shut. She rested her battered face on her mother's shoulder. She looked unmarried.

Chacaltana wondered what to do about unmarried rape victims in the legal system. At first he had asked that rapists be imprisoned, according to the law. But the injured parties protested: if the attacker went to jail, the victim would not be able to marry him and restore her lost honor. This imposed the need, then, to reform the penal code. Satisfied with his reasoning, the prosecutor decided to send the criminal tribunal in Huamanga another brief in this regard, attaching a communication pressing for a response at the earliest opportunity. A harsh voice with a northern accent pulled him out of his reflections:

"Prosecutor Chacaltana?"

A short man wearing glasses, badly shaven and with greasy hair, stood beside him eating chocolate. His medical jacket was stained with mustard, creole sauce, and something brown, but he kept his shoulders clean and white to conceal the dandruff that fell from his head like snow.

"I'm Faustino Posadas, the forensic pathologist."

He held out a chocolate-smeared hand, which the prosecutor shook. Then he led him down a dark corridor filled with suffering. Some people approached, moaning, pleading for help, but the doctor pointed them to the first waiting room with the nurse, please, I only see dead people.

"I haven't seen you before," said the doctor as they walked into a different pavilion, with another waiting room. "Are you from Lima?"

"I come from Ayacucho but lived in Lima since I was a boy. I was transferred here a year ago."

The pathologist laughed.

"From Lima to Ayacucho? You must have behaved very badly, Señor Chacaltana . . ." Then he cleared his throat. "If . . . you'll permit me to say so."

The Associate District Prosecutor had never misbehaved. He had done nothing bad, he had done nothing good, he had never done anything not stipulated in the statutes of his institution.

"I requested the transfer. My mother is here, and I had not been back in twenty years. But now that there is no terrorism, everything is quiet, isn't it?"

The pathologist stopped in front of a door across from a room filled with women in labor in the obstetrics wing. He transferred the chocolate to his other hand and took a key out of his pocket.

"Quiet, of course."

He opened the door and they went in. Posadas turned on the white neon lights, which blinked for a while before they went on. One of the bulbs continued to flicker intermittently. In the office was a table covered with a sheet. And beneath the sheet was a shape. Chacaltana gave a start. He prayed it was nothing but a table.

"I . . . only came to receive the relevant docu . . ."

"The certificate, yes."

Dr. Posadas closed the door and walked to a desk. He began to rummage through papers.

"I thought it would be here . . . Just a moment, please . . ."

He continued rummaging. Chacaltana could not take his eyes off the sheet. The doctor noticed and asked:

"Have you seen it?"

"No! I . . . took the statement of the officers in charge."

"The police? They didn't even see it."

"What?"

"They told the owner of the place to put the body in a bag before they went in. I don't know what they could have said."

"Ah."

Posadas stopped rummaging through his papers for a moment. He turned to the prosecutor.

"You should see it."

Chacaltana thought the proceedings were taking too long.

"I only need the rep . . ."

But the doctor walked to the table and lifted the veil. The burned body looked at them. It had clenched teeth but little else in that black mass was recognizable as being of human origin. It did not smell like a dead body. It smelled like kerosene lamps. The light flickered.

"They didn't leave us much to work with, huh?" Posadas smiled.

Chacaltana thought again about going to see his mother. He tried to recover his concentration. He wiped away perspiration. It was not the same perspiration as before. It was cold.

"Why is it kept in obstetrics?"

"Lack of space. Besides, it doesn't matter. The morgue doesn't have a refrigerator anymore. It broke down in the blackouts."

"The blackouts ended years ago."

"Not in our morgue."

Posadas went back to the papers on his desk. Chacaltana walked around the table, trying to look elsewhere. The burning was irregular. Although the face still had certain characteristics of a face, the two legs had become a single dark extension. Toward the top of the remaining side were some twisted protuberances, like branches of a fossilized bush. Chacaltana felt a wave of nausea but tried to disguise something so unprofessional. Posadas stared at him with slanted, suspicious little eyes, like the eyes of a rat.

"Are you going to carry out the investigation? What about the military cops?"

"The gentlemen of the armed forces," the prosecutor corrected, "have no reason to intervene. This case does not fall under military jurisdiction."

Posadas seemed surprised to hear it. He said dryly:

"All cases fall under military jurisdiction."

There was something challenging in Posadas's tone. Chacaltana attempted to assert his authority.

"We still need to verify the facts in the case. Technically, this may even turn out to be an accident . . ."

"An accident?"

He gave a dry laugh that made him cough and looked at the corpse as if to share the joke with him. He tossed the chocolate wrapper on the floor and took out a pack of cigarettes. He offered one to the prosecutor, who refused with a gesture. The pathologist lit a cigarette, exhaled the smoke with another cough, and said in a serious tone:

"A male apparently between forty and fifty years old. White— at least, whitish. Two days ago he was taller."

The Associate District Prosecutor felt obliged to display professional distance. He felt cold. Tremulously he said:

"Any . . . clue as to the identity of the deceased?"

"There are no physical marks or personal effects left. If he was carrying his national ID, it must be in there."

Chacaltana observed the body that seemed to dissolve as he looked at it. A black paste saturated his memory.

"Why do you discount an accident?"

Posadas seemed to be waiting for the question with indulgent pride, like a teacher with the dunce of the class. He left his desk, took up a position beside the table, and began to explain as he pointed at various parts of the body:

"First, he was doused with kerosene and set on fire. There are remains of fuel all over the body . . ."

"He might have perished in a fire. Someone was afraid to report it and hid the body. The campesinos tend to fear that the police . . ."

"But that wasn't enough," Posadas continued, apparently not hearing him. "He was burned even more."

He allowed the silence to heighten the dramatic effect of his words. His rat's eyes were waiting for Chacaltana's question:

"What do you mean more?"

"No one is left like this just because he's been set on fire, Señor Prosecutor. Tissues resist. Many people survive even total burns by fuel. Automobile accidents, forest fires . . . But this . . ."

He inhaled smoke and exhaled it over the table, at the height of the black face. The man lying there seemed to be smoking. The light flickered. The doctor concluded:

"I've never seen anybody so burned. I've never seen anything so burned."

He went back to his papers without covering the deceased. The report he was looking for was under a lamp. He handed it to the prosecutor. It had chocolate smears at one corner of the page. Chacaltana glanced at it rapidly and verified that it did not have three copies, but he thought he could make them himself, it would not be a serious breach. He waved good-bye. He wanted to get out of there quickly.

"There's something else," the pathologist stopped him. "Do you see this? These stubs like claws on the side? Those are fingers. They twist like that because of the heat. They're only on one side. In fact, if you observe carefully, the body looks unbalanced. At first glance it's difficult to see on a body in this condition, but the man was missing an arm."

"A one-armed man."

Chacaltana put the paper in his briefcase and closed it.

"No. He wasn't one-armed. At least not until Tuesday. There are traces of blood around the shoulder."

"He was injured, perhaps?"

"Señor Prosecutor, his right arm was removed. They tore it out by the roots or cut it off with an ax, or maybe a saw. They went through bone and flesh from one side to the other. That isn't easy to do. It's as if a dragon attacked him."

It was true. The part corresponding to the shoulder seemed sunken, as if there were no longer an articulation there, as if there were no longer anything to articulate. Chacaltana asked himself how they could have done it. Then he preferred not to ask himself more questions. The light flickered again. The prosecutor broke the silence:

"Well, I suppose all this is recorded in the report . . ."

"Everything. Including the matter of the forehead. Have you seen his forehead?"

Chacaltana tried to ask a question in order not to see the forehead. He tried to think of a subject. The physician did not take his eyes off him. Finally, he lied:

"Yes."

"His head seems to have been farther away from the heat source, but not by accident. After burning him, the killer cut a cross on his forehead with a very large knife, perhaps a butcher's knife."

"Very interesting . . ."

Chacaltana felt dizzy. He thought it was time to leave. He wanted to say good-bye with a professional, dignified gesture:

"One last question, Dr. Posadas. Where could a body be burned so severely? In a baker's oven . . . in a gas explosion?"

Posadas tossed his cigarette on the floor. He stepped on it and covered the body. Then he took out another chocolate. He bit into it before he replied:

"In hell, Señor Prosecutor."

sometimes i talk to them. allways.

they remember me. and i remember them because i was won of them.

i still am.

but now they talk moor. they look for me. they ask me for things. they lick my ears with their hot tungues. they want to touch me. they hurt me.

its a signal.

its the moment. yes. its coming.

we will burn up time and the fire will make a new world.

a new time for them.

for us.

for everybody.

Associate District Prosecutor Félix Chacaltana Saldívar left the hospital feeling out of sorts. He was pale. Terrorists, he thought. Only they were capable of something like this. They had come back. He did not know how to sound the alarm, or even if he should. He wiped away perspiration with the handkerchief his mother had given him. The dead man. His mother. He could not go to see her in this state. He had to calm down.

He walked aimlessly. In an automatic reaction, he returned to the Plaza de Armas. The image of the burned body flickered in his mind. He had to sit down and drink something. Yes. That would be the best thing. He walked toward his usual restaurant, El Huamanguino, to have a *mate*. He went in. In one corner, a television set was playing a black-and-white pirated copy of *Titanic*. A girl about twenty was behind the counter. He did not even see her. She was pretty. He sat down.

"What'll you have?"

"Where is Luis?"

She seemed offended by the question.

"Luis doesn't work here anymore. Now I'm here. But I'm not so terrible."

The prosecutor understood he had made a faux pas. He tried to apologize, but just then not many words were coming out of his mouth.

"A *mate*, please," was all he could manage.

She laughed. Her small white smile was timid.

"It's lunchtime," she said. "The tables are for having lunch. You have to eat something."

The prosecutor looked at the four other tables. The place was empty. He missed Luis.

"Then bring me a . . . an . . ."

"The trout's very good."

"Trout. And a *mate*, please."

The girl went into the kitchen. Her clothes were not flashy. She seemed simple in her jeans and Lobo sneakers, her hair pulled back in a braid. The prosecutor thought that perhaps, after all, the deceased was a case for the military courts. He did not want to interfere in the antiterrorist struggle. The military had organized it. They knew it best. He looked at his watch. He should not delay too long. His mother was waiting for him. It took the girl fifteen minutes to come out with a fried trout and two potato halves on a plate. In the other hand she carried the cup of *mate*. She served everything amiably, almost delicately. The prosecutor looked at the trout. Blackened, it seemed to observe him from the plate. He separated it down the middle. One of the sides seemed like a spreading wing, an arm. He let it go. He tried to drink a little *mate*. With his spoon he moved aside the coca leaves on the surface and raised the steaming cup to his lips. It burned him. He quickly put the cup down on the table. Suddenly, he was very hot. Behind him he heard a sweet laugh.

"You have to be patient," the girl behind the counter said.

Patient.

"Everything is slower here, it's not like Lima," she went on.

"I'm not from Lima. I'm Ayacuchan."

She lowered her eyes and smiled again.

"If you say so . . ." she said.

"Don't you believe me?"

Her only answer was to restrain a little laugh. She did not look him in the eye. He saw her for the first time. She was slim and very refined in her embroidered blouse.

"Are you familiar with Lima?" he asked.

She shook her head.

"But it must be nice," she added. "Big."

The Associate District Prosecutor thought about Avenida Abancay, its buses vomiting smoke, its pickpockets. He thought about the houses without water in El Agustino, about the ocean, about the zoo, the Parque de las Leyendas and its consumptive elephant, about the bare gray hills, about a game he had seen between the Boys and the U. About a door closing.

About an empty pillow.

"It is big," he replied.

"I'd like to go there," she said. "I want to study nursing."

"You would be a very good nurse."

She laughed. So did he. Suddenly, he felt relieved. He looked at the trout again, which had not stopped looking at him.

"Didn't you like it?" she asked.

"It's not that. It's just that . . . I have to go. How much is it?"

"I can't charge you. You didn't eat anything."

"But you worked."

"Come back when you're hungry. The food is nice."

He said good-bye to her with a smile that was also nice. He observed that it had been a long time since he had spoken to a stranger. In Ayacucho, the residents did not talk to one another, and they charged for everything. They were suspicious. On the other hand, the girl's pleasantness had made him notice how lonely he felt in this city where he had no friends even though he had been back for a year. People his own age whom he remembered from childhood had left or had died during the eighties, when they were in their twenties, a good age for the first and perhaps the worst time for the second. He walked up the street toward his house. He realized he was almost running. His house was old but in good condition, it was the same one he had lived in when he was a boy, and had been rebuilt after the disaster. He went in and hurried to the bedroom in the rear. He opened the door.

"Mamacita?"

Félix Chacaltana Saldívar walked to the chest of drawers where his mother kept her clothes and costume jewelry. He took out a skirt and blouse and laid them on the bed. It was a beautiful bed, small, with a canopy of carved wood.

"I should have come in this morning. I'm sorry. It's just that there was a homicide, Mamacita, I had to run to work."

He brought the broom from the kitchen and quickly swept out the room. Then he sat on the bed, looking at the door.

"Do you remember Señora Eufrasia? She used to drink *mate* with you? She's sick, Mamacita. I sent her a Virgin so she'd get better. You pray too. I only pray a little."

He felt sheltered in an old, warm mist. He caressed the cloth of the sheets.

"And pray for the man who died today, too. I will. That way the fear goes . . . I think the terrorists are coming back, Mamacita. It isn't certain, I don't want you to worry, but this is very strange."

He stood and passed his hand along the clothing he had laid on the sheets. He smelled it. It had the scent of his mother, a scent kept for many years. He opened the window to air out the room. The afternoon sun shone directly on his mother's bed.

"I have to go now. I only . . . I only needed to come here for a while. I hope that doesn't annoy you . . . It doesn't annoy you, does it?"

He crossed himself and opened the door to go back to his office. He gave a last look inside. It hurt him to verify once again, as he had every day for the past year, that there was no one in the room.

As he returned to the office he felt calmer, unburdened. His mother's room relaxed him. He spent hours there. Occasionally, often at night, he would recall some new detail, a photograph, an altarpiece that had decorated his mamacita's room in his child-hood. He would hurry to look for it in the market and order it if there was no copy exactly like the one in his memory. Little by little, the room had become a three-dimensional portrait of his nostalgia.

When he reached his desk, he found an envelope containing an invitation to the institutional parade on Sunday. He made a note of it in his date book, wrote an account of the complaint for the police, and made copies of the forensic report for each envelope. The chocolate smudges were well hidden on the photocopies. They looked like ink. Then he wrote a request for information to the Ministry of Energy and Mines asking what source could have produced sufficient heat to burn the body. And another request to the municipality of Quinua asking that they send him copies in quadruplicate of missing persons reports dated subsequent to January 1 of the current year.

He spent the rest of the afternoon taking care of other pending matters, such as the complaint of a citizen against his neighbor, whom he accused in his statement of being a faggot. The prose-cutor composed a reply to the report stating that homosexuality in any of its variants does not constitute a misdemeanor, infraction, or serious crime since it is not duly specified as such in the penal code. However, he added, if the individual engaged in relations with a human or judicial person without verifying that it was a concomitant voluntary act by the aforesaid person, he might commit a crime against honor as specified under the classification of violation.

He asked himself how to sanction the violation of one man by another. He realized he could not marry them because there was no relevant procedure to do so. Perhaps the situation deserved another brief.

SUNDAY, MARCH 12 / TUESDAY, MARCH 21

————————

The institutional parade at Lent had been established by decree in 1994 at the request of the archbishop. It began with the several branches of the armed forces passing before the dais in the Plaza de Armas and saluting the competent authorities of the state, the Church, and the military high command. After the hussars and the rangers, and always to the music of the National Police Band, various schools and institutions paraded past while an official introduced them over the loudspeakers:

"The María Parado de Bellido School: established by ministerial resolution 000578904 and governed by municipal statute 887654333, for two years this school has been training young Ayacuchan seamstresses and serving the interests of national handicrafts. The Daniel Alcides Carrión Institute: created by ministerial resolution . . ."

Associate District Prosecutor Félix Chacaltana Saldívar liked parades, the sonorous passing by of national symbols. The uniforms made him feel secure and proud, the young students allowed him to trust in the future, the cassocks guaranteed respect for traditions. He enjoyed hearing the National Anthem and the March of the Flag under the brilliance of trumpets and military braid. He sat proudly in the officials' box, dressed in his best black suit, his good tie, and a handkerchief in his pocket. The year before, after his arrival, he had participated by reciting a poem by José Santos Chocano, and the crowd had applauded loudly the seriousness of his recitation and the solemnity of his diction.

He did not like as much what came afterward, when the parade ended and the functionaries gathered for a fraternal celebration in the municipal ballroom. The year before, he had been invited to the celebration because of his poem. This year, perhaps it was a mistake. Although he felt proud to be considered one of the high-ranking officials, he never really knew what to say on those occasions. The competent authorities circulated around him, holding glasses of rosé, without ever stopping beside him. Many of the mid- and low-ranking functionaries spoke to him for a while but looked elsewhere, searching for someone more important with whom to converse. It was easier to communicate with them in writing.

As the celebration progressed and the alcohol made the rounds, the subject became limited to enumerating the women each man desired and the details of a hypothetical sexual encounter. For the moment, Associate District Prosecutor Félix Chacaltana Saldívar did not want to desire any woman. He tended to respond to these catalogues by nodding and wondering when he could say something, a word at least, trying to think of some woman who had attracted his attention. As a consequence, he normally preferred not to be present, to stay home tending to his mother's room or reading to himself the poems of José Santos Chocano. He liked small places, where no one heard his voice. But now he had a reason to go. He had to speak to Captain Pacheco, who had not yet responded to his inquiries. A case as important as this one ought to move to the highest levels as quickly as possible.

As he reached the ballroom, he met Judge Briceño, a short, nervous man with the little eyes and teeth of a guinea pig. They greeted each other. The judge asked:

"And how are things going in the Office of the Prosecutor? Are you getting used to Huamanga?"

"Well, as it happens, right now I am pursuing a case of the utmost importance . . ."

"I want to buy a car, Chacaltana. Even if it's a Tico. But a judge has to have a car. Don't you agree? I mean, am I right?"

"Absolutely. The case I am pursuing has to do with a recently deceased individual who . . ."

"A Tico or a Datsun? Because some 1990 Datsuns have come in that have hardly been driven . . ."

The judge discoursed on the topic for ten minutes, until Chacaltana caught sight of Captain Pacheco near the national pavilion in the ballroom, chatting with an official wearing a sky-blue tie and an officer in uniform. Judge Briceño noticed where he was looking.

"I see that you're aiming high," he said in a complicitous tone.

"Excuse me?"

"Commander Carrión," the judge indicated. The prosecutor understood that he was referring to the military man in the group.

"Of course, I have sent him some reports," he replied.

"Oh, yes? Why? Are you looking for a promotion?"

"What? No, no." And then he had second thoughts. "Well, one always wishes to serve with more efficiency . . ."

"Of course, efficiency. That's fine. He's the one who decides here."

The prosecutor had heard that lie several times but was certain that moving up in the ranks of the Ministry of Justice was independent of any pressure or interference. He tried to say so in response but could not really find the words to formulate a reply.

"Of course," he agreed at last, involuntarily.

The judge talked about two other car models until he spotted someone more important and left the prosecutor alone. Then the prosecutor approached Pacheco's group and greeted him with martial courtesy. No one introduced him or stopped talking. The prosecutor raised his voice slightly to address Captain Pacheco:

"Excuse me, Captain, hello . . . I stopped by your office this week with regard to the unfortunate homicide that . . ."

Pacheco was talking about the advantages of FAL rifles over a limited impact weapon. He seemed annoyed by the interruption.

"Yes, yes, I haven't been able to get back to you, I've been so busy. I'll send you a report soon, Chacaltana."

"I have already written a report, but I need yours to collate the forms."

The army officer laughed. The functionary seemed uneasy. The police officer did not want to change the subject. He repeated:

"I'm sorry, really. I'll send you the report as soon as possible . . ."

"In any event, I am interested in knowing if any missing persons were reported in the past few months in the municipality of Quinua."

His question resonated uncomfortably with the group. The army officer, who was observing the prosecutor with an ironic look, decided to intervene:

"With Carnival alone ninety percent of faithful husbands must have disappeared."

Everyone laughed except Associate District Prosecutor Félix Chacaltana Saldívar, who insisted:

"I need that datum to complete my report. If you could forward that to me as soon as . . ."

He noticed that they had stopped laughing. The army officer looked at the prosecutor in surprise. The police captain was obliged to make introductions. First he introduced the civilian, Carlos Martín Eléspuru, of the Intelligence Service. Then Commander Alejandro Carrión Villanueva.

"Yes. I have sent you several reports," the prosecutor said in greeting.

The prosecutor did not believe a military man could be concerned with promotions, but perhaps he could facilitate the process. His presence might serve to motivate the police officer to act efficiently with regard to the case. The captain would not refuse to do what was required in the presence of a military man. But the commander looked seriously at the prosecutor.

"Information regarding disappearances is classified," he said.

"If you want that information you'll have to ask me for it. I won't give it to you, but send in your request."

"It is just that if there is a missing person, it could be the dead man we found."

The commander seemed irritated by this civilian's impertinence. Eléspuru remained silent. The commander picked up another glass that the waiter brought on a tray. The rose-colored liquid gleamed. Suddenly, a smile appeared on his face:

"Ah! You're the one investigating the case of the cuckold!"

New laughter from everyone except Félix Chacaltana Saldívar.

"The cuckold, Señor?"

The commander took a good-humored sip of his drink.

"The man burned in Quinua. The cuckold must have been pretty angry, don't you think?"

"I am afraid it is too soon to know what happened, Señor."

"Please, Chacaltana. Three days of Carnival and a man dies. Jealousy. A fight over broads. It happens every year."

"No family member has claimed the body."

"Because they never talk. Or haven't you noticed that yet? The campesinos always avoid coming forward, they hide."

"That is precisely the reason they would not kill this way, Commander. Not so violently."

"Oh, no? You'd have to see me after a three-day drunk."

The prosecutor pondered the legal basis for that reply. While he was thinking, the commander seemed to forget him. He joined in the laughter of the other two and continued talking. He said something about the mayor's wife. They laughed. When Chacaltana had begun to seem like a decoration on the national pavilion, he decided to respond to the commander.

"Excuse me, Señor. But I am afraid your reasoning lacks juridical foundation . . ."

The commander broke off speaking. The man in the sky-blue tie looked uncomfortable. Captain Pacheco began to talk about how attractive the Lenten festivities were turning out. He spoke in a very loud voice. The commander did not stop looking at the prosecutor, who felt totally convinced of his argument. Yes. He was doing it well. Perhaps when the commander had confirmed his professional zeal, he would consider some kind of recommendation for him. The commander said:

"And what do you suggest?"

The police officer closed his mouth again. The prosecutor saw his opportunity to emphasize the gravity of the case and display his powers of deduction:

"I would not presume to discount a Senderista attack."

He had said it. The silence that followed his words seemed to reach the entire ballroom, the entire city. The prosecutor imagined that with this information they would take the case more seriously. It was a matter of the highest security. Civil law and the Ministry of Justice would collaborate for the common goal of achieving a country with a future. The commander seemed to reflect on his attitude. After a long while, he interrupted the silence with a laugh. Pacheco hesitated for a moment, but then he began to laugh too. And then the man in the sky-blue tie, Eléspuru. After them, the rest of the ballroom and the universe began to laugh just a little and then very loudly, until the air thundered.

"You're paranoid, Señor Prosecutor. There is no Sendero Luminoso here anymore."

And he turned away to end the conversation. With the pride of an archivist, the prosecutor countered:

"It has been twenty years since the first attack . . ."

The commander gestured with his hand as if he were brushing away the prosecutor's words.

"Bullshit! We finished them off."

"That first attack was carried out during an election . . ."

The military man began to lose patience:

"Are you arguing with me, Chacaltana? Are you calling me a liar?"

"No, but . . ."

"You aren't one of those politicized prosecutors, are you? You aren't an Aprista or a Communist, are you? Do you want to sabotage the elections? Is that what you want?"

In the face of the unexpected turn in the conversation, the prosecutor opened his eyes very wide and was quick to clarify matters.

"Not at all. If there is a boycott against the elections, rest assured I shall open an investigation as soon as I receive a formal complaint, Commander."

The commander looked at the prosecutor in disbelief. He thought he was an impossible man. Then he laughed again. This time he laughed slowly, paternally.

"You're pathetic, little Chacaltita. But I understand you. You haven't been here very long, have you? You don't know these half-breeds. Haven't you seen them hitting one another at the fertility fiesta? They're violent people."

The prosecutor had been at that fiesta several times. He remembered the blows. Men and women, it did not matter. All of them hitting in the face, where it bleeds the most. They believed their blood would irrigate the earth. He remembered the bloody noses and black eyes. The prosecutor usually classified the fiestas as "consensual violence for reasons of religious belief." Many strange things were done for reasons of religious belief.

"And the Turupukllay?" the commander continued. "What do you think of that? Isn't that bloody?"

The prosecutor thought about the fiesta of the Turupukllay. The Incan condor tied by his claws to the back of a Spanish bull. The bull bucking violently as it bleeds to death, shaking the enormous, frightened vulture that attacks the bull's head with its beak and tears open its back. The condor tries to break free, the bull tries to strike it and knock it off. The condor tends to win the fight, a flayed and wounded victor.

"That is a folkloric celebration," he said timidly. "It is not terror . . ."

"Terror? Aha, I understand. And the Uchuraccay massacre, do you remember?"

Chacaltana remembered. He had the feeling it was a very recent memory. But it was almost twenty years old. The corpses, the pieces of their bodies covered with earth, the interminable interrogations in Quechua, pounded at his memory. He felt relieved that things had changed. He did not want to say anything. They seemed distant words that it was better to keep distant.

"I'll remind you about Uchuraccay," the commander continued. "The campesinos didn't ask those journalists anything. They couldn't, they didn't even speak Spanish. The journalists were outsiders, they were suspicious. They lynched them right away, dragged them through the village, stabbed them. They were so battered they couldn't let them go back. They killed them one by one and hid their bodies the best they could. They thought nobody would notice. What's your opinion of the campesinos? Do you think they're good? Innocent? That all they do is run through the fields with feathers in their hair? Don't be naive, Chacaltana. Don't see horses where there are only dogs."

Chacaltana had turned pale. He tried to articulate a reply:

"I only . . . I thought it was a possibility . . ."

"You think too much, Chacaltana. Get one thing into your head: in this country there is no terrorism, by orders from the top. Is that clear?"

"Yes, Señor."

"Don't forget it."

"No, Señor."

"I want to see your report when you finish with this case. Keep me apprised of what you find out. Perhaps it's still not the right time to cede responsibility to civil jurisdiction."

The commander turned his back and left. Félix Chacaltana Saldívar, Associate District Prosecutor, could not obtain the required police report that afternoon.

On Monday the 13th, Prosecutor Chacaltana woke with a start

at 6:45 a.m. He was perspiring. He had had a nightmare. He had dreamed about fire. A huge blaze that spread through the city and then the fields until it destroyed everything. In the dream, he was in his bed and began to feel that it was raining inside his bedroom. When he got up, he discovered that it was raining blood, that every millimeter of his room was oozing warm red liquid. He tried to escape but the house was flooded, and he could not move through the dense liquid.

When he began to drown and taste the blood in his mouth and lungs, he woke up. He went to the bathroom. There was no water, but the prosecutor had a barrel in reserve for these occasions, which allowed him to wash his private parts and wet his head. He opened it with a trembling hand. It was a relief to verify that there was nothing but water in the barrel. He washed, then combed his hair back as his mother had taught him to do when he was a boy, as he had combed his hair every day of his life. Immediately afterward he went to his mother's room and opened the window. He let in the air and greeted her. Then he took a picture of Señora Saldívar de Chacaltana to have breakfast with him. He chose a photograph that showed him at the age of five, hugging her. She was smiling.

While he ate his breakfast of bread and cheese and *mate,* he told the picture about his plans for the day and all the documents he hoped to complete. He did not forget that he would have lunch at El Huamanguino to pay his debt to the girl at the counter. For the rest of the morning at the office, the words the commander had said to him the day before resounded in his head. A fight over broads. If the commander said it was a fight over broads, it was a fight over broads. The commander had fought so much that he would know. Yet in the prosecutor's opinion, something did not fit. But Chacaltana was a serious, honest bureaucrat. He was not supposed to have an opinion. Besides, the commander had asked him for his reports. He would read them personally. It was a great opportunity. He thought about Cecilia, his ex-wife. Perhaps this would show her what he was worth. He did not really care about her anymore; it was simply a question of pride. He could be somebody.

Without warning, when it was almost time for lunch, the commander's words began to mix in his head with images from the pathologist's table until he could not concentrate on what he was doing. In a mental flash he saw the face of the dead man wreathed in smoke, the slit up to his shoulder, his black hair. Violence. Jealousy. The word "terrorist" formed in his mind again. It took him back to electric pylons exploding. Ambulance sirens. He thought about his mother to fill his mind with another image. But he succeeded only in evoking the image of fire.

To distract himself, he decided to go out exactly at lunchtime and not fifteen minutes later, as he usually did. He left the Office of the Prosecutor and went to the previously mentioned restaurant. The same girl as the last time was working behind the counter, but now she wore black slacks and low-heeled shoes. The blouse was the same. Pink. With embroidery. This time she wore her hair pulled back in a bun.

"How nice that you came back. Your table's ready."

Now he had a table, as if he were a regular customer. It was the only place in the world other than his house where he had a table. It was the same one as the last time, beside the door. In fact, the table was already set. Again the restaurant was empty. She announced:

"Today we have deep-fried guinea pig."

The prosecutor nodded his agreement. While she went to the kitchen, he looked at the television on the wall. On the screen, a woman was hitting a man, the two of them surrounded by an audience that cheered the hair-pulling and biting. The prosecutor found out that she was his fiancée and that he had deceived her with her sister, her cousin, and her great-aunt. He did not want to see any more. Twelve minutes later, the girl came out of the kitchen. She served him the guinea pig and an Inca beer. The Associate District Prosecutor brought the flatware to the plate and saw the rodent's face. Its mouth was open and it had long, aggressive front teeth. It seemed to Félix Chacaltana that the guinea pig wanted to eat him. He put down the knife and fork.

"It's not that hot," the girl said defensively.

"Thank you. It is just that . . . I was thinking."

"You think a lot, don't you?"

You think too much, Chacaltana.

"No, it is . . . I just work."

"And what were you thinking about? If you don't mind my asking."

She laughed as if she had asked a very naughty question. Associate District Prosecutor Félix Chacaltana Saldívar tried to think up a convincing lie.

"A dead man," he said.

His mother had already told him he did not know how to lie. The girl did not seem surprised. She began to wash some dishes.

"There are a lot of them around here," she said.

"Yes."

"I talk to them."

"Are you serious?"

"With my papa and mama. I go to see them in the cemetery and talk to them, I bring them flowers."

"Of course. I do the same thing. With my mother. Her memory is always with me."

Suddenly, he felt comfortable in this place. As if he were home. She turned around. She did not stop washing but gestured toward the guinea pig with her nose.

"Aren't you going to eat?"

"Yes . . . Yes. Right away."

He tried to pick up a piece of meat with the fork. The bones were mixed up with the skin. The best thing was to eat with his hands. Touch it. And bite it. On the screen, the same man was still being hit, now by two women at the same time.

"What would you like them to do with you when you die?" the girl asked as she dried some flatware.

"What?"

"I wouldn't want to go to the cemetery. It's like . . . having a house where you don't live. And my family would have to go all the way out there. In the end they'd get lazy and stop going."

"Maybe they can bury you in your house."

"No. My house is very small." She dried her hands. "You don't like the guinea pig, do you?"

"Yes I do! Very nice. It is just . . . just that I would like a *mate* with it . . . please."

"Today we only have coffee."

"Coffee would be fine."

"Coffee with guinea pig? You're very strange, Señor . . ."

"Félix. Call me Félix."

"Don Félix."

"Just Félix. Please."

She took a jug of boiling water off the fire and poured a cup. She placed it on the table and beside it the little pitcher of coffee essence. The prosecutor poured the liquid into the hot water. The coffee color began to spread in the water, like dark blood. The prosecutor hated Ayacuchan coffee. Watery. Weak.

"I'd ask to be cremated," she said.

"What?"

"To be cremated. Turned into ashes. Then my family could have me at home when they wanted to see me."

An oven. Fire. A crematory. A furnace that feeds on people. It was simple, really.

"And where would you do that?"

"In the Church of the Heart of Christ. They have an oven. And it's closer to my house than the cemetery."

"They have that? Churches don't have ovens."

The prosecutor asked as if he were a tourist. She laughed again.

In a corner of her mouth she had a silver filling that glistened in the light.

"This one does. What about you? You'd be buried, wouldn't you?"

"I have to go."

He stood with the feeling that something was boiling in his head. Perhaps he had time to stop by that church before his lunch hour was over. In any event, if not he could claim the pressure of work. He had not made note of it in the morning, but perhaps he could send a memo correcting his statement regarding justified absences. Perhaps the proof that they were not terrorists would be there. Jealousy. It had to be jealousy. It had to be demonstrated that it was jealousy. She watched him get up from the table. She seemed disappointed.

"You could at least taste it before you say you don't like it!"

"Oh, no . . . you do not understand. It is just that I am in a terrible hurry. I promise that tomorrow . . . What is your name?"

"Edith."

"Edith, of course. I promise that tomorrow I'll come and really eat lunch. Yes, I promise."

"Sure, go on."

The prosecutor tried to say something clever. All he could think of was jealousy. He left the restaurant, reached the corner, and remembered that he ought to pay the bill. He did not want her to think he was an opportunist. He turned and walked toward the restaurant. Then he thought that if he paid, she would think he was not returning the next day. In the middle of the street, he wondered what he should do. He looked at his watch. He would go to police headquarters and to the church. It would be better not to be distracted from his work. He looked toward the restaurant one last time. Edith was cleaning his table. He waited for her to look up. To wave good-bye to him. She finished the table and then swept up a little. She looked at the sky. The sky was clear.

Then she disappeared again into the interior. The prosecutor thought about the oven. Edith had cooperated with the law without realizing it. He retraced his steps to the restaurant. He went in. She was surprised to see him return. He said:

"Thank you. Thank you very much."

"You're welcome."

She smiled. He realized then that he was smiling too. Feeling calmer, Félix Chacaltana Saldívar continued on his way.

He stopped by police headquarters, where the same sergeant as last time received him:

"Good afternoon, I am looking for Captain Pacheco."

"Captain Pacheco?"

"That is correct."

The sergeant wrote down the prosecutor's information again on a piece of paper and went into the office. He came out nine minutes later:

"The captain is very busy right now but asks that you send him a written request, and he'll study it carefully."

"It is just that . . . the police ought to carry out this investigation. I cannot move forward if I do not see that you are moving forward too."

"Of course, I understand. I'll let the captain know."

The Church of the Heart of Christ was beyond the Arch, almost where the mountain began. The principal nave was completely overlaid with wood and gold leaf, and the stained-glass windows were representations of the Stations of the Cross. In one corner there was an altar to Our Lady of Sorrows with the seven daggers in her bosom. On the other side, near the sacristy, was an image of Christ dragging the cross to Golgotha. There were short red candles before each holy image. The image of the crucified Christ looked down on the main altar. Félix Chacaltana stared at his somber nakedness, the drops of blood running down his face, the wounds of the nails on his hands and feet, the gash in his side.

A hand touched his shoulder.

The prosecutor jumped. Behind him was a priest still dressed in the vestments of the Mass. He carried several objects of silver and glass. He was about fifty years old and had very little hair.

"May I help you? I'm Father Quiroz, the pastor of Heart of Christ."

The prosecutor accompanied the priest as he put away the implements of the Mass in the sacristy, explaining the situation. On the wall hung a chiaroscuro image of Christ raising his hands to God. His perforated hands. The crown of thorns circled his head like a red and green tiara. Chacaltana wanted to say something agreeable:

"How beautiful your church is," was what occurred to him.

"Yes, it's beautiful now," the priest responded as he placed the wafers in a plastic box. "We've restored it recently with money from the government, this church and all the others. There are thirty-three churches in this city, Señor Prosecutor. Like the age of Christ. Ayacucho is one of the most devout cities in the country."

"Religion is always a consolation. Especially here . . . with so many dead."

The priest polished the paten and chalice carefully.

"Sometimes I don't know, Señor Prosecutor. The Indians are so impenetrable. Have you ever seen the churches of Juli, in Puno?"

"No."

Quiroz took off the green and gold chasuble and the cordon that tied the stole around his waist. He folded the cloth articles and placed them delicately in a chest in order not to wrinkle them. Each gesture seemed like another ritual of the Mass, as if each movement of his hands had a precise meaning. He said:

"They are open-air churches, like corrals. The Jesuits built them during the colonial period to convert the Indians, to have them attend Mass, because they worshipped only the sun, the river, the mountains. Do you see? They didn't understand why worship was held in an enclosed place."

"And did it work?"

The priest locked with a key each of the chests in which he had placed articles. He carried the keys on a large ring.

"Oh, yes, to keep up appearances. The Indians were delighted to attend Mass, and at Mass . . . They prayed and learned canticles, they even took Communion. But they never stopped worshipping the sun, the river, and the mountains. Their Latin prayers were only memorized repetitions. Inside they continued worshipping their gods, their *huacas*. They deceived the Jesuits."

Father Quiroz stood facing the prosecutor. He was tall. Félix Chacaltana thought he ought to contribute something to the conversation. He wondered what Commander Carrión would say. He asked:

"What would you have recommended?"

"One reaches the true spirit only through suffering. Pleasure and nature are corporeal, worldly. The soul is full of suffering. Christ endured blood and death to save us. Penance is the only way to reach the heart of man. Shall we go down now?"

The prosecutor nodded. He had not understood very well what the priest had said about suffering. In general he did not like suffering. They left the church and walked down a short alleyway that led to the small parish house. In the living room there was an accumulation of old furniture, cardboard boxes, and church decorations. Quiroz made an embarrassed gesture. He said:

"Forgive the disorder. I usually see people in the parish office. I'm the only one who comes in here and that's only to sleep. The oven is down below."

The prosecutor remarked:

"I did not think Catholics had crematories."

"We don't. The body should reach the day of the Final Judgment to be resurrected with the soul. The basement of the parish house was a storeroom. The recent crematory was built in the 1980s at the request of the military high command."

"The high command?"

They stopped at a heavy wooden door. The priest took out another key and opened it. In front of them were damp unlit stairs. Holding on to the walls, they climbed down to the basement. It smelled of incense and enclosure.

"Too many dead. The city was often under siege, and the cemeteries were full. One had to dispose of the bodies."

"And why did they do it here?"

"In wartime, every request from the military is an order. The high command considered us the ones who took care of people after they were dead. According to them, the logical thing was for us to take care of the oven."

Down below a faint light came from a small, high window of opaque glass that faced the alley. The priest turned on the overhead light. It was a white neon bulb, like the one at the morgue, but round. When he turned it on, more boxes appeared piled up in a corner. And beside them, in the stone wall, was an opening with a metal door and lining. A chimney, which must have gone up to the roof of the house, protruded on one side. As if it were a baker's oven, the priest showed him how it operated. The body was introduced vertically into the oven, lying on a grate. The fire was fueled by gas and distributed uniformly around the body until it was reduced to powder. The ashes were collected in a metallic tray that was reinforced to withstand the heat, and from there they went down to the urn or jar where they would rest forever.

"We haven't used it for a long time. The people here are very tied to the earth. And I don't like the idea of destroying the body, either. Only God should dispose of bodies."

The prosecutor placed his hand inside the opening. He touched the walls, the door. They were cold.

"Could it have been used recently without your consent?"

"Nothing is done here without my consent."

The priest adjusted a cross hanging on the wall. It was a black cross without the image of Christ. Just a black cross on a gray surface. The prosecutor did not want to think about the cross burned into the forehead of the corpse.

"And on the night in question did you notice anything unusual? Any noise? Anything unexpected?"

"I don't know, Señor Prosecutor. I don't know which is the night in question."

"I thought I told you. Forgive me. It was Wednesday the 8th. Just after Carnival. The body was found on the same day it died."

The priest made an ironic face.

"How appropriate."

"What do you mean?"

"Ash Wednesday. It's time to purify bodies after the pagan festivities and begin Lent, the sacrifice, the preparation for Holy Week."

"Ash Wednesday. Why Ash?"

The priest smiled pityingly.

"Ah, secular public education. Nobody taught you the Catechism at your school in Lima, Señor Prosecutor? On that day a cross of ashes is marked on the foreheads of Catholics, as a reminder that we are dust and will turn to dust."

His mother had taken him to church from time to time and that sign had been put on him by a cold, black hand. He touched his forehead, as if he wanted to wipe away the mark.

"To remember that we are going to die?" he asked.

"That we are going to die and will be resurrected to a purer life. Fire purifies."

Without knowing why, the prosecutor felt as he had days earlier in the office of Dr. Posadas. Faint. He wanted to cancel the visit. There was no jealousy here. He decided to ask something that had no answer, something that would leave the crematory like a dead-end street, something to be forgotten.

"What . . . other persons have access to this place?"

"As I told you, this place is hardly used. I have the only key. Do you consider me a suspect?"

"Oh, no, Father, please. But I think perhaps someone could have tried to make the corpse disappear in your oven. Do you know if anyone could have had access to a copy of the key?"

The priest reflected for a few seconds.

"No."

The Associate District Prosecutor felt more and more relieved with each answer. There was nothing else to do here. To be certain he had fulfilled the duties of his position, he insisted:

"Some worker or civilian who offered his services, for example?"

"Well, a few weeks ago I had to dismiss a cleaner. He had stolen a chalice. A rather dim-witted Indian, actually. I don't consider him capable of planning anything. But if he had wanted to, he might have had access to the key, I suppose."

The prosecutor unwillingly took out his notebook. He regretted having insisted on the question.

"Aha. His name?"

"Do you think he brought a corpse here at night and then carried it through the streets only partially burned? I don't believe that poor soul of God . . ."

"It is just routine. I will verify it for my report."

"If I remember correctly, his name was Justino. Justino Mayta Carazo."

"Thirty-one."

"What?"

"Nothing, forget it."

The Associate District Prosecutor again felt perspiration on his forehead. He wanted the police here. He looked at the oven again. He wanted to be buried when he died.

in this city the ded arent ded. they walk the streets and sell candy to the children. they greet the adults. they prey in the churches.

sometimes there are so many i wonder if im ded too. maybe im skinned and cut up, my peeces at the bottom of a pond. everything i see is only what my eyes see and maybe there not here anymore.

maybe i dont know it anymore.

but hes really ded. really. his ashes cant wander around. his arm isnt an arm anymore. his skins got nothing to cover. thats why he talks to me that way. thats why he complanes. and i tell him you cant do anything anymore, you son of a bitch. ha. you cant do anything anymore.

too many sins. all there in your chest like the worms that eat you. the fire. but you cant do anything anymore. your cleen.

thanks to me.

i came from hell to save you. i cleened your blood and your semen out of the sewers so there wont be more sins like you. bastard. i did it for you. your skins good for feeding the dogs. your spit. your spit.

some day men—ded men—will look back and say the 21st sentury began with me.

but you wont see the 21st sentury now.

your cleen.

because of me.

Associate District Prosecutor Félix Chacaltana Saldívar spent the rest of the week trying to locate Justino Mayta Carazo for the pertinent interrogation. He had recovered somewhat from the grim impression made by the crematory. In fact, he was calmer. He thought the commander was right. Unmistakably a fight over broads. Mayta Carazo had tried to make the evidence disappear, but a body takes a long time to turn into ashes. He must have seen that he would be found out and pulled the body out in time. The cross on the forehead was to mislead the authorities. In the end he said that he had found the body to deflect the suspicions of the police. No terrorists, just a crime of passion. With motive and opportunity. The commander would be pleased with his investigation.

In order not to waken his fears, the prosecutor sent to the domicile of the suspect three subpoenas and two summonses to appear as a witness. At the same time, he sent Captain Pacheco an account of the facts so the police could locate the suspect. By means of briefs, he inquired about him in the municipality of Quinua and in the appropriate parish.

On Friday he still had not received a reply. The messenger service at the Office of the Prosecutor informed him that they had not sent out a single envelope all week because the messenger was sick. Maybe he'd feel better next week. Or maybe not. The prosecutor thought that if matters were put off too long, the commander would forget about his case. He himself wanted to forget about it as soon as possible. The case seemed to inflame his memories. That night he discussed the situation with his mother:

"I really don't know, Mamacita. If I don't resolve this case, they won't give me another good one. I've learned by now that you have to fight your way up."

He remembered a voice saying: You're an incompetent with no future, Félix. You'll never amount to anything. It was not his mother's voice, but he remembered it clearly. He remembered an empty pillow, like his mother's. He remembered the Lima fog at the windows of the enormous building where he worked, on Avenida Abancay. He did not want to go back there.

"I'm going to look for Mayta myself. I'm going to prove to the commander that I'm an exemplary prosecutor. Even if it fucks me up, excuse my language, the fact is this case makes me very nervous."

On Saturday the 18th he got up at seven and had breakfast with a photograph of his mother in Sacsayhuamán, in her native Cuzco. It was a sunny, tranquil photo, as if meant to begin a good day. After saying good-bye, he closed the windows of his mother's room because he would be out late. He went to the jitney stop and took public transport. He sat between a woman carrying a hen and two boys who looked like brothers. When they left Ayacucho he enjoyed the view of the dry, interminable mountains and the river far below. The sky was clear. On the road to Quinua, the landscape became greener and more lush in places. At the end of the trip, the doors of the houses decorated with little ceramic churches indicated that he was close to his destination.

The prosecutor got out of the jitney beside a soccer field where about ten boys without shoes were playing. The two who had ridden with him ran to join the others. He realized too late that his trousers were covered with their snot. He cleaned it off with his handkerchief, passed the shops for tourists, and entered the village. He asked a street vendor:

"Mamacita. I'm looking for Justino Mayta Carazo. Have you seen him?"

The vendor did not take her eyes off her altarpieces and weavings. She said:

"Well, who's he I wonder?"

"Don't you know Justino? Don't you live in the village?"

"Well, what's he look like I wonder?"

"Do you know where this address is?"

"Not too far, right over there."

Then she mumbled a couple of phrases in Quechua. The prosecutor understood that "not too far" could mean "two days away." He remembered how difficult it is to question Quechua speakers, especially if they also do not feel like talking. And they never feel like talking. They are always afraid of what might happen. They do not trust anybody. Street by street he looked for the address he had written down on a piece of paper. Finally he came to a narrow house that seemed to have only one room downstairs and another upstairs, with one window. He knocked at the door. He had the impression that someone was watching him from the upstairs window, but when he looked up he did not see anything. After a long wait, an old woman opened the door a crack. In the darkness all he could see was one of her eyes and part of her long black braid.

"Well, what is it I wonder, Señor?"

"Good morning, Mamacita, I am looking for Justino Mayta Carazo. I am from the Ministry of Justice."

She closed the door and when she was inside she asked him to show his identification. The prosecutor passed it to her under the door. He thought he heard whispering inside. He waited a while longer until the woman opened the door again and asked him to come in. The house was scantily furnished with a table and two chairs. It had no light and no bathroom. The sofa was on bricks instead of legs and had a blanket thrown over it. Two children watched curiously from the hand ladder that went up to another bare brick space.

"Justino isn't here," said the woman. "He left."

"Where could I find him?"

"Well, where is he I wonder? He left."

"When did he leave?"

"A while ago now."

"Do you mind if I take a look around the house? It is . . . an official investigation."

She looked upward. She said nothing but did not try to stop him either. The prosecutor checked the small first floor, but there was nothing of interest. He began to climb the creaking ladder. The children watched him in silence. He greeted them, but they did not respond. They simply stared at him. He climbed up with difficulty because the ladder seemed about to fall. One of the boys coughed. The prosecutor got a splinter in his hand. He licked the puncture. Then he heard the thud. It was like a large sack of potatoes landing on the street. He went up two more rungs and was on the second floor. The upstairs window was open. He turned to go down but missed his step and fell to the bottom of the ladder. When he stood up, he felt a pain in his leg but went to the door and looked out. He caught sight of a man racing around the corner. For a second he wondered if following him was the responsibility of the Associate District Prosecutor or if he only had to pass along the information. Then he remembered the fire. He thought that pursuit was the responsibility of the National Police, and if he ran after the man, he could be liable for usurpation of duties. He looked at the woman:

"Who was that?"

"Who?"

"The one who left here."

"Nob'dy left here. Nob'dy."

He knew it would make no sense to accuse the woman of obstruction of justice. He went to the offices of the municipality. He was going to slip his official documents under the door but remembered that no one could sign the receipt certificate on a Saturday. He considered his official activities over for the day.

Before returning to the city, he decided to visit the Quinua plain. He climbed the highway until he reached the flatland crowned in silence that extended between the mountains in front of him. He was out of breath after the climb, but he was no longer limping. And it was peaceful. The only thing up there with him was the huge marble monument to the Liberators erected by the military government of Velasco. He imagined the heroic battle that had given the nation its freedom. He thought of the sound of weapons tearing apart the eternal silence of the plain. In the distance, past where the plain ended, he could see the tops of trees moving in the wind, and a stream. He was overcome by a feeling of pride and freedom. He sat down next to the monument to look at the landscape. He used his handkerchief to wipe the perspiration from his forehead, searching out parts of the cloth that had not been dirtied with snot. He noticed that he could not hear anything. Not a sound. He felt a whistling in his ears, the acoustic illusion produced when there is silence around us. The plain was transmitting the music of death.

He spent several minutes breathing the clean sierra air until he decided to go back. When he stood, he heard breathing behind him. He had just started to turn when he heard another thud, this time a fist landing directly on his jaw, and then another dry thud, like the handle of a shovel or something like it landing on the back of his neck. He felt everything going black around him, he did see a red wool mountain hat, a pair of shoes with tire soles running, racing away from him, and a man hurrying across the plain while silence invaded everything.

He woke as it was growing dark, a sharp pain in his head. Above him the sky was turning red, announcing the darkness, as if it were bleeding onto the setting sun. He touched the back of his neck. It felt warm and wet. He stood, returned to Quinua, and took another jitney to Ayacucho. When he reached home he hurried to wash his wounds. He did not know if he should file charges, he did not know why he had been hit. He had never been hit in his life. Or had he? No. He had never felt a blow. He told himself he would be able to think more calmly the next day. This case was becoming a headache. He went to bed, not without first bringing into his room a photograph of his mother in the rocking chair, smiling warmly. He wondered who would take care of her if anything should happen to him. He was afraid for her. He did not want to leave her alone, not again.

He thought that if it were a case of terrorism, it would be under military jurisdiction. If not, the police ought to intervene. His work had ended honorably, with the greatest effort on his part, even with wounds received in the line of duty.

But for the next two nights, nightmares gave him no peace.

Added to his dreams about fire were dreams about blows, dry thuds, and a woman's screams. On Sunday he had to sleep in his mother's bed to feel safe. On Monday he woke shaken by the blows in his dreams. As soon as he opened his eyes, he was certain the institution of the police would take charge of the case that same day.

In the afternoon, after he left the Office of the Prosecutor, he went to police headquarters. He had a bandage on the back of his neck covering the wound.

"Good afternoon, I am looking for Captain Pacheco."

The sergeant on duty was the same one as before. Chacaltana wondered if he lived in that desk.

"Captain Pacheco?"

"That is correct, yes."

Nervously the sergeant went into the side office. He stayed for six minutes. Then he came out.

"Unfortunately the captain isn't here right now. He's gone to the barracks with respect to certain operations."

"Do you know when he will be back?"

"I have no specific knowledge in that regard."

It was late. The prosecutor thought about the work piling up in his office for the next day: sending his regrets for two banquets, and preparing a memorandum for the provincial prosecutor regarding sexual crimes in the region. Prosecutor Chacaltana considered the request from the provincial prosecutor as a way to finally recognize his work in the field and his thinking about this social misfortune. Furthermore, he had to write a document concerning electoral transparency before the next elections. It was very difficult for him to make the decision, but he had no time to lose. And he did not have anything better to do to fill the hours after work. After thinking it over for a moment and finding a chair to sit on that had fewer holes, he said:

"I will wait for him here."

He sat down. The sergeant was not expecting that answer. He seemed nervous. He looked at the office. Then he looked again at the prosecutor.

"No, the fact is . . . The captain won't be back for hours. Maybe he won't come back at all. But I'll inform him that you . . ."

"I am in no hurry, but I do feel some urgency."

"He left word that he'd send you a report with regard . . ."

"I prefer to see him, thank you."

The sergeant's look turned into an entreaty. He sat down and took a deep breath. So did the prosecutor. The sergeant let half an hour go by before he spoke again, with a yawn.

"I don't think he's coming back anymore today, the captain."

"If he comes tomorrow morning, I will still be here. Or Thursday. Or whenever."

He was surprised by his own decisiveness, but it was true that the functioning of the mechanisms of inter-institutional communication in Ayacucho left much to be desired. He thought that perhaps in this way he might be able to improve them. He could be very bold if he put his mind to it. He shifted in his seat and let time pass. At 8:00, two gendarmes came in and the sergeant had them go into the office. They came out at 9:00, cheerfully saying good-bye to someone inside. At 10:30, the sergeant repeated that he would inform the captain that the prosecutor had stopped by. At 10:31, the prosecutor replied that it would not be necessary because he would be in the reception area when the captain arrived. At 11:23, he took off his jacket and arranged it over his body as if it were a blanket. At 11:32, he began to snore with a muffled whistle. Finally, at 12:08, the sound of a door wakened him. Captain Pacheco came out of the office, looked at the prosecutor with hatred, and kept walking to the bathroom. He stayed inside for seven more minutes, after which he came out drying his hands to the sound of the toilet flushing. The sergeant stood to greet him:

"Good evening, Captain! I didn't know you were here. The prosecutor came to the office to . . ."

"Shut up, damn it. Go in, Chacaltana. You want to talk? We'll talk."

The Associate District Prosecutor followed him into the office, victory shining in his smile. Captain Pacheco sat down heavily behind his desk, beside the national flag, beneath the photograph of the president. On the wall hung the coat-of-arms of the police with its motto: "Honor is their shield."

"Before you begin, allow me to say that you are really a pain in the balls," he said by way of official greeting. "What happened to your head?"

The prosecutor was afraid to say that he had been beaten. He would not be respected if he said that.

"Nothing, I fell. And I am sorry for recent events, Captain, but I have sent a brief to your off . . ."

"Yes, yes, yes. Mayta Carazo. I've seen it."

"Unfortunately, your response in this regard seems to have been lost and never came into my possession . . ."

"I didn't send you a response, Chacaltana. And I'm not going to send you one. Is that what you wanted to hear?"

"No, Captain. I need your cooperation and collaboration to close the case of . . ."

"Chacaltana, are you an Aprista or an imbecile?"

"Excuse me, Captain?"

"Didn't you hear Commander Carrión when he spoke to you?"

"Yes, Captain. And I believe, in fact, that I have found confirmation of his suspicions . . . I have evidence that indicates that the aforementioned Justino . . ."

"I don't want to know what evidence you have. I don't want to know anything having to do with this case. Elections are just around the corner. Nobody wants to hear about terrorists in Ayacucho."

"Permit me to express my surprise at your words . . ."

"Look, Chacaltana, I'll be totally frank with you, and I hope this is the last time we talk about this subject. The police are controlled by the Ministry of the Interior, and the interior minister is a military man. Doesn't that tell you something?"

"That does not constitute an irregularity. Members of the armed forces are authorized to . . ."

"I'll try to say it so even you can understand: They make the decisions here. If they don't want an investigation, there's no investigation."

"But it is our duty . . ."

"Our duty is to shut up and do what we're told! Is it so difficult for you to get that into your head? Listen, I have no interest in helping you because I don't feel like it. But even if I did want to help you, I couldn't. So don't get me involved in this because you'll fuck up my promotion. Please, I'm begging you! I have a family! I want to go back to Lima! I can't be bothering Commander Carrión."

In the hierarchical gears that constituted the mind of Associate District Prosecutor Félix Chacaltana Saldívar, there was no place for the possibility of not being promoted because of following procedures. To the contrary. He tried to explain the point, but the captain interrupted him:

"Why don't you write a report and close the case once and for all? Attribute it to a fire or a car accident . . . And everybody's happy."

Chacaltana opened his eyes in genuine surprise.

"But I . . . I cannot do that . . . Doing that without the police report is illegal, Captain."

The captain buried his head in his hands. He closed his eyes. He moved his lips gently, as if counting to one hundred in silence. When he was calmer, he said:

"Chacaltana, this is an emergency zone. A large part of the department is still classified as a red zone. Laws are legally suspended."

"Moreover, the survivors of the deceased could demand . . ."

"He has no survivors! Nobody knows who he is! The case has not been leaked to the press. Nobody will complain, the Indians never complain. They don't care. And neither do I."

The picture of the president seemed to tremble at his back when he said that. Then the office sank into silence. On his desk, the captain had national ID–size photographs of his family, two children and a wife. Chacaltana liked families. But at that moment he rose to his feet in genuine indignation.

"I also want to close this case as soon as I can, Captain, but your report has to reach me because procedure demands it. I cannot conclude the process without a report. I am keeping a record of how the details of the proceedings are being executed."

Chacaltana walked with dignity toward the exit. The captain leaned back in his chair. Just before Chacaltana opened the door, the captain said:

"Is that all?"

Chacaltana stopped. He did not turn around. He knew he had won.

"It is why I have come."

Chacaltana said this in a firm tone of voice, standing rigid beside the door. The captain demanded confirmation:

"If I give you a report written by my experts and signed by me, there won't be any more problems?"

"The only problem we have is the administrative irregularity that does not allow us to close the case."

The captain sketched a smile. Then he stopped. He frowned. Chacaltana maintained the imperturbable face of the professional prosecutor. The captain gave a clear laugh.

"Fine, Chacaltana, I understand. I'll speak to my people and get my men together. You'll have your report tomorrow first thing in your office. Thanks for the visit."

In reality, that was the only thing the Associate District Prosecutor was waiting to hear.

He left police headquarters with the feeling that he had engaged in a great battle and won. Still, he understood the misgivings of the police. He should not forget they were living in a red zone, and that always made people more suspicious.

At that hour everything in the city was closed. No one was in the streets except for an occasional patrol, a leftover of the curfews. He walked through the silent blue night to his house, breathing the clean provincial air. When he reached his house he went to his mother's room. It was cold because the window had been open all day. He apologized as he closed it.

"I'm sorry, Mamacita. I left you alone all day. It's just that this case is very difficult, Mamacita. Very sad. The deceased has no survivors. Can you imagine? How sad."

Still speaking, he took from a drawer the warmest wool pajamas and laid them out on the sheets.

"If you die without anyone to remember you it's like dying twice. Where can this man's family be? Who'll remember something nice about him, or turn down his bed at night, or give him his pajamas? Nobody at all, Mamacita. Nobody to look at his photograph or say his name at night. Do you see how it is? When someone ceases to exist like that, it's as if he never had existed, as if he had been a ray of sunlight that leaves no trace afterward, when night falls."

He caressed the pajamas and the sheet. Then he picked up a photograph from the bureau, the one of his mother alone, with her sweet young gaze. He carried it to his room and put it on the table beside his bed, to feel less alone after he closed his eyes.

The next morning, in fact, the police report was lying on his desk. The prosecutor opened it and looked it over. It was very badly written, full of redundancies and spelling mistakes, but the content was simple and legally valid. The police version differed from his hypothesis but contributed definitive proofs suggested by their experience in the investigation of malefactors and homicides. Throughout the day he verified certain data. They were correct. He called police headquarters, where Captain Pacheco answered the phone personally, certified his procedures, and offered all the cooperation at his disposal.

The prosecutor had no ambition to play a leading role. He did not want to engage in controversy or doubt the good faith of institutions. If the competent authorities offered a more solid version of events than his, he accepted it. His job was to facilitate the operation of the forces of law and order, not stand in their way. True, he did feel proud about the change in attitude he had caused in Captain Pacheco, who had overcome his resistance and collaborated, finally, with the greatest efficiency. In the long run, the captain would realize the advantages of cooperation among institutions in times of peace. And thank him.

He accepted the police report as valid and decided to close the case with the information at his disposal. He wrote a report that did not satisfy him on account of its excessive length. He threw it in the wastebasket. He wrote another page but found it full of simplifications and omissions. Again he threw it out and wrote a third page, being especially careful about syntax and punctuation:

simple, nothing excessive, sober. As he corrected the commas and tildes, he felt relieved. Images of the burned man would not bother him again. And above all, the channels of inter-institutional communication had proved themselves effective. One more sign of progress.

On Tuesday, the seventh day of March, 2000, when festivities to celebrate Carnival were in progress, an electrical storm was pragmatically verified visually in the highlands of Huancavelica, producing a significant amount of material and personal damage in unpopulated areas.

Subsequently, the aforementioned meteorological phenomenon moved in the direction of the province of Huamanga, where its verification has not been duly corroborated as a consequence of the alcoholic condition of the inhabitants of said province during the abovementioned celebration.

The deceased in question, a one-armed man whose identity could not be established, demonstrating that this is a matter of a traveler and/or foreign tourist, presented himself, due to the abovementioned meteorological conditions, to take shelter for the night in the residence of Nemesio Limanta Huamán (41), who refused the aforesaid permission, although due to the fraternizing that took place on the above-referenced dates, he has no memory in this regard.

Despite the refusal of Nemesio Limanta Huamán (41), the deceased in question had recourse to his prerogative to take shelter for the night, thus committing the crime of breaking and entering and unlawful use of private property, entering the hayloft, said appurtenance serving as well as a repository of kerosene and other combustible liquids utilized in the process of small-scale farming and animal husbandry.

The deceased in question remained in the environs of the

hayloft for a period of two days when, in an effort to evade the consequences of his crime, he hid in the straw to avoid being seen by the inhabitants of Quinua, a reason that contributes to the explanation of the general lack of memory with respect to his presence in this locality.

On Wednesday, the eighth day of March, 2000, at approximately the hour of dawn, an electrical charge, caused by unfavorable meteorological conditions, produced in the form of a lightning bolt a fire in the residence of Nemesio Limanta Huamán, precisely in the locale of the hayloft where the abovementioned deceased in question was taking shelter for the night. Struck on his shoulder by the meteorological phenomenon, which opened a wound, and bursting into flames, the deceased in question revealed his ignorance of rural customs when he attempted to extinguish the fire with certain combustible liquids, which, combined with the action of the electrical charge, intensified the process of combustion and deteriorated into a blaze of considerable proportions which, however, due to the dampness of the element of straw, did not spread to other structures on the aforementioned property.

In conclusion, in the corresponding fall to the ground of the aforementioned deceased, his face hit the hay harrows, producing a sharp cruciform puncture wound on the frontal cranial area.

In witness whereof this is signed, on Friday, the seventeenth day of March . . .

Now it was perfect, with appropriate conjugations and correct pauses. Along with the relief of seeing the report completed, there was also the knowledge that there was no murderer loose in the province. No terrorists. The war was over. Not even a crime of passion. Certainly, concerned with the consequences of his being discovered, Justino Mayta Carazo had fled the prosecutor, who did not believe it necessary to denounce him because of that. His fear was also normal.

The prosecutor made the necessary copies and placed them in their respective envelopes. He sent them with the satisfaction of a job well done. He thought about his mother. She would be proud of him. He thought about Edith. In the turmoil of the case, he had forgotten to seek her out during the past week. He ought to stop by the restaurant. He suddenly felt his appetite return.

THURSDAY, APRIL 6 / SUNDAY, APRIL 9

"First of all, I want you to know we are very proud of you, Prosecutor Chacaltana. And that the Armed Forces of this Nation count on your Tireless Efforts on behalf of Law and Order."

It seemed to Prosecutor Chacaltana that all those words were spoken in capital letters, like the certificates, not to mention the medals and flags, covering the walls of Commander Carrión's office behind his immense desk chair. While a lieutenant served two cups of *mate,* Chacaltana noticed that the commander looked taller from the small armchair where the prosecutor had been seated.

"Thank you, Señor."

"I must confess we had our doubts as to whether civil justice could contend with a case of this kind. If you don't mind my saying so, not all bureaucrats are prepared to understand what goes on here. Those from Lima, even less so."

"I am from Ayacucho, Señor."

"I know. And that too fills us with pride."

Prosecutor Chacaltana wondered what one had to do to be from a place. What made him more from Ayacucho than from Lima, where he had always lived? He thought his place was where his roots and affections were. And Ayacucho was fine. And getting better.

The weeks following the presentation of his report had been unexpectedly pleasant. Suddenly Associate District Prosecutor Félix Chacaltana Saldívar seemed to have been promoted. He stopped receiving a subordinate's assignments, and even Judge

Briceño sent his congratulations in writing on the speed and efficiency with which he had resolved the question of Quinua without needing to alarm the public. The day after he closed the case, he received his new typewriter and enough carbon paper to make the copies he needed for all his cases. Even his dreams had become serene, a curtain of peace closing over his nightmares about fire. And at the end of the week, the commander had sent for him. It was unusual for the commander to meet with functionaries, and even more unusual for him to invite them to his office. The prosecutor felt content, but he did not want to take advantage of his position:

"I believe the entity that should really be thanked for its investigation is the National Police, which gave constant indications of efficiency and commitment . . ."

"You are an example of humility, Señor Prosecutor. Captain Pacheco has already informed me that this case would not have moved forward if it had not been for your decisiveness and courage."

"Thank you, Señor."

The commander leaned back in his chair and drank a little *mate*. He seemed relaxed. He did not look as menacing as he had the first time. The prosecutor attributed this to the fact that they were gaining confidence in each other. The commander continued:

"The majority of these cases are never resolved. Often proceedings are not even opened because nobody demands it. But it is always better to have everything archived and organized legally. Our best weapon is doing things well, don't you agree?"

"Of course, Señor."

Feeling authorized to do so, the prosecutor also took a sip of *mate*. He thought of Edith. He had not wanted to go to her restaurant with the bandage on his neck; he had not wanted her to see his injury. He did stop by one morning to say hello. She had welcomed him with her brilliant smile. He had promised to return and walked out backward so she would not see his wound. But that morning he had removed the bandage. And the scar did not look bad. Perhaps he ought to stop by when he left the commander's office so she would not think he was an opportunist. And to celebrate.

"That is precisely why I wanted to see you," the commander continued. "Now the time has come for us to concentrate on the elections. We need trustworthy people who believe in legality, and in Peru, to face the great challenges of the twenty-first century."

"I will be delighted to do whatever I can, Commander."

"As I am that you'll collaborate with us. But first I'd like to ask a few questions."

The commander took a folder from his desk. It was a thick file filled with papers and some photographs. The prosecutor recognized the documents. It was his work file, though it looked much thicker than a normal work dossier. The commander put on his glasses and turned several pages. He stopped at one:

"It says here that you personally requested your transfer to Ayacucho."

"That is correct, Señor. I wanted to return home."

"You left here after the death of your mother, is that so?"

"Yes, it is. I went to live with her sister, who resided in Lima."

"How did your mother die? Was she . . . a victim of terrorism?"

"No, Señor. She died . . . years before the start of all that . . ."

A dark mass agitated his memory. He tried to go on without trembling:

"She died in a fire. I was nine."

For the first time, the commander gave signs of having an emotion.

"I'm sorry," he said.

"It is all right, Señor. She will always be alive . . . in my heart."

"And your father?"

"I never knew him, Señor. I never asked about him. In a sense, I never had a father."

There was a photograph in his memory. His mother with a man, smiling. He looked white, perhaps a Limenian. It was in his mother's room, on the bureau. No. It was not there anymore. It never had been there.

"It also says that you're married."

"Yes, Señor."

"I don't think we've seen Señora Chacaltana here."

Félix Chacaltana Saldívar felt uncomfortable. He remembered a cup with no coffee, an empty space in bed, the absence of a voice at the bathroom door in the morning.

"There is no Señora Chacaltana anymore, Señor."

"Did she pass away too?"

"No, no! She simply left. A little over a year ago. She said I . . . had no ambition. Then I requested my transfer."

He wondered why he had said that to Commander Carrión. He had not asked for so many details.

"Not having ambitions is a good thing," the military man replied. "There are more than enough ambitions here. Children?"

With his glasses bent over the folder, the commander looked back and forth from his papers to the prosecutor, who seemed to grow smaller in his chair.

"No. I believe that was another reason she left."

"That doesn't constitute grounds for divorce."

"I did not ask for one. I thought that . . . there was no need. I did not want to marry again. Ever. Excuse me, Señor. Am I authorized to ask why . . . ?"

He did not want to say more. The commander removed his glasses and gave him a father's smile. What probably was a father's smile, at least.

"I'm sorry to ask you these personal questions. Believe me, they're necessary. But I don't need to know any more. I think you're perfect for the work we need. You have no family, and so you can travel. Further, you're a man who loves his home and respects the family, an honorable man."

The kind of man who dies with no survivors, thought Chacaltana. He asked himself who would smooth his sheets after he died.

"Will it be necessary to travel, Señor?"

"You'll see, Chacaltana. The elections are on Sunday and we need qualified personnel committed to the defense of democracy. Do you understand?"

He did not understand anything.

"Yes, Señor."

"In the villages that will be visited by reporters we'll need electoral prosecutors we can trust."

Chacaltana reviewed mentally the electoral laws and the statutes of the Ministry of Justice. He found a contradiction.

"Commander, the electoral prosecutors do not belong to the Ministry of Justice. They are functionaries of the National Election Board or the National Office of Electoral Processes . . ."

"Yes, of course. But we don't want to get involved in titles and words. That's for the politicians. After all, a prosecutor is a prosecutor, Chacaltana, for whatever his country requires of him. And you are perfectly qualified."

"It is a great honor . . . I do not know if I have time to take the corresponding training course or prepare myself . . . Besides, I have to speak to my superiors . . ."

"We have confidence in your ability, Chacaltana, forget about training courses. I'll attend to all the details: you can take a paid leave for granted, and don't worry about bureaucratic obstacles. The high command of the armed forces will take care of all the paperwork."

The commander took out another file. Inside was a signed accreditation as an electoral prosecutor with Chacaltana's photograph, some money for travel expenses, bus tickets, a booklet on electoral legislation, and other papers. Chacaltana felt like a priv-ileged individual.

"It is an honor that you have thought of me to . . ."

"You absolutely deserve it, Prosecutor Chacaltana."

"Where will you send me, and when?"

"To Yawarmayo. Your bus leaves in two hours."

"That soon?"

"The nation has no time to lose, Señor Prosecutor. And the elections are on Sunday. Any questions?"

"No, Señor."

"You can leave, then. I hope this is the start of a promising ca-reer, Chacaltana."

"Thank you, Señor."

He left the building with a quiver of emotion in his jaw. For the first time in many years he felt euphoria. He wiped the perspira-tion from his brow with his handkerchief. At last, his work was being recognized. He felt he had to share his success with some-one before he took the bus. Almost unconsciously, he found him-self at El Huamanguino. He greeted the waitress with a big smile.

"I bought some *mate* for you. And today there's a spicy *puca*," she greeted him in return.

"I did not come in for lunch. I . . ."

"The tables are for eating lunch. If you don't have lunch, you can't sit down."

"Bring me one, then."

He waited the prescribed length of time, longing to speak. A soap opera was playing on television, and a woman was weeping copiously for her man. This time, on the plate Edith served him, there were cracklings, a pig's foot, and warm potatoes.

"I am being sent on a trip," Chacaltana said proudly.

"Really?"

"Yes, yes. I did some good work. And I have been appointed to supervise the elections."

"Congratulations! That deserves a little glass of *chicha*."

"No thanks. I don't drink."

Still, she poured him a glass of sweetish, dark red liquid.

"You don't have any vices, do you? Your wife must be happy . . ."

"I don't have a wife, either."

"Ah. Are you going to try the *puca*?"

"It is just . . . just that I do not have time . . . but listen . . . When I get back . . . in a few days . . . I think I will be invited to some galas. High command affairs. Important engagements."

"And you won't come back anymore?"

She seemed sad when she said that. The prosecutor was encouraged to see that.

"On the contrary. I will come back. But I would also like . . . well . . ."

"Yes?"

"The authorities attend these events with their wives, their spouses."

"Of course."

"I would like to take you, Edith. If you would not mind."

He realized that now he, like Edith, was using the formal *usted*. She laughed.

"Me? Why me?"

"Because . . . because I do not know anyone else in the city . . ."

Now she frowned. He tried to rectify his mistake. He had lost the habit of saying certain things, but perhaps he had never said them.

". . . anyone as pretty as you."

"Now you're talking foolishness!"

"It is not foolishness."

"Are you going to eat or not?"

"It will not be possible. I am leaving now. I have to hurry and pack my bag. Will you go with me when I get back? Will you?"

She turned as red as a chili pepper. She laughed. She seemed to laugh at everything. And when she laughed, she appeared to shine. On television, the villainess of a soap opera threatened her rival because she was trying to take her man.

"Yes," said Edith.

The prosecutor felt that his day was complete. That his year in Ayacucho was complete. He felt happy as he stood up. Surreptitiously, he left the money for lunch on the table so she could not refuse it. He approached her to say good-bye. She was holding a rag. He opened his arms. Then he lowered them. He did not want to take liberties. He held out his hand. She took it. He said:

"Thank you. We will see each other soon."

She nodded and seemed embarrassed. The prosecutor hurried to his house.

"Mamacita, I don't have time to explain everything to you, but I'm happy." He took the underwear he found and put it in an old sports bag. "You'll see how well everything turns out, Mamacita. I'm sure that after this they'll pay me more and I'll buy you new pajamas, you'll see." He packed ties and shirts and took two jackets and a pair of trousers from their hangers. "And then Edith. You'll meet Edith. You'll like her. Good-bye, Mamacita."

He closed the doors and windows and hurried to the terminal. Halfway there he stopped and went back. He found the house keys in the suitcase and went in. He hurried to the back room, took a photograph of his mother when she was very young, posing for the camera in an embroidered dress. He noted carefully that there was no photograph of her smiling with a man who looked as if he came from Lima. He confirmed it. He kissed the photograph, put it in his bag, and went out again.

There was mass confusion in the terminal. The four o'clock bus was full, and his name did not appear on the reservation list. A woman with four children shouted at him for trying to steal her place. The driver ordered him to get off and stop causing trouble. Finally, after fifteen minutes of arguing, a surly employee of

the bus line asked him to take the night bus. Prosecutor Chacaltana thought he would have more time to eat with Edith and say
good-bye to his mother, and he agreed. Then it occurred to him
that if the military people saw him outside the station, they would
think he was abandoning his post, and so he sat down to wait
seven and a half hours for the departure of the next bus after making certain that this time his name was on the reservation list. He
used the time to review the electoral laws and the regulations for
observers.

That night, his bus left only fifteen minutes late. Another sign
that Ayacucho was moving with a firm step toward the future.
Yawarmayo was seven hours to the northeast, toward Ceja de
Selva. Although the darkness did not allow him to see anything
through the window, the prosecutor made the trip guessing at the
unpaved roads the bus was rattling along, the flat-top hills that
surrounded the city, and then the progressive change of the countryside from dry sierra to the wild green of the mountains. From
time to time he dozed off and was awakened by the jolting of the
bus over some pothole. A moment came when he did not know
if he was asleep or awake, if his happiness was real or dreamed.

Until he opened his eyes.

The bus had stopped. He looked at the time: four in the morning. He saw the fogged-over glass in the windows. He wiped his
so he could look outside. Lashed by the wind, the rain fell hori-
zontally. It was hailing. He noticed that the person sitting beside
him had disappeared, along with a good number of other people.
The lights were turned on and the bus was half empty, occupied
only by women with sleep-crusted eyes. From the door, someone,
perhaps the driver, was shouting:

"They said for all the men to get out! Only the men!"

The prosecutor did not understand what was going on. He
tried to catch a glimpse of something in the darkness outside. The
interior lights of the bus allowed him to make out only some

hooded silhouettes and the projection of bayonets slung over their shoulders.

He had a rapid memory of the last time he had visited Ayacucho to see his mother before he came back to live there. It had been in the early eighties, when he was a recent appointee to the ministry. Before it reached the city, his bus had been stopped by a terrorist group that had asked all the passengers for their identification. The military men wearing civilian clothes ate their papers. The prosecutor also swallowed his identity card from the Ministry of Justice. The terrorists had taken all the electoral identification cards from the bus and then torn them up in front of the owners:

"You no longer have documents," they shouted, "you can't vote, you're not citizens! Long Live the People's War! Long Live the Communist Party of Peru! Long Live President Gonzalo!"

They made everyone repeat their slogans and left after stealing the little the passengers had with them. They wore balaclavas and carried weapons. Like those who had stopped the bus now.

At the door, the driver called again for the men. Two others who had been asleep walked to the door, rubbing their eyes. The prosecutor wondered if he ought to swallow his identification as an election inspector. But the document was encased in plastic. It was impossible to chew. He hid it under his seat and stood up. He walked to the door. When he climbed down, a man in a black balaclava began to shove him and drag him to the line that the others were forming. The rain fell like a whip against his face. He verified with relief that the man pushing him wore the green uniform of the army. He tried to identify himself:

"I am Associate District Prosecutor Félix . . . !"

The other man responded with a shove. When his turn came, a sergeant faced him, also hidden behind his balaclava. Between the mask, the rain, the fear, and his dreadful Spanish, he could hardly be heard when he shouted:

"shhhhwmmmmyrccccrrrt!"

Accustomed to roundups, the prosecutor took out his national ID. The other man scrutinized it carefully and looked the functionary in the face. It was difficult to read the expression in his eyes. He returned the document and shouted again:

"shhhhwmmmmmyyrrrrccccrt!"

The prosecutor showed him his military identification. The other man nodded and returned it to him. The first man pushed him back to the bus. The prosecutor climbed in, feeling calmer, thinking that his safety was guaranteed day and night by the armed forces.

The bus started moving again and Félix Chacaltana Saldívar retrieved his election identification and went back to sleep. He woke in the light of dawn with the image of a river running down the slopes of the hill the vehicle was descending. As the rain clouds dispersed, the sky recovered its comforting brightness.

The bus stopped at seven in the morning. The prosecutor climbed down and picked up his suitcase from among the sacks of potatoes and cages of animals. There was no terminal. The bus had stopped only to drop him off. The town was two hours away. It was the same length of time until the public offices opened. The prosecutor was supposed to go to the National Office for Electoral Processes and to the National Police. He thought he would arrive in time to have breakfast. He walked along a dusty road, his baggage on his back. He crossed the river and two hills that turned out to be higher than they had seemed at first. He would stop periodically to make certain his suit was not wrinkling or becoming covered with dust.

Finally he reached a valley. In the distance he could see Yawarmayo. As he walked toward it, he thought he saw someone at the entrance to the village. He thought the appropriate authorities were waiting for him. He waved his hand. The person did not return his greeting. When he came to the edge of the village, no one was there. No business was open. No certainty that there was a single restaurant or a single person. Not even a piece of asphalt. Only streetlights in the distance, still on in spite of the daylight.

The streetlights seemed to be decorated with wreaths or some kind of colored decoration. He thought it was probably a remnant of Carnival or an ornament for Holy Week. He dusted off his trousers and readjusted the hanger with his suit, his file, and his sports bag. He continued walking.

Only when he stood at the foot of the streetlights could he see up close what hung from them. Dogs. Some strangled, others beheaded, some slit open, their internal organs dribbling from their bellies. He dropped the bag. A chill ran down his spine. The dogs wore signs that said: "This is how traitors die," or "Death to turncoats."

The prosecutor felt dizzy. He had to lean against a wall. He felt alone in the middle of the street where, he noticed again, no one else was walking this morning.

He was still there half an hour later. He had failed to find an open door. He did not know what to do, where to go. Until the first shadows appeared on the street. They belonged to police, walking heavily and carrying ladders to take down the dogs. They leaned their ladders against the streetlights and removed the animals following an established order, more bored than repelled, as if accustomed to a routine of canine corpses. Félix Chacaltana thought about the commander's words. Don't look for horses where there are only dogs.

The detail, as far as Chacaltana could tell, consisted of five skinny men with puffy eyes. None could have been more than nineteen. None looked at him. He walked up to one, who was holding a ladder:

"Good morning. I am looking for Lieutenant Aramayo."

The policeman gave him a suspicious look. The prosecutor showed him his identification. A dog fell down, almost on his head. A cloud of flies followed it. Behind him, the prosecutor heard a commanding voice:

"Damn it, Yupanqui. Don't throw around the dogs that spatter. Motherfucker . . ."

The prosecutor deduced it was the voice he was looking for. He turned and saw an officer of about fifty whose belly overflowed the khaki shirt of his uniform.

"Lieutenant Aramayo?"

"What?"

"I am the election inspec . . ."

"Shit, Gonza! With your hands! Like a man!"

Two lampposts further on, a policeman was trying to push the dog with a wire to see if it would fall without his needing to touch it. With a resigned face, he let go of the wire and continued untying the animal with both hands. The prosecutor tried to make himself heard:

"I have come with regard to observing the election."

The lieutenant seemed to have just noticed the visitor. He looked him up and down with a distrustful expression.

"To do what?"

"To obser . . ."

"Papers. I want to see your papers."

He showed him his identification card. The lieutenant studied it on both sides. He asked:

"Who sent you?"

"The National Office of Pro . . ."

"Who sent you, Chacaltana?"

"Commander Carrión, Señor."

The policeman's eyes lost their contempt.

"Come have breakfast with me. And you, Yupanqui! I want to see this all cleaned up within the hour."

The local police station had only one floor, divided into two separate spaces. In one, waiting on a desk, were two tamales, a little cheese, bread, and café con leche. The mattresses where the police had spent the night were still on the floor. The lieutenant divided everything in half and invited the prosecutor to sit down. Once again, Chacaltana was not hungry. But the lieutenant ate like a horse.

"This . . . Is it normal?" asked the prosecutor.

"What? The tamales?"

"The dogs."

"Well, that depends, Señor Prosecutor. What's normal for you?" he asked, swallowing a piece of bread he had dipped into the milk.

"I did not know that . . . Sendero was still operating in the area."

The lieutenant's laugh went down the wrong way when he took a swallow from the cup.

"Operating? Ha, ha. Yes, a little. More like fucking us up."

"I have come to attend to the subject of the elections. You know that observers will be coming and . . ."

"It would be fine, damn it, if somebody would observe something around here."

He laughed again, displaying a piece of half-chewed tamale. The prosecutor interrupted. Recently he had not really been able to know exactly what his conversations were about. He tended to lose the thread. He tried to recapitulate:

"And how long ago did you verify this outbreak?"

"What outbreak? This isn't an outbreak, Chacaltana. This has been going on for twenty years."

"Ah."

"They offered me a transfer to Lima and the rank of captain if I agreed to suck the dick of some commander in the capital. But I refused. So they sent me here to fuck me over. Here where you see me, Señor Prosecutor, the most honest thing in this shit village is me. Are you going to eat that?"

"No, you go ahead."

The lieutenant finished off the second tamale in almost one mouthful. The prosecutor continued to obtain information:

"And haven't you asked for reinforcements?"

"Reinforcements? Of course. We also asked for a swimming pool and a couple of whores. And here we are."

The lieutenant lit a cigarette and belched. The prosecutor thought this was how he had concluded the conversation regarding the subject of Sendero.

"Well. With respect to the electoral program, I have been reviewing the law. I wonder if the tables have been prepared for the prisoners to vote and the . . ."

"The prisoners? You want us to let out the prisoners? Forget about them. They don't vote."

"But the electoral law specifies that . . ."

"Ha, ha. You tell Commander Carrión that you want to take the lousy terrorists out of their cells. You'll see where your electoral law gets you."

"Permit me to read to you what it says in this regard in this brochure; I have a copy for you . . ."

The lieutenant did not even look at the brochure. He stared into the visitor's eyes and adopted an attitude of seriousness and resolve.

"No, permit me to tell you what you're going to do. In the first place, I don't want you to go around attracting attention. No official vehicles or distinctive markings: absolutely no jackets, uniforms, or insignias. You'll make yourself a target and I'll be blamed for it. The last inspector who came through here thought he was a real tough guy. He came in making a lot of noise. He drove a car with polarized glass and two bodyguards. The damn terrorists saw polarized glass and said, 'Whoever's inside that car has to be important.' Seventy bullet holes from FAL rifles in the body of the car. And hand grenades. The bodyguards, dead. The inspector, seriously wounded, I think he lost an eye. He never came back here, the dumb prick."

Félix Chacaltana Saldívar could not think of anything to say. He looked at the remains of the tamales, a piece of chicken skin hanging from one of them. He sat looking at the lieutenant as he finished his cigarette. The lieutenant did not say anything else either. In any case, the prosecutor put the brochure on the table for him before he stood up.

"Well," said Chacaltana, "having made the necessary introductions, it is time to look for a place to stay."

"Find Yupanqui, the guy taking care of the dogs. He's a prick, but he'll help you."

Once more the prosecutor put his bag and the hanger with his suit on his back. When he was almost at the door he heard the police officer's voice again:

"Listen, Chacaltana, do you know . . . I mean, are you aware of where they've sent you?"

"This is the village of Yawarmayo, isn't it?"

The lieutenant smiled and exhaled the last mouthful of smoke.

"No, Chacaltana. This is hell. In the name of the National Police, I bid you welcome."

He found Yupanqui a few streets away. He had just finished putting all the dogs in large black bags meant for humans, which the rest of the men dragged away to incinerate outside the village. Yupanqui explained to the prosecutor that there were no hotels in the village, but he could stay in a private house, where they were always glad to take in a visitor. He took him the length of the village to a house that was a little larger than the rest. When they reached the entrance, he shouted:

"Teodoroooo!"

And he pounded on the door while he continued to shout. At times he would turn to the prosecutor with an apologetic smile. When Chacaltana was about to suggest that perhaps no one was in the house, the door opened, revealing a man with his wife and three children. It was as if they were all petrified, looking at the visitor. The policeman said something to them in Quechua. The man responded. The policeman raised his voice. The man shook his head vehemently. Then the entire family responded by shouting, all at the same time, but the policeman shouted back and took out his club. The prosecutor thought he was going to hit them, but he did nothing more than shake the weapon in the air in a menacing way. In the middle of the argument, he turned to Chacaltana and said in Spanish:

"Do you have dough?"

"What?"

"I said do you have money? Any amount."

The prosecutor took two one-sol coins from his pocket. When they saw the coins, the members of the family suddenly fell silent. The policeman gave them the coins and indicated to Chacaltana with a gesture to put his things down on the floor. Then he left. A place to stay had been arranged.

Chacaltana remained standing, facing his hosts. There was no place to sit. Only a pot on a pile of burned wood and some weavings on the floor.

"Good morning," he said, "I hope I am not causing you any inconvenience."

The others looked at him and said nothing.

"May I leave my things here? They are not in the way? . . . Would you happen to know where the National Office of Electoral Processes is located? No?"

He tried to think of where he could hang his suit. A cross hung from the only nail in the house, and he did not want to take that down, out of respect for the family. He folded the suit as carefully as he could and left it in a corner, on top of the bag. Then he said good-bye respectfully and went out to proceed with his labors. No one said good-bye to him.

The National Office of Electoral Processes, according to what he was told at the police station, had been set up in the house of Johnatan Cahuide Alosilla, who owned some fields under cultivation outside the village and would be in charge of the polls and the counting of votes. As soon as he entered, the Associate District Prosecutor saw a poster of the president, like Captain Pacheco's, but bigger. He introduced himself. Johnatan Cahuide, the head and sole functionary in the office, greeted him pleasantly. He assured him that everything was ready for the elections. The prosecutor remarked:

"Excuse me, Johnatan, but we will have to take down that photograph of the president. The law stipulates that electoral advertising is forbidden two days prior to the ninth of April."

"That? That's not electoral advertising. This is an office of the state. It's a photograph of the chief."

"But the chief is a candidate."

"Yes, but there he doesn't appear as a candidate but as the president."

The Associate District Prosecutor—now Provisional Electoral Inspector—promised himself that he would review the relevant clause in the law.

"How many people are going to vote here?"

"Three thousand. Tables will be set up in public school Alberto Fujimori Fujimori."

"That is the name of the school?"

"That's right. The president founded it almost in person."

"And do you think we could cover over that name? The law stipulates that electoral advertis . . ."

"That isn't electoral advertising. That's the name of the school."

"Of course. Has the training been completed for the poll workers?"

"Yes." Johnatan Cahuide showed him the registration sheets. "The authority approved two people."

"Two?"

"That's right, Señor Chacaltana. Most of the poll workers have to travel by mule for two days and bring their family because they don't have anybody to leave them with. And so they don't come. We're lucky if they come on Sunday to vote."

"But are they informed about the candidates . . . about their rights?"

"The army boys . . ."

"The personnel of the armed forces." The prosecutor corrected him.

"That's right. They go up there and tell the campesinos they have the technology to know who it is they vote for. That is, they'll all vote for the president."

"But that is . . . that is false and illegal."

"Well, yes. They're bastards, those army boys," replied Cahuide with a mischievous smile.

The prosecutor wondered if the official himself had completed the relevant training courses.

After eating lunch with him, the prosecutor went alone to see the school where the voting tables would be set up. The Alberto Fujimori Fujimori School was small, with two classrooms and a courtyard in the center of the building. There would be two tables in each of the classrooms. He made some notes, but in general he thought the location was adequate. He returned to the street. Since the dogs had been taken down, the village was coming back to life. Campesinos walked by with their tools, and women went down to the river to wash clothes. At times the prosecutor managed to forget about the morning's episode.

When he turned a corner, he bent down to tie his shoe. Out of the corner of his eye he thought he saw the same figure he had glimpsed in the distance as he was approaching the village. A campesino, closer to him now. He turned to look at him, but no one was there. He thought perhaps he had only imagined it. He walked to the corner. Only women were out on the dirt streets of the village.

That night, he returned to his lodgings. When he walked in,

the entire family was crowded into the back room, not speaking. The prosecutor's things were where he had left them, intact, beside a woolen blanket.

"Good evening," he said.

No one answered. He did not know if he should undress in front of all of them. He found it embarrassing. He took off his jacket, tie, and shoes and lay down in his place. It did not take him long to fall asleep. He was very tired. In his dream, his mother was crossing the mountains in the cold sierra night, between enormous bonfires that lit up the countryside. She walked with a sweet gaze and a smile filled with peace. She seemed to be approaching her son, who waited for her with open arms. But when she was very close, she turned away. She began to walk toward one of the fires. Félix Chacaltana ran to stop her, but it was as if he were running in place, not moving forward, while she approached the flames without losing her smile. He shouted, but she did not turn around. He felt tears rolling down his cheeks as she walked closer to the bonfire. It seemed to him that his tears were made of blood, like the tears of the Virgins. When she placed her foot on the flames, he heard the explosion.

He sat up in a sweat, his heart pounding. He supposed the explosion had been part of his dream. He turned toward Teodoro's family, who had not moved from their corner. When his eyes grew accustomed to the darkness, he saw them looking at him, crouching in their corner like frightened cats. They were not asleep. Perhaps they had not been asleep all night. He wondered if he might have called out during his nightmare.

He turned toward the wall and tried to go back to sleep, but he heard noises, echoes, distant shouts. The sound seemed to come from everywhere but remain distant. He tried to understand what they were saying. The tone of voice, the timbre, sounded familiar. Then he heard the second explosion.

The family had not moved from their place.

The prosecutor stood up:

"What is going on?"

No one in the family replied. Huddled together, this time they gave him the impression of a nest of snakes. The prosecutor began to lose patience.

"What is going on?" he shouted, picking Teodoro up by his shirt. He felt the man's alcohol breath on his face. Teodoro began to speak in Quechua. His voice sounded like a lament, as if he were apologizing for something.

"Talk to me in Spanish, damn it! What is going on?"

The quiet lament continued. His wife began to cry. So did the children. Félix Chacaltana let Teodoro go and went to the window. There was fire in the mountains. Lights. The image of his mother was fixed for a moment in his mind. He opened the door and went out. Now he heard the shouts more clearly. They were the same shouts he had heard many years before, on the bus that had taken him to Ayacucho. Slogans. Enormous bonfires topped the mountains at each of the cardinal points. Up above, just behind him, the figure of the hammer and sickle outlined in fire hovered in the night over the village.

The prosecutor ran to the police station. No one passed him in the street. Not even any people looking out the windows. The houses seemed like mass graves, blind, mute, and deaf to what was happening in the hills. He reached the station and pounded on the door:

"Aramayooooo! Aramayoooo! Open up!"

No response. Only howls from the hills. Long Live. The Communist Party of Peru. President Gonzalo. They seemed to grow louder and surround him, suffocate him. He wondered if the terrorists would come down and where he would hide if they did. He beat on the door again. Finally it opened. The five policemen and the lieutenant were inside. The lieutenant's shirt was open and he held a bottle of *pisco* in his hand. The prosecutor walked in shouting:

"It's an attack, Aramayo! They're all around us!"

"We've seen it, Señor Prosecutor," the police officer responded calmly.

His passivity hurt Chacaltana more than the shouts from the mountains. He grabbed him by the front of his open shirt, just as he had grabbed Teodoro earlier.

"And what are you going to do! Answer me! What are you going to do!"

The lieutenant did not lose his serenity:

"Chacaltana, let me go or I'll smash your face in."

Chacaltana became conscious of his hysteria. He released the police officer, who offered him some *pisco*. The rest of the police were on the floor, petrified, holding their weapons. They were so young. Outside, the shouts continued. The hammer and sickle were reflected in the window of the police station. Chacaltana took a drink, returned the bottle, and collapsed into a chair. He apologized. Aramayo walked slowly and deliberately to the window.

"The show's ending," he said. "They'll start to quiet down."

Chacaltana buried his face in his hands.

"Is it always like this?"

The lieutenant took another drink from the bottle.

"No. They're pretty calm today."

One of the police burrowed beneath his sheets. Aramayo said:

"I don't think there are any dogs today. At the most some graffiti. Tomorrow we'll have to go out early to wash them off. Your buddy Carrión is coming to visit us."

Chacaltana felt a flash of relief. He said:

"Excellent. The high command should know what is going on . . ."

Aramayo interrupted him with a laugh.

It seemed to Chacaltana that his laughter was morbid. With his back still turned to the prosecutor, the lieutenant said:

"The high command doesn't see us, Señor Chacaltana. We're invisible. Besides, the command doesn't command. Lima's in charge here. And the guys in Lima won't find out there's a war until they get a bullet up the ass."

He walked heavily to his mattress. He put the bottle to one side and lay down.

"But don't worry, Señor Chacaltana," he said with a yawn. "They'll realize it sooner or later. And they'll come, naturally they'll come. They'll send commissions, members of congress, reporters, military men, they'll put up a monument to peace . . . The only problem is that for this to happen, we'll all have to be dead."

No one else spoke that night. The prosecutor curled up beside the door. He did not have the strength to move. He heard the volume and frequency of the shouts gradually diminish. Hours later, when sleep overcame him, the hammer and sickle were still burning in the mountains.

He opened his eyes. The police station was empty and the sun filtered in through a window over his head. His body ached, and he needed a shower. He rubbed his face to get rid of the sleep in his eyes and shake off his drowsiness. As he was trying to comb his hair, trying to see his reflection in the window, Aramayo came in:

"Good morning, Señor Prosecutor, did you sleep well?"

"It's not funny, Aramayo."

Aramayo laughed, displaying his missing canines.

"Carrión's in the village. Poor Yupanqui had to climb the mountain to get rid of the remains of the bonfires. The others have spent the morning painting the walls. You'll see how pretty the village looks. Like Miami."

He handed him a basin of cold water so he could wash his face. The prosecutor missed his toothbrush. He said:

"I have to speak with the commander."

"The elections are tomorrow, so you won't have to spend many more bad nights. You can go back tomorrow night with the military transports carrying the urns."

The prosecutor dried his face with his shirtsleeves and said:

"I am not the point. Somebody has to tell the commander what happened. Before they kill everybody."

He looked at himself again in the window glass. He seemed a little more presentable. He walked to the door. Before he stepped outside, the lieutenant blocked his way with his arm.

"Don't tell them anything, Señor Prosecutor."

"What? You need reinforcements. You have to immediately ask for . . ."

"There's nothing to ask for."

"Let me try. The commander will understand."

"The security of this village is my responsibility. If you complain to the high command you'll make a problem for me."

"You already have a problem, Lieutenant. Didn't you notice that last night?"

He had to push away the lieutenant's arm in order to pass. The lieutenant looked as if he were about to speak again, but the prosecutor's eyes dissuaded him. As he was going out, Chacaltana heard the policeman's voice behind him.

"You don't know what a real problem is, Chacaltana."

He did not want to hear him. When he walked out, he recognized the smell of fresh paint on some facades. Under the yellow, green, and white colors, the slogans in red paint were still visible. He looked for Carrión. His presence was felt in the number of armed soldiers walking the streets and standing guard at the corners. On the square were the jeep and the truck that had brought them here. Wherever the greatest density of soldiers was, that is where Carrión would be. And the greatest density of soldiers was in the National Office of Electoral Processes, where the commander was talking to Johnatan Cahuide. The prosecutor did not need to identify himself to approach them, and they greeted him with the remains of a breakfast and smiles. Carrión said in good humor:

"Dear little Chacaltita, my trustworthy man! Have some coffee."

"Commander, we have to talk, Señor."

"Of course. Johnatan Cahuide has been telling me about your efficient and meticulous work . . ."

"We have to talk about that too. I have reason to believe that certain prominent members of the military in this zone are preparing a fraud behind your back."

Carrión's smile suddenly froze. Cahuide gulped. The commander put his cup down on the table and shifted in his chair.

"What did you say?"

"It is true. Perhaps a training course in democratic values is necessary for members of the armed forces who . . ."

"There you go again with training courses, Chacaltana, what a pest you are."

"There are indications that . . ."

"Chacaltana . . ."

"The soldiers are campaigning in favor of the government . . ."

"Chacaltana . . ."

"Even coercing the vote of the peasants . . ."

"Chacaltana, damn it!"

They were silent. Carrión got up from his chair. Johnatan Cahuide looked at the prosecutor in terror. Carrión shouted at two soldiers in the doorway to get out, and he closed the door. Then he sat down. He let a few seconds go by while he calmed down.

"What are you doing, Chacaltana?"

"Presenting an oral report, Señor," the prosecutor replied, surprised at the question.

At that moment the door opened and in came the functionary with the sky-blue tie whom Chacaltana had seen next to Carrión on the day of the parade. He was wearing the same tie and a badly pressed suit. The commander introduced him as Dr. Carlos Martín Eléspuru. With almost no voice, the man gave a somber greeting and sat in another chair. He poured some coffee. The prosecutor was still standing. Carrión had regained his composure and brought the newcomer up to date.

"Prosecutor Chacaltana has been . . . alarmed at the alleged behavior of some soldiers in the elections. Where did you get this information, Señor Prosecutor?"

Chacaltana looked at Cahuide, who gave him a pleading glance.

"Statements by the residents, Señor," he replied.

Carrión put on that paternal smile again.

"Please, my dear Chacaltana, the residents can't even speak Spanish. I don't know what they tried to tell you, but don't worry about it."

"Excuse me, Señor, but in elections . . ."

Carrión interrupted him:

"The people here don't give a shit about the elections, don't you know that?"

"But the fact is that according to the law . . ."

"What law? There's no law here. Do you think you're in Lima? Please . . ."

Carrión sat down. The man in the sky-blue tie passed him a paper, which the commander read calmly. They began to talk quietly. They seemed to have forgotten about the prosecutor. Chacaltana cleared his throat. They continued, not looking at him. Chacaltana had the impression that they did not want to look at anything else either, not anything that was real, not anything standing beside them, clearing his throat. He made a decision and spoke:

"Permit me to say, in that case, I do not understand what my function here is."

Eléspuru and the commander stopped reviewing their papers.

Carrión looked as if he were summoning all his patience in order to respond:

"Reporters will come to fuck over the armed forces. You have come to defend us. You can go."

Eléspuru, as if he were thinking of something else, poured himself more coffee. He looked at the prosecutor. Chacaltana decided to say everything once and for all, make a last-ditch stand, the way heroes did:

"There is something else, Señor. Last night . . . a terrorist outbreak was verified in the zone."

Eléspuru seemed to pay attention for the first time. Now he looked at the commander, who smiled with certainty.

"An outbreak. Don't exaggerate, Señor Prosecutor. We know there are a few clowns around here who set off fireworks, but they're harmless."

"But the fact . . ."

"Did they kill anyone?"

"No, Señor."

"Did they hurt anyone? Did they occupy any houses?"

"No, Señor."

"Threats? Disappearances? Damage to private property?"

"No, Señor!"

"Were you afraid?"

He had not expected that question. In his mind, he had not wanted to formulate that word. He hated that word. He found himself obliged to acknowledge mentally that nothing serious had occurred last night.

"A little, Señor."

The commander laughed louder. Eléspuru smiled as well.

"Don't worry, Señor Prosecutor. We'll leave a patrol here for any eventuality. Don't let yourself be intimidated. We sent you because you're a brave man. There may be a subversive or two left, but essentially we've gotten rid of them."

Eléspuru looked at his watch and signaled to the commander, who stood up.

"It's time to bring this meeting to an end. We'll see each other in Ayacucho."

The prosecutor shook the hand that the commander offered him. It was a hard hand that squeezed his as if it were going to break it. Looking into his eyes, the commander said:

"Tomorrow is a very important day, Chacaltana. Don't betray our trust. That won't be good for you."

"Yes, Señor. I am sorry, Señor."

Eléspuru said good-bye with a gesture, not offering his hand or letting his voice be heard. When they went out, Johnatan Cahuide said:

"Now you're really fucked, brother."

They spent the rest of the morning making final preparations for the elections the next day and arranging the material in the school. At noon they went to have lunch at Cahuide's house. As they were eating a corn and pork stew, the prosecutor asked:

"How were you appointed to the position in the National Office?"

"I was head of the president's campaign in the region. Then they called me for this job."

Head of the campaign. Yet Cahuide was so sincere that the prosecutor did not even want to hold the regulations in one hand and remind him of his duties. "Cahuide, do you realize that you are a huge walking electoral irregularity? You should be proscribed."

"Are you going to proscribe me?"

No. He was not going to proscribe him. In the past twenty-four hours, the things that needed to be proscribed had grown dim.

"I will not do anything to you, Cahuide. And I could not. I am not here to avoid fraud, am I?"

"I'm not going to commit any fraud. And I know these things

aren't seen very often, Chacaltana. But no one has organized any-thing. There's no need."

"There's no need?"

Johnatan Cahuide offered him more stew. He served himself as well.

"Félix, eight years ago, if I went out they would kill me. Not now. The damn terrorists killed my mother, they killed my brother, they took away my sister so the damn soldiers could kill her afterward. Since the president took office, they haven't killed me or anybody else in my family. You want me to vote for some-body else? I don't understand. Why?"

Why? Chacaltana thought that the question did not appear in the manuals, the brochures, or the regulations. He himself had never formulated it. He thought that one should believe in order to build a better country. The person who asks does not believe, he doubts. One does not get very far with doubts. Doubting is easy. Like killing.

The two men sat in silence, thinking, until they heard the sound of motors and shouts in the streets. The sounds were much closer than the ones the night before. Cahuide closed the window. Cha-caltana tried to look out.

"What is going on now?"

"Don't get involved, Félix, don't fuck around anymore."

"I have to know what is going on."

"Félix. Félix!"

The prosecutor went outside, followed by Cahuide. In the streets, young men were running, pursued by soldiers hitting them with their clubs. The jeep and the truck had closed off the two principal exits from the village. Patrols of soldiers with rifles were stationed around the perimeter. At times they fired into the air. The pursuers did not carry firearms but they did have clubs that they used to beat the fugitives who had fallen to the ground. Far-ther away, two soldiers broke down the door to a house. The wails of a woman were heard inside. A few minutes later, they came out with two boys about fifteen years old. They had twisted their arms against their backs and kicked them to make them walk.

"What is all this?"

Cahuide tried to make Chacaltana go back inside the house.

"Let it go, forget it."

"How can I forget it? What are they doing?"

"Don't be an asshole, Félix. This is a press."

"Press conscriptions are illegal . . ."

"Félix, stop thinking like a law book. Did you want security measures? Now you have security measures."

"Where are they taking them?"

"They'll perform their obligatory military service. And that's it. They'll have work. There's nothing to do here. What do you want them to do? Study engineering? It's better for them. Félix. Félix!"

Chacaltana was hurrying to the police station. He remembered that electoral law prohibited detentions twenty-four hours before elections. He knew he would seem ridiculous, but he could not think of anything else to do.

Near the station was another military truck, toward which soldiers were shoving the young men they had hunted down. If they refused to climb in they were forced to by blows with a club to the face, stomach, and legs, until they had been hurt so much they could not refuse anymore. Three meters from the door of the police station, two soldiers stopped the prosecutor. He tried to resist and showed his identification, but they barred his way. One put his hand on his revolver. The prosecutor calmed down. He said he would wait. Farther away, in the dust raised by the skirmish, he could see the commander with the official in the sky-blue tie and Lieutenant Aramayo. Eléspuru seemed unperturbed and looked away while the commander shouted something at the lieutenant. The police officer looked down and nodded, appearing repentant, like a little boy admitting his mistakes, while the furious commander criticized him. After shouting several times in the confusion of the roundup, the commander walked away. He gestured to an officer, and his jeep drove up. He and Eléspuru climbed in. Only then did the prosecutor manage to break through and approach the vehicle.

"Commander! Commander!"

Carrión sighed. The prosecutor's presence exhausted him. He barely looked at him as he came up sweating, covered with dust in spite of his handkerchief and the clean, pressed suit he had worn for the occasion. Chacaltana panted as he spoke to him:

"Commander, this operation must be stopped. This is . . . it is . . ."

"Take it easy, little Chacaltita. We're picking up people without documents and those wanted for questioning. So they won't frighten you."

The commander laughed, but not like a father. The jeep drove away, and behind it came the two military trucks filled with villagers and soldiers. In five minutes, even the town's dust was still, as if it were dead. A few meters away, the lieutenant followed on foot, chewing on his rage. The prosecutor tried to talk to him; he wanted to offer his cooperation in finding help at the highest level. But when he reached his side, the lieutenant spat in his face:

"Chacaltana, you motherfucker! I told you not to say anything! You're very brave. Huh? You want to be a hero? All right, then. We'll see who helps you when you come crying in the night. Your fucking mother will protect you. It's really easy to be a hero here."

"But Lieutenant! The correct thing was . . ."

He could not go on. The continuation of that sentence was obscure, perhaps impossible. The lieutenant turned his back and went into the station. Chacaltana looked for a glance of support in the other policemen, who responded to him by dispersing, one by one.

The prosecutor returned to Cahuide's house. He knocked on the door several times, but no one answered. He went up to the window. Cahuide was there. From the interior he looked back at him with a mixture of pity and fear. The prosecutor did not insist further. He crossed the half-deserted village feeling the distrustful looks piercing him from the windows. They did not answer the door in the house where he was staying either. This time, he did not even go up to the window. He continued walking until he reached the countryside.

As he walked, not doing anything, he thought about Edith. He missed her, her silver tooth, her table settings in a restaurant where he had never eaten. He thought that, for the moment, Edith was the only person waiting for him. He did not know if he should tell his mamacita about it. He stopped at a stream to skip stones the way his mother had taught him when he was little. He became sad. The way things were going, Edith would have no good reason to respect him. He would not be promoted. Perhaps that was better. If Yawarmayo was a promotion, he preferred to stay where he was. He took a deep breath. For a few moments he enjoyed the peaceful light and air in the countryside. He forgot where he was.

As the ripples disappeared on the surface of the water, images reappeared as geometrical reflections: a branch, a projecting rock, a tree trunk. The images of the countryside seemed small, insignificant, so different from the disordered, foul-smelling visions of the capital. Among the decomposing figures he saw the face of his ex-wife. Perhaps she was right, perhaps Chacaltana had never had any ambition and the best thing for him was to sit in an office in Ayacucho and write reports and prepare recitations of Chocano. Ayacucho was a city you could walk all around on foot; he liked that. And it was a safe place, sheltered from roundups and bombs in the night. His ex-wife's face was turning into his mother's face. The prosecutor would have liked to do something to make her proud of him.

He decided to go back. He took a last look at the stream. The figures continued to play on the water. One of them was becoming fixed as the surface settled down. At first it appeared to be a strange bird, but then the prosecutor looked more carefully. That was not a bird. It was the shadow of a man.

He did not look up. He wanted it to be nothing but an optical illusion. He had already seen enough in the past two days. His eyes were not accustomed to seeing so much. Slowly, he moved toward a spot where the stream narrowed. He jumped to the other side in order to leave. The shadow did not move. He took a few more steps. About two hundred meters away, two campesinos, each with a machete, approached on foot. He wanted to call to them but was afraid of provoking the shadow. He thought about moving closer to them. After a few more steps, he could not control himself any longer. He shouted:

"Excuse me! Señores!"

The campesinos turned toward him. They made a move toward him but then seemed to think better of it. They stopped. The prosecutor greeted them from a distance. They looked at him with curiosity. They said something to each other. He smiled at them. They resumed walking and moved away, speeding up the pace. The prosecutor wanted to follow them or call to them. It occurred to him to identify himself as an electoral observer. He realized that the best thing was to let them go. He listened to the sound of the branches as they moved. He tried to hurry too and reach the village. At that moment, he was hit on the back of his neck by a falling body.

The blow made him lose his footing. He almost fell in the water but held on to the branches of a bush and managed to crawl out from under the pressure of the man, who rolled a few meters and stood to throw himself at the prosecutor. Félix Chacaltana recognized the dwarfish silhouette he had seen the day before at the entrance to the village. As he tried to stand, he caught a glimpse of the old shoes with the tire soles and, above all, the same red *chullo* cap he had pursued days before in Quinua. Justino Mayta Carazo did not give him time for more before he leaped at his throat.

The prosecutor managed to hit him in the face with a branch and run toward the steep rocks. He found himself facing a stone wall. Justino came bounding after him. Chacaltana began to climb. He felt that each rock pierced his hands, that his feet were slipping on the falling rocks. He did not want to look down. He simply let himself be hit in the face by some of the stones dislodged from the wall as he advanced. The rocks ended in an embankment. The prosecutor took several seconds to reach the top, feeling that at any moment he might slip down to the bottom. But spreading before him at the top was a large ascending plain surrounded by another stone wall. He ran. Justino had climbed up very quickly but seemed to be limping slightly after his fall from the tree. The prosecutor sensed that Justino was gaining on him, but the slopes of the rise were too steep for him to descend any of them. He veered to the right, trying to reach the next wall in order to climb it. He tried and failed, feeling that altitude and exhaustion were overwhelming him. His heart was pounding, he needed air. He reached the slope and clung to the rocks with his hands. He began to climb, supporting himself on occasional projections. He hung from a cornice and pushed himself forward. The vertical surface seemed impossible to conquer. He spent his last breath in the effort and managed to rest on a rock and move a meter up from the ground. When he tried to take the second step, his foot rested on a false projection and slipped. The rock he was on gave way, and his entire body hurtled toward the ground in a small avalanche of stone and soil. He fell on his back.

The campesino picked him up from the ground and pinned him against the wall. Chacaltana had time to think of something to say:

"Señor Justino Mayta Carazo, you are liable for contempt and lack of respect for the law."

The other man shouted something in Quechua. His voice betrayed more fear than courage.

"I assure you that I will bring you up on charges for your assault on my physical well-being . . ."

Frothing at the mouth and sputtering in Quechua, Justino began to squeeze Chacaltana's neck. For a moment, the prosecutor had the sensation that the air was escaping his lungs, his throat, his mouth trying to articulate that he was merely an electoral official. The campesino did not let him go; on the contrary, the pressure became harder and harder. With his right hand, the prosecutor felt around him until he found a stone, lifted it, and with all his remaining strength hit Mayta in the face. The campesino fell to the ground. The prosecutor needed to catch his breath before he got to his feet. He gulped in all the air he could. He felt as if his chest were about to explode. Off to one side, Justino raised his hand to his face. The prosecutor was afraid he would attack him again. But the campesino in the red *chullo* began to sob gently.

"I ain't done nothin', Your Worship! My brother's the one. He does everythin'! Everythin'!"

"Honestly, I don't understand what you're saying," the prosecutor managed to say.

"My brother, it's my brother, Your Worship! I ain't done nothin'!"

Chacaltana understood he could not say much else in Spanish. He understood what Pacheco and Carrión were alluding to when they said these people do not speak, do not know how to communicate, it was as if they were dead. The campesino did not crawl on the ground. His body was square and solid from working the land, but he did not seem to threaten him now, it was more as if he were pleading. He had moved from aggressor to victim to unmoving man. The prosecutor thought that now he would let himself be taken away peacefully, having understood the principle of authority that made him subordinate to the Ministry of Justice. He wanted to take the campesino someplace where there was a translator. His testimony had to be something important. He thought about calling Ayacucho. But he would not find a telephone he could use. The campesino sank progressively lower and lower until he was sobbing at his feet. The prosecutor decided he would oblige the police to receive him and take his statement. They could not refuse. Sobbing and whimpering, the campesino kept talking about his brother. The prosecutor wondered to which jurisdiction Yawarmayo belonged and which judge he would appear before. Suddenly a new possibility occurred to him that he had not considered previously. Or, rather, he had assimilated the obvious. He looked again at the wretched man groveling on the ground. He asked him:

"You were . . . you were going to kill me, weren't you?"

It had never occurred to him that someone might want to kill him. Perhaps Justino had intended to burn him and make his body disappear. He felt the impulse to hit him, to kick him until he bled. He realized he could not. Justino's pathetic suffering had disarmed him. The killer had been consumed in his own attack. Without warning, the wretch lamenting on the ground filled him with fear and pity, just like the mountains, the stream, the clean, dry air.

He grabbed Justino by the back of the collar and lifted him up.

"I am going to take you to the police station. The lieutenant will have to listen to me now."

But Justino had other plans. As soon as he found himself on his feet, he gave the prosecutor a surprise blow in the stomach with his elbow. Chacaltana had the air knocked out of him, and could not respond. Justino punched him in the face and then kicked him to the ground. In one jump he was on the stone wall and began climbing again. Down below, Associate District Prosecutor Félix Chacaltana Saldívar could do nothing but watch him disappear up the mountain while he tried to warn him that now he was committing the crime of assault and flight.

As soon as he recovered his strength, he returned to the village, thinking that the police still had time to pursue Justino. In the station he found Yupanqui and Gonza playing cards. He went in short of breath, panting. He had a bruise on his face.

"I found a terrorist. I have his name and description. I know where he has gone. We can still catch him."

Yupanqui threw a card on the table. He did not even turn to look at him.

"Go away, Señor Prosecutor."

"Listen to me! He is a killer. I can prove it."

Yupanqui had won the hand. He smiled and picked up the cards from the table, along with three one-sol coins. Gonza made an annoyed face. Yupanqui said:

"If you don't leave, we'll have to throw you out."

"I want to speak to Lieutenant Aramayo."

Yupanqui shuffled and began a new deal. Chacaltana insisted:

"I want to speak to . . . !"

"Don't raise your voice, Señor Prosecutor. The lieutenant isn't here. As far as you're concerned, he won't ever be here again."

The prosecutor left the police station. He walked to Teodoro's house, looking at the mountains, as if he might discover Justino's hiding place there. He understood that the enemy was like the hills: mute, immobile, mimetic, part of the landscape.

He had to knock a long time on Teodoro's door before they let him in. His things were still there but opened and disturbed. His suit was wrinkled and thrown under his bag. He was surprised to realize he did not care. Teodoro said something to him in Quechua. It did not sound like a lament. It sounded like a reproach. The prosecutor took a couple of coins from his pocket and put them on the ground, in front of the owner of the house, who said nothing else to him. Chacaltana appreciated the progress he had made in his ability to communicate. He lay down right away, in his clothes and shoes. Although it was just getting dark, he felt exhausted.

At night, he again heard the sound of bombs and saw the light of fires coming from the mountains. He did not turn to look at Teodoro's family, and he did not try to leave the house. The first shouted slogans seemed like the echoes of an old movie. Then, everything seemed like the background music to a nightmare.

He thought about his mother.

That night, he did not dream.

The next morning, he got up early to go to his work. At seven, police were still painting the facades of houses. No dogs had been hung that night either.

Voting began at eight, with six members absent from the table and a total ignorance of electoral procedures on the part of the other six. Some voters were recruited for the tables, and they tried to get out of their duties until two soldiers energetically asked them to sit down. No agent or representative of any political party was accredited. The entire police force guaranteed security in the area surrounding the Alberto Fujimori Fujimori School.

At about noon, a civil service helicopter appeared in the sky and landed at one end of the village, making the plants shake in the wind from the rotors. The villagers enjoyed watching it descend. The children went up to play with it. Civilian journalists climbed out with cameras and tape recorders. They were all white, Limenians or gringos. They looked very serious. They greeted the police and Johnatan Cahuide and went into the school to verify the normal process of the elections. They spoke with the two table members who knew Spanish. The table members asked if the president had come in their helicopter.

While the journalists were taking the usual photographs, a reporter went out to the square and lit a cigarette. One of the villagers came up and asked him for one. And then another villager. And another. In five minutes, the reporter was surrounded by villagers who wanted to smoke. Prosecutor Chacaltana considered it appropriate to move them away. He approached and asked them to allow the reporter to do his work in peace. When they were alone, the reporter said:

"It seems that everything's calm, doesn't it?"

"It seems so, yes."

"There haven't been any problems the last few days? This zone is completely pacified?"

Prosecutor Chacaltana thought that perhaps it was his last opportunity to tell what he knew. The reporter could publish it and let them know about it in Lima, where they surely would become indignant and send a commission or demand an investigation. Perhaps the commander simply was not aware of what was going on, but if the order came from Lima, he would make new inquiries. He wanted to talk about Justino Mayta Carazo and his mysterious appearances and disappearances, about the hammers and sickles burning in the Yawarmayo night, about the shouts from the hills and the shouts of the young men from the village when they were shut inside the military trucks. He opened his mouth and began:

"Well, sometimes . . ."

"Sometimes you'd think there had never been a war here."

The voice that interrupted him belonged to Lieutenant Aramayo, who had come up to them wearing an amiable, satisfied smile.

"As you can see," the police officer continued: "A good climate, a peaceful countryside, people freely exercising their right to vote . . . What else could you ask for?"

"You're right," said the journalist. "I ought to move here. Lima can be an unbearable city."

"I can well imagine," Aramayo replied with complicity. "Can I steal a cigarette from you?"

Prosecutor Chacaltana did not say anything for the next twenty minutes. Then the journalists returned to their helicopter and left. The winds did not allow planes to fly into Ayacucho after two in the afternoon. They were running out of time. From the ground, the prosecutor could see the cameras taking their final shots from the helicopter windows.

At four o'clock, when it was time for the voting tables to close, polls had called the opposition candidate the victor. Some gave him more than half the votes. At the National Office and among the military a strange uneasiness was spreading. Until five o'clock, Cahuide kept receiving phone calls and preparing the packages for the military truck. Officers ran back and forth, indifferent to the prosecutor, who had been transformed into one more object that had to be taken away, one that made no noise.

Four hours later, the truck was approaching Ayacucho with the radio playing. Filtering through the salsa and vallenatos that the soldiers had tuned in to for the trip was the announcement of the first official returns. All the polls had been wrong. The real winner was the president. It was about to be decided if there would be a recount. The soldiers driving the truck tuned in to music. Politics bored them.

That night, two hours before they arrived, Chacaltana remembered Aramayo's words when he said that in Lima they did not want to see what happened in his village. But he also asked himself why (lately he was asking himself why a good deal) the lieutenant had refused to inform the journalists and the high command. He thought that perhaps he was ashamed. It is not easy to admit that you are dead.

MONDAY, APRIL 10 / FRIDAY, APRIL 14

On the eighth day of March, 1990, on the occasion of a Senderista assault in which the electrical installations of the region were blown up, a detachment of armed forces appeared at the domicile of the Mayta Carazo family, located at Calle Sucre 14 in the municipality of Quinua, to carry out the appropriate inquiries with regard to Edwin Mayta Carazo, twenty-three years old, suspected of terrorism.

For reasons of security the detachment, led by Lieutenant Alfredo Cáceres Salazar of the Army of Peru, exercised its prerogatives and broke into the aforementioned residence with no prior warning, its members hooded and armed with antisubversive H&K combat rifles, at which time they discovered in the interior the family composed of the abovementioned suspect, his brother Justino, and the mother of both men, Señora Nélida Carazo widow of Mayta, who were spending the night at that site.

After the detachment entered the site, the two Mayta men, who offered no resistance, were subdued with the butts of the weapons for the sake of greater security, while Nélida Carazo widow of Mayta was removed from the area of operations by two troops who, according to their statement, proceeded to place her against an exterior wall of the property at gunpoint, under orders that she not shout or attract the attention of the neighbors. The request of the troops seems to have been heeded, since none of the residents of Calle Sucre has confirmed the version of the family, the majority of the residents stating that they were absent from the location, having left for various reasons related to work from midnight until three in the morning, the hours in which these events were recorded.

By order of Lieutenant Cáceres Salazar, the troops proceeded to inspect the domicile in search of explosives or Senderista propaganda. After examining the interior of the property and removing the appropriate pieces of furniture without success, they interrogated both suspects, who denied having knowledge of any terrorist activity. Lieutenant Cáceres maintained, however, that terrorists who do not appear to be terrorists are those who present the greatest danger to national security, and consequently proceeded to seize the possessions of the family and arrest the suspect Edwin Mayta Carazo, leaving his brother at large in consideration of the fact that in the course of the interrogation the femur of his left leg had been fractured.

At the same time, the mother of both men, Nélida Carazo widow of Mayta, attempted to enter the house and join her offspring, at which point the troops of the Army of Peru found themselves obliged to detain her to prevent her from interfering with the official duties of the authorities. Subsequently, as indicated by the relevant medical certificate, Nélida Carazo suffered a fractured jaw with complications in the parietal osseous structure.

The operation having been concluded, the suspect Edwin Mayta Carazo was driven in a military vehicle to the military base of Vischongo, several hours distant from the location of his domicile, where the required interrogation was carried out.

The detainee denied repeatedly the existence of any connection to Sendero Luminoso, which convinced Lieutenant Cáceres Salazar even more firmly of the aforesaid detainee's involvement in the abovementioned assaults because, as he has stated, it is characteristic of terrorists to always deny their participation in these events. As a consequence, and in order to increase the cooperation of the detainee, he put into effect an investigative technique that consists of tying the suspect's hands behind his back and letting him hang suspended from the ceiling by the wrists until the pain permits him to proceed to confess his criminal acts.

Subsequently, since the detainee insisted on denying his culpability, the military troops then undertook another technique of inquiry designated by the name "submarine," which practically submerges the head of the suspect in a basin of water several times until he is close to drowning, causing his receptivity to the questions of the authorities to increase significantly. According to the statement of the authorities, the detainee continued to deny his participation in Sendero Luminoso. Despite the efforts of the authorities, cooperation on the part of the aforementioned suspect was not achieved.

Finally, in the face of the repeated denials of Edwin Mayta Carazo, Lieutenant Cáceres Salazar decided to give him his freedom, leading to the aforesaid detainee's release from prison the following day as indicated in the daily records of the military base at Vischongo.

The whereabouts of Edwin Mayta Carazo have been unknown since that day. His family denies having seen him again, as do his friends and acquaintances, all of which reinforces the thesis that he has become clandestine as a member of a terrorist group, in all probability Sendero Luminoso, despite the fact that terrorism was eradicated and continues to be eradicated at the present time, April, 2000.

In an oral declaration to this official, his brother Justino admitted that Edwin engaged in dangerous acts, the nature of which he did not specify. As a consequence, this Office of the Prosecutor recommends the appearance in person in the shortest feasible time of Edwin Mayta Carazo, Justino Mayta Carazo, and Lieutenant of the Army of Peru Alfredo Cáceres Salazar to make their statements to the court.

Associate District Prosecutor Félix Chacaltana Saldívar read the report for the tenth time. This time he did not throw it in the wastebasket. But he did hesitate. He was concerned. The syntax was not bad, though perhaps too direct, showing little respect for traditional forms. For example, the ages of those involved were missing, since he had not been able to verify them in every case. But the prosecutor was concerned above all that it would be inadmissible to reopen the case, and as Captain Pacheco had told him, the police would not be the competent body to handle a problem of terrorism.

He thought again of Justino's words: My brother's the one. He does everything. Perhaps the prosecutor should have let those words go without thinking more about the matter, perhaps he should have closed his eyes, should have forgotten. Forgetting is always good. But the entire subject of Yawarmayo was a buzzing that vibrated in his ears, the back of his neck, his stomach.

Besides, he did not do anything all day. Since his return from Yawarmayo, he had turned into a ghost at the Ministry of Justice. No one had assigned him work, not even an indictment, not even a memorandum. His pending assignments had been transferred to other offices during his trip. The Provincial Prosecutor had given him no explanation. His colleagues claimed not to know anything. For his part, Judge Briceño called him aside to congratulate him in a complicitous way for being Commander Carrión's new protégé. He said that was the best way to buy a

Datsun. The prosecutor thanked him for his congratulations without really understanding them, and hours later, in the bathroom, he heard the same judge at the urinal telling someone that Carrión had ordered the prosecutor isolated because he no longer had any confidence in him. "That prick is fucked," the judge concluded. More than the ordinary intrigues of the Judiciary, what bothered Prosecutor Chacaltana was the feeling of emptiness. For twenty years he had been busy writing every morning and now, suddenly, he felt useless, as if his office were an ice bubble isolating him from the world. He was bored.

He spent the rest of Monday trying to toss a wad of paper into a wastebasket. From time to time, like a flash of lightning, memories of Yawarmayo and Justino came to him. My brother's the one. He does everything. What brother? What does he do?

He did not want to have lunch with Edith, at least for as long as he had no sign of support or promotion from his superiors. When he said good-bye, he had told her that he would invite her to the gala affairs of his superiors. He would not go back now and say he could invite her only to an empty office. He felt he had let her down, that she would feel disappointed by him. He had lunch in his office, some rice and chicken he had brought from home in a thermos, and the rest of the afternoon was devoted to his wad of paper. That night he slept badly.

Tuesday passed in exactly the same way. Along with his nightmares he suffered sweating and nausea.

On Wednesday the 12th, at 9:35, spurred by the need to do something, he decided to look for Justino's name in the archives of the Office of the Prosecutor. Perhaps he would find something useful or at least give the impression of doing something useful. He had learned that really working was not as important as letting it be seen that one was working. In Lima, where there was more competition, Prosecutor Chacaltana would remain in his office until ten at night even if he had nothing to do in order to

avoid the impression that he was going home too early. In Ayacucho, functionaries left earlier than that, but gossip circulates
more quickly in small cities.

The archive was in an enormous windowless room filled with
papers and boxes, and the prosecutor spent the entire morning
there meticulously searching through records of the 1980s and
old, dusty documents for the family name Mayta Carazo. It did
not appear in the archives filed according to name. And it was
not among the files of those detained or interrogated with regard
to either terrorism or common crimes. When he was about to give
up, the prosecutor decided to look through the dismissed or dis-
continued cases. He found the complaint filed by Edwin's mother
after his disappearance. This must be the same woman who
opened the door for him in Quinua on the day he was attacked.
The charges had been withdrawn the day following the complaint
without the signature of the complainant.

With the information contained in the complaint, he could
check Edwin Mayta Carazo's background in the section called
"rejected complaints." Finally, he found a clue: Justino's brother
had once been accused of being a member of a cell operating near
Huanta, but nothing had ever been proved. After some electric
towers were blown up, a resident denounced two other members
of that same cell. Then, the army began to look for Edwin to
make the relevant inquiries.

Along with the information on Edwin were the names of the
other members of the cell. Two of them, a man and a woman,
were listed as "whereabouts unknown." The third, Hernán Durango González, alias Comrade Alonso, was serving a life sentence in the Huamanga maximum security prison.

The prosecutor became aware that never in his life had he
spoken to a terrorist. He wondered if it would be valid for the investigation, if he could accept as evidence the statements of a
criminal who had committed treason. Then he realized it did not

matter. There was no evidence because there would be no trial or judgment. The subject of the corpse in Quinua was a closed case.

That afternoon, after eating lunch at a stand on the street, he went to the prison. He thought that if he at least closed the case for himself, his nightmares would end.

The Huamanga maximum security prison, with a capacity for three hundred prisoners, housed 974 criminals, 252 of them accused of terrorism or treason. As he approached it on foot, the prosecutor looked at the walls ten meters high and the watch towers at the corners. There was nothing and no one within a radius of three kilometers, so that any movement in the surrounding area could be detected before it got too close to the compound. In order to go in it was necessary to show one's national identity document at the gate and have one's name entered into the visitors' book. After the first checkpoint, a long corridor led to another sentry post.

"Today isn't a visiting day," the second guard said dryly.

The prosecutor showed his identification. The guard did not even look at it.

"Today isn't a visiting day," he repeated.

The prosecutor wanted to avoid unnecessary arguments. He thanked him for his kindness, picked up his document, and proceeded to retrace his steps. He was already outside when he remembered that he had nothing to do in his office. He thought about his wad of paper. And his nightmares. He turned around and showed his identification to the first guard, who wrote his name again in the visitors' book without saying anything. He walked down the corridor again until he reached the second checkpoint.

"Call the functionary of the National Penal Institute. I am on official business," he said with self-assurance.

The guard grunted, as if annoyed that someone would disturb the peace of his Wednesday. Then he stated:

"There is no functionary."

"Excuse me, but this is a penal institution, and there has to be a functionary from the . . ."

"Colonel Olazábal is in charge here. If you want to talk to him, you have to send a fax to the General Administration of Police requesting an interview."

The police. Chacaltana knew that in many penitentiaries there were police instead of functionaries because the Institute could not manage all the prisons and had no troops at its disposal. He felt frustrated as he left again, thinking that perhaps he could also send a written request to the National Penal Institute asking for an official introduction. Then he reconsidered: his case was closed, and the system of inter-institutional message delivery had not proved to be very efficient. In spite of his confidence in institutions, he understood that no one would give him an appointment. But he also understood suddenly that he himself was also an institutional authority. He was already outside the prison when, resolute and sure of himself, he turned, showed his national identity document once more to the silent guard at the entrance, and appeared again before the second guard, who seemed drowsy as he grumbled something, perhaps his surprise at seeing one human being so many times in a single day at his post.

"Call Colonel Olazábal," the prosecutor demanded. "I will talk to him."

"He's busy. I already told you that you have to send a fax to . . ."

"Then give me your name and badge number, because I will mention you in the fax."

Suddenly, the policeman seemed to regain consciousness. He no longer looked drowsy.

"Excuse me?" he asked slyly.

"Give me your information. I will make a note of it here and inform Colonel Olazábal of your negligence in assisting in investigations ordered by your superiors."

The guard was not grumbling now. Instead, he grew pale and leaned to one side to hide his badge:

"Well no, Chief," he said, and the prosecutor noted that he had called him "Chief" and that his voice was gentler now, "that isn't really true, I have my orders and I follow them. It isn't my intention to neglect . . ."

"I am not interested in your stories, Corporal. I told you to give me your information or I will communicate with Colonel Olazábal. It is up to you."

The prosecutor asked himself if he could be accused of lack of respect for authority, insubordination, and treason. He told himself he could. But suddenly he felt he was doing something different, perhaps something important, at least for himself, for his dreams. The guard looked at him with hatred, rose to his feet, and left his box. He returned fifteen minutes later. With a gesture he ordered the prosecutor to follow him.

Between the entrance building and the cell blocks there was a second ten-meter-high wall, topped by barbed wire and separated from the exterior wall by a no-man's-land, a gray, arid area eight meters wide where anything that moved would be shot.

To Associate District Prosecutor Félix Chacaltana Saldívar, the no-man's-land seemed like a first inkling of hell: the prisoners locked behind the grating in the cell blocks, their empty stares that had not seen anything but those walls for ten years, the police playing cards and wiping the sweat from their necks with the braid on their uniforms, knowing it was not a good place for promotions and eventually spitting out their frustration at the prison bars. For sixteen prisoners serving life sentences in Cell Block E, that enclosed, desertlike strip of land was simply the last piece of relatively free terrain they saw, so they would never forget that they would never walk there again.

They climbed to the second floor of the entrance building. Standing at the top of the stairs, a tall white officer, almost completely bald though still a young man, was waiting for them. He had on a short-sleeved shirt and wore no kepi. The entrance guard gave him a military salute. He called him Colonel Olazábal. The colonel asked him to leave them alone.

"We haven't been informed of any inspection," he said disagreeably.

The prosecutor attempted to justify himself:

"I am not here for a formal inspection. This is only a personal interview."

"I'll reply only with my superior present."

"It is not with you but with the inmate Hernán Durango González."

"I cannot allow unscheduled interviews without orders."

The prosecutor felt he was confronting the final wall before he could see his suspect. He observed the pistol in the officer's belt. He thought that he had a weapon too. A double-edged one. He said:

"Call Commander Carrión, please. He will tell you what you want to know. But he will not like anyone questioning his authority."

Then, it was as if the colonel had stumbled. His eyes opened wide, his entire body became rigid except for his face, which he tried to stretch into a smile. The prosecutor continued:

"I am working on an investigation for the General Staff regarding . . ."

"You don't need to tell me," the colonel interrupted. "Our doors are always open for the commander."

Suddenly everything moved faster. The officer left him with a corporal who would take him to his prisoner. With him as an escort, Prosecutor Chacaltana crossed the no-man's-land and entered the cell blocks. They turned to the right. In the long corridor of Cell Block E they passed faces filled with stony, silent curiosity. They reached a central courtyard. Between the barred windows were worktables for handicrafts and manual labor. Some of the prisoners were putting together fishing rods or making weights.

"Did you come to review our sentences?" asked one of the inmates.

"Quiet, damn it," said the corporal. And then he shouted into the air: "Hernán Durango González!"

The prosecutor saw the prisoners' eyes all fixed on him, on this man in a suit and tie who could be anybody, perhaps a lawyer. The prosecutor took charge of the situation. He felt pity. He said to the prisoner:

"I will try to have your case reviewed, Señor. Write down your information for me and I . . ."

The policeman laughed. He said to the prosecutor:

"You're going to have this motherfucker's case reviewed? It's already been reviewed. He killed twenty-six people, six of them children. All in cold blood. Review it again if you want."

The prisoner did not respond. He seemed annoyed. Another prisoner approached from the other side, thin, dark, with icy eyes. He said he was Hernán Durango González. He preferred to be called Comrade Alonso. The corporal handcuffed the terrorist and led him and the prosecutor to an office in the entrance tower, where they could have a private interview. While the prosecutor was thinking about what to say, the prisoner spoke first:

"If you're going to ask me for information in exchange for benefits, forget it. I won't betray my comrades."

The prosecutor had expected this direct challenge, the first effort at intimidation. He had read about it in countless manuals on the antisubversive war. He had also read the response. The scorn:

"Your comrades? Your comrades no longer exist. They have all been arrested. The war is over. Don't you watch TV?"

Hernán Durango González fixed his eyes on the prosecutor's. He seemed to be engaged in a staring contest, waiting for the prosecutor to look away. The terrorist's gaze was difficult to endure. No. He could not lower his eyes. He tried to conceal the shudder that ran down his spine. He had been told that confessed terrorists attempt to impose themselves in interrogations, that one needs a good deal of personality or a couple of blows from a rifle butt to tame them. He tried to look up, to not be deflected from the subject:

"I have come to ask you about a person you knew: Edwin Mayta Carazo."

The terrorist seemed surprised.

"Edwin?"

"Do you remember him?"

Durango seemed to recover and try to gain ground.

"I won't talk."

"He was arrested ten years ago. After he was freed, he became clandestine."

"Freed?" In spite of the smile formed by his mouth, the terrorist maintained a gaze as steely as a bullet. "He was arrested by Dog Cáceres. Cáceres didn't free suspects. He got rid of them."

The prosecutor remembered that he should not debate, that he should not be provoked into an argument. He had been told that terrorists argued only to confuse, lied as a distraction, shielded themselves behind the worst falsehoods. The prosecutor took a deep breath:

"That is what is recorded in our files."

"And are Cáceres's murders recorded in your files? And when he said better a hundred dead half-breeds than one live terrorist?"

"I have not come to talk about . . ."

"Do you know how Lieutenant Cáceres trained his men? He made them kill dogs and eat their intestines. The soldier who refused would be treated like a dog. That's how Cáceres got his name. Where's that in your files?"

The prosecutor remembered the dogs in Yawarmayo. He tried

to move the memory out of his head, as if he were brushing away a mosquito.

"Señor Durango, for now I will ask the questions."

"Ah, right. I forgot who it is you work for."

The prosecutor wanted a glass of water. He realized there was nothing in the office where they were, no water, no bathroom, no decorations, only two chairs and a desk that was clear except for a small Peruvian flag. He decided to continue:

"According to the information at my disposal, it is not clear if Edwin in fact was part of Sendero Luminoso or if he was innocent . . ."

"And you? Are you innocent? And your superiors? Are they innocent?"

"I am referring to the question of whether he committed acts of terrorism . . ."

"Of course. If you kill with homemade bombs it's called terrorism, and if you kill with machine guns and hunger it's called defense. It's a play on words, isn't it? Do you know what the difference is? We don't care. But your people piss with fear without a machine gun in their hands."

Almost twenty years earlier, in his last visit to Ayacucho, the prosecutor had flown over the area surrounding Huanta in a military helicopter as the guest of a captain who was a friend of his. In the middle of the flight over the mountains, a man came out of the scrub carrying a red flag. He was alone. And he ran in front of the helicopter displaying the flag. The soldier on board had a Star machine gun. He fired. The pilot changed the route to follow the flag. The man on the ground ran as fast as he could, pursued by bursts of machine-gun fire that tried to catch him before he returned to the underbrush. But when the man with the flag reached some bushes that could have hidden him, he kept on, he continued running through the clearings with his flag like red spittle in the face of the military. He did not hide and went on for hundreds of meters, scorning the natural hiding places along the way and followed by the dust raised by the bullets coming closer and closer to his heels. After five minutes of pursuit, the bullets hit him, first in the legs and then, when he had fallen, in the back and chest as he dedicated his final movements to keeping the flag in the air. The shooter congratulated himself as if he had shot down a bird, and continued firing as he shouted insults at the man down below who would never hear them now.

"Why did he do that?" the prosecutor asked on that occasion. "Why did he let himself be killed that way?"

"To show that he doesn't care about dying," the pilot replied.

Then the helicopter turned back toward the place where the flag had appeared, and riddled the underbrush, the trees, the bends in the river, the plants with bullets. The prosecutor asked again:

"And why are you shooting now at nothing?"

"To see if we hit any of the kids who saw him. That's part of their training. Sendero is full of thirteen-year-old children who get excited when they see these things. Each dead man with a flag like the one we've seen produces ten to twelve assassins ready to do the same thing."

He remembered that episode for a moment before he collected his thoughts and answered Hernán Durango González:

"I will not permit you to compare the troops of the armed forces to . . ."

"There is no comparison. They're the watchdogs for their masters."

"You people are defeated. You no longer exist."

"Are you in the habit of talking to people who don't exist?"

The prosecutor thought about his mother. He hesitated.

"You . . . You are defeated. And let me remind you that you are a prisoner."

"We're there, Señor Prosecutor. We're hunkered down. This

prairie will catch fire, as it has for centuries, when a spark ignites it."

It will catch fire. The phrase made Prosecutor Chacaltana nervous. He repeated to himself that he should not engage in discussions or justify himself. He replied:

"I have come simply to ask you about Edwin Mayta Carazo. Not to listen to your speeches."

The terrorist seemed to relax his gaze for a moment. He looked out the window. The windows in the offices had fewer bars than the ones in the cells. He spoke:

"You ought to visit maximum security prisons once in a while, Señor Prosecutor. Is this the first time you've come to one?"

"Well . . . yes. I previously did not have cases of this . . ."

"You ought to visit the cells. You'd see interesting things. Maybe it would rid you of that mania for distinguishing between terrorists and innocents, as if this were heads or tails."

The prosecutor did not want to say what he said. But he could not avoid it.

"I am afraid I do not understand."

"There's a man in prison for distributing Senderista propaganda, but he's illiterate. Innocent or guilty?"

The prosecutor mentally shuffled through the legal code searching for an answer as he stammered:

"Well, in a technical sense, perhaps . . ."

"Another's in prison for throwing a bomb at a school. But he's retarded. Innocent or guilty? And those who killed under threat of death? According to the law they are innocent. But then, Señor Prosecutor, we all are. Here we all kill under threat of death. That's what the people's war is about."

There were too many questions together. The prosecutor's capacity for looking into regulations collapsed.

"I have limited myself to asking what you know about a suspect."

"And I've limited myself to telling you, Señor Prosecutor."

A silence like a tombstone fell between them. The prosecutor could not think of anything else to ask. He was confused. Perhaps he should not have come to the prison. He was not obtaining any useful information. He had already been warned that to interrogate a Senderista you need cunning, balls, and a club. The prosecutor was very thirsty. When he was about to end the interview, the terrorist asked:

"Now you tell me. How is your mamacita?"

Félix Chacaltana felt each muscle in his body contracting in a heavy, gray nausea. Durango had expressionless eyes, the contemptuous eyes the prosecutor had seen in every dirty terrorist who had been arrested.

"What?"

"I know you keep her memory alive. She died, didn't she?" Durango continued.

"I . . ."

"You were very little, weren't you?"

"How do you know that?" the prosecutor asked, perhaps only to reverse the roles in their encounter. Suddenly, it had seemed that he was the one being interrogated.

"The party has a thousand eyes and a thousand ears," said Durango, smiling with inexpressive eyes fixed on those of the prosecutor. "They're the eyes and ears of the people. It's impossible to lock up and kill all the people, somebody's always there. Like God. Remember that."

Associate District Prosecutor Félix Chacaltana Saldívar felt faint when he left the office, and he had a lump in his throat. Suddenly he felt more than ever that the case of the dead man in Quinua had something to do with him more concretely than he had imagined. He went into a bathroom in the guard building and washed his face. Since there was no toilet paper, he dried himself with his handkerchief while he smoothed the rebellious hairs in his combed-straight-back hairdo. He took a breath. He tried to relax a little. He opened the door and came face-to-face with Colonel Olazábal. He was startled. Olazábal, however, seemed attentive.

"How did it go? Did you get the information you wanted?"

"Yes, more or less . . ."

"You can come back whenever you like."

"No . . . I don't think that will be necessary."

He hoped it would not be necessary.

"Can I offer you something to drink? Coffee? *Mate*?"

"No, thank you. I think I ought to be going now."

"I hope you'll give my regards to Commander Carrión."

"Yes, of course."

The prosecutor began to walk down to the exit. The police colonel was close behind him.

"And communicate to him my desire to support all his initiatives."

"I will do that, yes."

"Señor Prosecutor . . ."

"Yes?"

Associate District Prosecutor Félix Chacaltana Saldívar felt he should stop and face him. It was very difficult for him to do so. He wanted to leave. He was a little sorry he had insisted on the investigation. There are things better left alone and forgotten. There are things that are conjured up when you mention them, words that should not be said. Or thought.

"Do you think . . . Señor Prosecutor . . . that you could speak to Commander Carrión about something?"

"Tell me what it is. I will let him know."

"I've been in a maximum security prison for ten years now. Within the chain of command, I ought to have a better position in the police region. I'd like at least to change my fate. Could you have the commander approve my transfer?"

Now the prosecutor felt that the look on the colonel's face came from a place light years away from his problems. He promised to do what he could and left the building, walking as quickly as he could, almost running, although he maintained the dignity appropriate to an official of his rank. As he crossed the plain that separated the prison from the city, he felt he was being watched. He turned. There was nobody for three kilometers around.

When he returned to the Office of the Prosecutor, he wrote his report.

Now, as the sun was setting, he continued his meticulous revision of the document, asking himself if it was worth sounding the alarm or if there was no alarm to sound or if talking about it would cost him his rank and his job. He understood the reasoning of Lieutenant of the Army of Peru Alfredo Cáceres Salazar and his investigative methodology, but it was not clear to him that Edwin Mayta was a terrorist. Perhaps he was merely thinking too much about the entire case. Perhaps Justino had simply lost his mind after his brother's arrest and thought the prosecutor had something to do with it. In any case, the prosecutor recapitulated, the whole problem is limited to one corpse and has already been resolved, there are plenty of corpses in Ayacucho and it is better not to poke your finger into any in particular because pus is gushing out of all of them. There was no terrorist threat. Terrorism was finished. The rest was nonsense propounded by the terrorists themselves in order to confuse people. He put the report in a drawer, under the pencils and forms for requesting supplies. Then he looked at his watch. It was time to go. He gathered his things and left punctually. He felt strangely nervous. Out on the street the tourists arriving for Holy Week were beginning to give a livelier image to the city. Most came from Lima but there were even some gringos, Spaniards, perhaps a Frenchman or two, the kind who travel through the Andes with backpacks. Prosecutor Chacaltana decided to stop at the restaurant and see Edith and relax a little. Perhaps it was also time to apologize for his absence. He had begun in a very impetuous way with her and then had disappeared. That was not how gentlemen behaved.

In the restaurant, for a change, she was alone. The prosecutor sat in his usual place, but Edith did not seem to be in a very good mood.

"Where have you been eating lunch?" she said. "You don't come here anymore."

"I just have a lot of work. But that does not mean I don't want to."

"Sure, now it seems you're too important to come here. We have stewed tripe. Do you want some?" she asked without enthusiasm, as if he were just another customer in a crowded restaurant. He thought the best thing would be to agree and improve the mood of his hostess. Fifteen minutes later she put the plate down on the table and went to one side, her back turned, to wash glasses. An American sitcom was on television. Two blond girls fought nonsensically over a tall, good-looking boy who did not know which one to choose.

"I even bought a dress for the parties you invited me to," Edith said.

With a gesture she indicated one of the chairs, where a pink lace dress was hanging, covered with embroidered arabesques and decorations. She had kept it there for days to show to the prosecutor when he came in. By now it even smelled of the kitchen. The prosecutor thought it was pretty. And he felt guilty for having made her spend her money. He was not hungry. His eyes moved back and forth between his plate and the young woman, and he did not know where to rest them. He wanted to say that he was very busy, that it was not always possible for him to have lunch, given all his meetings, dinners, and work-related travel. Finally he said:

"I'm not important."

"What did you say?" She stopped and turned around. Her straight hair hung loose over her shoulders, her neck, her forehead.

"I'm not . . . important at all, Edith. I don't have a car. And I won't have one. They won't invite me to the parties for high-placed officials. In fact, I don't think I'm very good at those parties. When I try to speak no one listens. Perhaps it's because I never understand what's going on at parties . . . I don't think I even understand what's going on in this city or this country. Recently I've thought I don't understand anything about anything. And not understanding frightens me."

It embarrassed him to tell a woman that he was afraid. But the words had left his mouth automatically, like a burst of bullets from a Star machine gun in a helicopter flying overhead. He had not been able to control them. That, perhaps, was what frightened him most. Knowing there was something he could not control, something inside him, terrified him more than what he could not control on the outside, what depended on whispers in bathrooms, on galas, on offices decorated with flags, on parades. He had lowered his eyes to his untouched plate, so that only the scent of Edith's cheap shampoo made him aware that she had approached him and almost touched him.

"Nobody understands anything here," she said. "But nobody admits it, either. You have to be brave to say that."

"I'm a coward, Edith. I always have been."

Suddenly the prosecutor felt warmth on his hand, an agreeable, protective feeling he had not experienced for a long time. It took him a few seconds to move his eyes away from the tripe and discover it was Edith's hand that had interlaced fingers with his. They remained silent for several minutes while the tourists made more and more noise as they searched for bars where they could spend the evening. Two Limenians came into the restaurant.

"Do you sell beer?"

"We're closing," she replied.

The prosecutor wanted to tell her not to stop working because of him. The tourist business would be very good for the restaurant, and in any event, his problem was not that serious. In fact, he was not even sure what "his problem" was, and it was not worthwhile for her to worry so much about it. But the pressure of those slim fingers on his and the odor of tripe coming from that small woman seemed to have sealed his lips. When the tourists left, Edith locked the door, put the prosecutor's plate in the refrigerator, and went out with him. They walked in silence to the prosecutor's house. Chacaltana remembered what it was like to walk down the street with a woman beside him, the feeling of four legs walking in rhythm, not like guards marching but with a free step, calm and slow. From time to time they smiled for no reason.

"During Holy Week I'll work at the restaurant in the mornings too," she said. "There'll be lots of tourists. You can come for breakfast if you want. Because you eat in the mornings, don't you?"

"Call me Félix."

"I have a small farm with my cousins in Huanta. I work here now because the harvest is over. I'll come back next year."

"Every year."

"Every year. Time is like that here. Everything is repeated over and over again. Planting, harvesting . . ."

"Maybe life can change. When somebody disappears, nothing is the same anymore. When somebody falls in love, nothing is the same either. Some things are forever."

"I hope so."

When they were in his house, the prosecutor offered her a *mate*. They sat in the living room to talk. The prosecutor wondered if her impulsive visit to the house was a sign she would end up in his bed. Then he realized he did not really want to go to bed with Edith, at least not that night. That night he felt like talking to her, being lulled by her voice and her patience, perhaps embracing her. That was all. At least, that was what he thought.

"How did your parents die?"

"It was the terrorists," she replied.

"It was a horrible time, wasn't it?"

"I don't want to talk about it."

Nobody wanted to talk about it. Not the military, or the police, or civilians. The memory of the war had been buried along with its dead. The prosecutor thought the memory of the eighties was like the silent earth in cemeteries. The only thing everyone shares, the only thing no one talks about.

"Do you go to visit your parents often?"

"I go all the time. I feel alone without them. I've always felt alone."

"I still see my mother."

She smiled without understanding. He decided to show her what he had never shown anyone. Perhaps she would understand. He took her hand and led her to the back room. When he opened the door, her eyes lit up. The interior looked like a room from twenty years ago, the room of a señora with its mirror, its furniture of old wood, even the old-fashioned creams and colognes used by grandmothers. She walked around the room, touching everything gently, as if acknowledging the presence of his mother through touch.

"This was her room?"

"My house burned down when I was a boy. When I came back, I reconstructed her bedroom here just as I remembered it. It was pretty, wasn't it?"

She did not answer. He asked himself if she would understand. He had never shown the bedroom to anyone. Perhaps it was a mistake to let her see it. It was like undressing in public.

"She . . . is my strongest memory of Ayacucho," he said.

"It's as if she were still alive."

"She is . . . in a way."

Edith looked at the photographs.

"And your father?"

Prosecutor Chacaltana shook his head. He smiled as she admired the fabric of the sheets and the aroma of damp wood.

"It's important to remember," she said. "They remember us."

A warm breath emanated from the interior of the bedroom. The prosecutor knew that his mother liked this girl and welcomed her into her embrace, as if she were a new daughter. He approached the bed and kissed her. It was a gentle kiss, barely a brush of their lips. She did not resist. He repeated the gesture slowly, trying to grow accustomed again to the touch of someone else's skin. He took her hand and led her to the living room. It seemed disrespectful to kiss her in the bedroom. They lay down on the sofa in the living room and continued kissing gently, exploring each other. After a few minutes, he slipped his hand under Edith's blouse. She let him do so, embracing him. He lifted her blouse and lowered his head. He kissed her navel, her belly, and moved up until he was licking her breasts. They were small breasts, just like her, barely rising from her recumbent body. He felt a remote heat that had almost been banished from his memory. He continued moving up to her throat. Now she let him do what he liked without responding. The prosecutor noticed that he had an erection. He tried to move his hand below her waist. She stopped him firmly. Edith's eyes were half-closed but attentive. Perspiration beaded in the space between her upper lip and her nose, like a liquid mustache. She was trembling.

"I'm sorry." The prosecutor withdrew.

"I don't want you to think badly of me afterward," she said.

He sat up. He was aware he ought to respect her and he did not know what to do. Solitude is dangerous. It accumulates until it becomes uncontrollable and explodes. He thought that in the end he would ruin everything. He wanted to offer her a *mate*. Perhaps an alcoholic drink would be better, but he did not have any. He spent several minutes trying to say something before too much time went by. He managed to articulate:

"It's just that with you I feel less absurd. You're one of the things I don't understand, but the only one I like not understanding."

She smiled and kissed him. He accepted the kiss and returned many more but avoided touching her too much.

The next morning, the prosecutor felt revitalized, happy: for the first time in a long while he had not had nightmares. As he crossed the parade of confraternities going to the Church of the Magdalena to prepare the vestments of the holy images for Friday, he felt that the city was recovering its life as they passed by. He reached the office earlier than usual, with a picture of his mother and an ID photo of Edith that she had given him the night before, toward the end, as he walked her home. He placed both images in a picture frame on his desk and opened the windows to air out the office. He happily greeted the embittered secretary of the Provincial Prosecutor and sat down to do some work.

There was no work to do.

Determined not to waste time, he took out the report on Edwin Mayta Carazo that he had put in the drawer and looked at it again. All in all, it did not say anything so terrible. A detachment of troops had carried out its normal routine duties ten years ago and then released the suspect. And that was all. Perhaps it might prove useful in subsequent investigations: everything indicated that this Edwin was part of the group harassing the police outpost in Yawarmayo. It seemed correct to have written it although there was no open case. Its effect had been positive and had eased his dreams, as he had hoped. He thought about his ex-wife. He realized her memory was beginning to disappear, to fade into oblivion. One needs a present in order not to have to think about the past. The prosecutor had one. That day it seemed to him that Ayacucho had one, that the city needed only a little more air, a little more light.

As he hummed an old *huayno* that he recalled hearing his mother sing, he put the report back in its drawer and turned the key twice. He spent the rest of Thursday playing with the wad of paper, feeling that an enormous weight had lifted from his shoulders. When he left the office, the bands were beginning to play. In the churches they were burning broom while men walked through the streets with bulls that shot off fireworks. Fire bulls. Chacaltana smiled. For the first time in days, fire seemed to be an omen of celebration and joy.

On Friday the 14th, at 5:30 a.m., the Associate District Prosecutor opened his eyes to the sound of excessively loud pounding at the door. He recognized the difference between blows from fists and blows from rifle butts. These were the latter. Without opening the door, he announced that he would dress and come out, but the soldiers insisted on coming in. With nothing to fear, the Associate District Prosecutor opened the door. There were three of them. Two were armed with FAL rifles. The third, an army lieutenant, carried a pistol at his waist. They were not aiming their weapons at him, but they indicated they were in a hurry. Commander Carrión's orders.

The prosecutor barely had time to wash a little and go with them. They had him climb into a jeep, flanked by the two soldiers. He saw that their rifles did not have the safeties on. He preferred not to say anything. The jeep drove out of the city and went up Acuchimay Hill, heading for Huanta. The prosecutor saw dawn break near the Christ of Acuchimay, while he imagined at his back the city topped with tiles and surrounded by dry hills, even though the last rains of the season were still falling. Christ protected the city spread out at his feet. The prosecutor wondered if he would protect him too. He wanted to know where they were taking him.

"Are we going to Huanta?"

"You are not authorized to speak, Señor Prosecutor."

He was not authorized to speak. Like the inmate at the Huamanga prison.

"Is it because of what happened at the prison? I used Commander Carrión's name to get in but . . . I know I committed an irregularity, but I believe he will understand . . . It was an official investigation . . ."

"Señor Prosecutor."

"What is it?"

"Be quiet."

He obeyed. Perhaps that had been his most imprudent act. A beginner's mistake. Certainly the commander would understand that. Perhaps he had simply read his report and sent for him to congratulate him. Yes. That was most likely. He had once called him "my trustworthy man."

They turned left onto an unpaved road and crossed a rocky terreplein that made the jeep bounce. They drove for another half hour until they stopped in front of a military reserve. After showing identification, they continued driving until the rough ground did not allow them to go on. They got out, holding the prosecutor by the arm. They walked, almost climbed the slope of a cliff where the prosecutor slipped several times and the soldiers picked him up with very little delicacy. The prosecutor knew there were no barracks nearby. He did not understand where they were taking him. When they reached the top of the hill, the prosecutor could see what was on the other side. An enormous hole ten meters across, hidden by the hills. A military cordon surrounded the wide pit. He knew without having to ask what was inside. On one side, directing the military detachment, was Commander Carrión. Someone told him the prosecutor was arriving. The commander looked very serious. The prosecutor tried to smile as pleasantly as he could.

"Good morning, Commander. I was surprised by your summons . . ."

"Come over here, Señor Prosecutor," was all the commander would say. "Look at this."

The prosecutor looked up at the hole. His feet refused to move. He heard a rifle being cocked behind him. He took a few steps, very slowly, before he felt the shove that hurried him toward the excavation. Behind his feet he heard a pair of military boots advancing. He approached the huge hole and stopped a meter from the edge. He felt another shove. He was sweating. He took out his handkerchief and wiped his forehead. He dared to turn around. The commander was about twenty meters from him. He motioned for him to look in. Around him, the soldiers had moved out toward the hills that surrounded the hole, as if not to see. The prosecutor felt another shove. He wondered if it was a hand or the barrel of an FAL. He turned to see the face of the soldier who had come with him. The soldier was pale and muttered:

"Turn around, damn it."

The prosecutor looked at the sky. The sky was clear, just a few black clouds in a corner, probably heading for Ceja de Selva. He looked down at the ground again. Slowly, he advanced a step and stretched his neck, looking into the circular blackness of the excavation.

The spectacle inside disconcerted him. At first he thought he saw only boxes, old ruined boxes, surrounded by cloth rotted by time and earth. But then, what he had thought were rocks and earth began taking on a more precise form before his eyes. They were limbs, arms, legs, some semipulverized at the time of their burial, others with bones clearly profiled and surrounded by cloth and cardboard, black, earth-covered heads one on top of the other, forming a mountain of human remains several meters deep. One could not even see the end of this accumulation of bones and dry bodies. The prosecutor fell to his knees and vomited. As he threw up the little he had in his stomach, he realized he was in a perfect position to join the bodies down below, the nape of his neck exposed, offered to the rifles, his body leaning over the hillocks of death, his mind lost in some moment of time when everything was even more dangerous, asking himself how long it would take that time to finish dying, how much longer it would take the memory to disappear, the pain to be extinguished, the wounds to scar over, the eyes to close.

He closed his eyes. It seemed that the bodies down there were mirrors that multiplied him into infinity. And he did not want to be multiplied.

Suddenly, he felt a tug. It was the soldier who had brought him there. Now he was picking him up, perhaps to make him more comfortable. He thought about Edith. He thought about fire. But the soldier made him turn and retrace his steps. Almost holding his hand, or rather his arm, almost dragging him while his legs were not sure they could support him, he took him back to the jeep where the commander was waiting for him and deposited him in front of the officer, like a child who is left at the door of a school.

"They found it last night," said the commander. "The news came just as I was finishing your report. It's the second mass grave that has been opened in three days."

The Associate District Prosecutor did not know what to say. He looked at the grave again, almost as a gesture of comprehension. Now, a peasant woman was coming down one of the hills on the other side. She tripped and rolled toward the foothills but got up and continued climbing down. Three soldiers on that side moved to block her way. The woman shouted something in Quechua. The prosecutor recognized her. It was the woman who had opened the door for him in Quinua, the mother of Justino and Edwin, Señora Carazo de Mayta.

"We've managed to keep the matter out of the press," the commander continued, as if he had not seen her. The prosecutor looked at the officer. He had seen her, his dark glasses reflected her as she approached the edge of the pit. The soldiers took her by the arm but she pulled free and kept running and shouting. She reached the edge. She seemed to want to throw herself in. One of the soldiers pulled on her skirt. Another struggled with her, trying to drag her away. The woman refused to move. She seemed stronger than the three of them together. The third soldier took out a pistol. She did not see it. Her back was turned, she was concentrating on the grave, on her shouts. The soldier aimed his weapon at her back.

"Let's go, Señor Prosecutor," said the commander.

The prosecutor could not look away from the woman and the soldiers. The commander put his hand on his shoulder. The prosecutor said:

"Stop them, Commander."

But the commander said nothing, gave no order, did not raise his voice to his subordinates. Thirty meters away, the soldier continued to hesitate, holding his weapon while the woman threatened to throw herself, head first, in among the corpses. He aimed at her back, then at the back of her neck, then at her leg. The other two tried to hold her still. They shouted something at her. The prosecutor heard: "Get out of here, Mamacita, there's nothing here you should see." The soldier with the weapon pointed the barrel at the sky. He turned to his companions. Then to the commander. The commander observed him but made no gesture. The prosecutor wanted to shout. Then he realized that nothing would change, that too many shouts serve only to hide the sound of shots. He held back his tears and said nothing. On the other side of the grave, the soldier put away his weapon and helped the other two drag the woman outside the perimeter of the security cordon.

"They would never kill a mother, Señor Prosecutor," said the commander. "Sometimes fear makes them go too far. Sometimes they've even hit one. But they never kill them. They wouldn't do that even under orders. It's stronger than they are. It's a natural law. They can't."

Two other soldiers came over to help. They picked the woman up and carried her past the hills. When the prosecutor climbed into the jeep to go back to Ayacucho, her shouts could still be heard among the hills. Or perhaps not, the prosecutor thought, perhaps they were only inside his head, saturated in his memories.

you behaved very bad, justino, you behaved very very bad. and i dont deserve it. i gave berth to you, i opened the black mouths of deth with you, and this is how you repay me. its not right, unnerstand? look in the mirrer, look at yourself. your a traiter.

dont look at me like that. its not my fault. its not even my desision. blood makes us strong, it doesnt hurt us. even an idiot like you can unnerstand the strenth of what were doing. were creating a new world.

but your weak. its normal. nobody can start a struggel and think hes going to win it very fast. unnerstand? itll take senturies, its allready lasted senturies. remembering is important. each life, each of the fallen, it piles up in history and dissolves in it, like tears in the rain. and its sap so that we can live, we who will die. its all the same to me, dont think its unjust.

do you hear it, justino? that voice. yes, its your brother. hes calling to you. do you hear him? didnt you want to see him? hes here, with us. down here, look at him. dont cry justino, men don't cry. leest of all men who have done what you did, what we did. we shed blood instead of tears, justino, you damn faggot. you almost deserve to live because your life is a slow painful death, but ill save you the effert, yes i will. thats what comrades are for, right? thats what were there for.

come here, thats right, like that . . . rest your head on my sholder. ill be with you every step of the way, i wont leave you alone. we wont leave you alone. well take you with us to the end of the rode. well take everybody who unites us to the end of the rode, everybody whose with us from the beginning of time. the moment comes closer and closer, justino. the moment of victory comes closer and closer. do you see the stains on the earth? do you see the red color of the puddels in the night? its your seed, justino, its you who waters the land so that from your guts the world weve fought so hard for will grow. enjoy it, because its the last thing your going to enjoy.

"You think we're a gang of killers. Isn't that right, Chacaltana?"

The commander's question came after a long silence, when they were already on the highway back to Ayacucho, between the mountains and the river. He was driving the vehicle himself. They were alone.

"I do not know . . . I do not know what you are referring to, Commander."

"Don't act like a prick, Chacaltana. I know how to read between the lines of reports. And I know how to read faces, too. Do you think you're the only one here who knows how to read?"

The prosecutor felt obliged to explain himself.

"We waged a just war, Commander." He said it like that, using the first person. "That is undeniable. But sometimes I have difficulty distinguishing between us and the enemy. And when that happens, I begin to ask myself what exactly it is that we fought against."

The commander let several more minutes go by before he spoke again.

"Have you ever been in a war, Chacaltana?"

"What did you say, Señor?"

"I asked if you've been in a war. In the middle of bullets and bombs."

The prosecutor remembered the incidents in Yawarmayo. Then he thought about the bombs, the power cuts in Lima, he remembered the night patrols, the ambulances, the buildings destroyed by explosives, the eyes of the police when they saw the mutilated, bloody bodies that came out of the wreckage. No. He had never been in a war. The commander continued:

"Have you ever felt surrounded by fire and known that your life at that moment is worth less than a piece of shit? Or have you found yourself in a town full of people and not known if they wanted to help you or kill you? Have you seen your friends falling in battle? Have you had lunch with people knowing it may be the last time, and the next time you see them they'll probably be in a box? Have you? When that happens you stop having friends because you know you'll lose them. You get used to the pain of losing them and simply try to avoid being one of the empty chairs that keep multiplying in the dining rooms. Do you know what that's like? No. You don't have the slightest idea of what that's like. You were in Lima, after all, while your people were dying. You were reading nice poems by Chocano, I suppose. Literature, right? Literature says too many pretty things, Señor Prosecutor. Too many. You intellectuals have contempt for military men because we don't read. Yes, don't make that face, I've heard your jokes, I've seen the faces of old politicians when we speak. And I understand. Our problem is that for us, reality is a pain in the balls, we've never seen the pretty things your books talk about."

Associate District Prosecutor Félix Chacaltana Saldívar became aware that he was considered an intellectual. In his way he had been in a war, as an unwilling witness, as the one who stays in the fortress of the capital until fire begins to bring down its walls and the smell of the dead contaminates the clean air. Suddenly, the commander stopped the jeep at a bend in the road and turned toward him:

"There wasn't one terrorist group here, or two. There was a war here, Señor Prosecutor. And in a war people die."

The commander was becoming agitated. His voice, always so authoritative, seemed to break at certain syllables as he brought his face very close to Chacaltana's. Perhaps that was why he didn't say anything else. The prosecutor tried to calm him.

"I'm with you, Commander. I understand what happened. I saw it too, from the other side."

The commander drew back his head. He took a deep breath. He no longer seemed furious. He seemed disoriented.

"The other side. Sooner or later they'll come from your side. Sooner or later they'll come from Lima, Chacaltana. They'll come for our heads. They'll sacrifice us, the ones who fought."

The commander was sweating. The prosecutor offered him his handkerchief. The commander looked straight ahead. He seemed very concentrated. The prosecutor did not dare to move the handkerchief too close to him.

"It was them or us."

The commander did not say anything else. Them or us, thought Chacaltana, until we are all the same, until there is no more distinction between us.

"I understand," he said.

The commander started the motor again. He seemed to gradually evanesce as they returned to the highway.

"It's important that you understand," he insisted, "because you still haven't seen anything."

They continued on to Ayacucho, and then to the military hospital, where they got out. They climbed the steps and crossed the waiting room together. No one asked where they were going or tried to stop them. No one went to an office to find out if they could go through. They entered the corridor that Chacaltana remembered very well from his last visit, passing several wounded people who did not approach them to ask for help. They had not walked very far before the prosecutor realized they were going to the obstetrics ward, to the closed office surrounded by women in labor. He thought of his mother as the cold illumination revealed the criminal pathologist.

"Please close the door quickly."

From the door, the dandruff on his shoulders was not noticeable. Only when they were at the autopsy table did the prosecutor notice that the pathologist seemed dirtier than last time. The smell was different too. This time it was clearly the smell of a corpse. Not too decayed yet, but already penetrating. Several cigarette butts and a few matches had accumulated under the table. This time there were no chocolate wrappers.

"Señor Prosecutor, I see you're not alone."

"Hello, Posadas."

This time nobody spoke about any paper. The commander's greeting was a gesture. The pathologist gave them two surgical masks smeared with Vicks VapoRub.

"You're going to need them," he said.

Then he stood and walked to the table covered with a cloth. The prosecutor brought his handkerchief to his mouth in anticipation of what lay underneath. The light flickered. No one had fixed it since the last time. No one would ever fix it. The pathologist uncovered the table. This time the body was not as decomposed as the last time. It was a recent corpse, unburned, the body still bruised by the onset of rigor.

"Completely drained of blood," Posadas remarked. "Observe the shoulder."

The chest was an enormous red vulva with several sharp metal protuberances pointing at the ceiling. On the left side a mass of bones, muscles, and arteries erupted. What did not erupt was an arm.

"The first time it was the right arm, now they've cut off the left. It seems these gentlemen want to make a puppet."

The commander came close to the face. It was a face stretched into a final shout, with open eyes trying to escape their sockets. He closed the dead man's eyes. Only then, safe from the pressure of those eyes on his, could the prosecutor recognize Justino Mayta Carazo.

"They just brought him in," said the officer. "He was found at dawn, right after the news about the mass grave."

At that moment the prosecutor did not remember fire but he

did remember blows, blows on the chest, one after another, like the dripping from the table, blows on the door at dawn, in a house without light.

"It is clear to us there are several of them," said the prosecutor. "Or at least two well-trained men. The things they have done in both cases cannot be done individually."

"Digging up graves can't be done alone either," added the officer.

The prosecutor asked for a glass of water. The physician took a bottle out of a refrigerator for specimens. The prosecutor decided not to drink that water. The physician handed it to him, saying:

"They're also trained. At least the one with the knife is. These are surgeries. He was stabbed seven times in the heart, with perfect precision. With all kinds of things: machetes, scouting knives, even a butcher knife. They had a good collection, apparently. They destroyed the heart without cutting the principal arteries and deliberately left the body facedown. Almost all the blood came out of his chest, the pulverized heart still managed to pump for a few minutes after death. He was being extinguished. It was slow, but to accelerate exsanguination they cut off his arm. It seems to be the same method as the previous time. It was removed by the roots."

"A two-handed saw, probably," said the commander. "Two people, you cut through the bone as if it were a piece of wood. You only need a little patience. What are those lacerations all over the body?"

"Beak marks," the physician explained. "They left the body where we found it, on Acuchimay Hill, for the buzzards to eat."

The prosecutor felt he ought to make a contribution to the discussion but was afraid that if he opened his mouth something would escape, tears, retching, inappropriate words. A puppet. A puppet constructed with human parts, a Frankenstein monster made of Ayacuchans. He tried to maintain a professional tone.

"Was . . . was there any recovery . . . of a Senderista . . . nature near the deceased?"

The pathologist seemed surprised by the question. His face reflected relief and at the same time terror. He turned toward the officer, who took a paper from his pocket and unfolded it. The prosecutor thought about suggesting more attentive care of evidence but preferred to concentrate on the note. He read:

KILLED BY THE PEOPLE'S JUSTICE
for rustling
Sendero Luminoso

They are back, thought the prosecutor.

The commander said:

"When all is said and done . . . you may have hit the nail on the head with your idea about the terrorists, Señor Prosecutor."

"Nail" was an unfortunate word. The prosecutor tried to focus his gaze on some less horrific part of the body. He stared at the feet splayed from walking through the countryside, the thick nails, green now.

Dr. Posadas lit a cigarette.

The second time the prosecutor entered army headquarters, he did not have to present any identification. With Commander Carrión, he crossed the central courtyard of the old building and climbed a wooden staircase to the second floor. There, at the end of a creaking wooden corridor, was the commander's office. Inside, the air seemed heavier than it had the first time. It made him think of the air in Lima, downtown, on Avenida Tacna at six in the evening. The commander poured two glasses of *pisco*. The prosecutor did not want to refuse. They sat facing each other, this time at the worktable. Sitting there, they were on the same level. The commander took the first drink.

"I don't like working with civilians too much, Señor Prosecutor. And let's be frank, in general you and I don't like each other much. But I'm very worried."

"Well, Commander, I believe we could establish inter-institutional bridges of the greatest . . ."

"Chacaltana, let's get to the point."

"Yes, Señor."

"We'll work together but under my command."

"Of course, Señor."

They were silent for a period of time that seemed like years. Finally the commander said:

"All right, say something, damn it!"

The prosecutor tried to be calm. He wondered if he was feeling palpitations, or if perhaps everything around him was suffering from palpitations. He tried to confine himself to the case:

"I have written a report that I will send to you, Señor. I will tell you in advance that I would ask for a statement from those involved in this report, to wit, Lieutenant Alfredo Cáceres Salazar of the Army of Peru and the civilian Edwin Mayta Carazo, both of whom can shed useful light on the connection of the deceased to . . ."

"See them? Mayta and Cáceres? You want to see them?"

"See them . . . and speak with them, Señor."

"Speaking with them will be difficult. As for seeing them, you already saw them. You met Edwin Mayta Carazo, at least a part of him, this morning when you looked into the grave. And you saw Lieutenant Cáceres Salazar thirty-eight days ago, when his burned body was found in Quinua."

The prosecutor felt blocked by the information, passed over.

"Señor?" he stammered.

"Yes, it was that motherfucker Cáceres. He was reported missing in Jaén a month before his body was discovered."

"Dog Cáceres?"

The commander gave a half smile, as if he were remembering an old comrade:

"They called him Dog, right? He was a shit of a man. A *sinchi*, a member of the counterinsurgency forces. They were kept rotting on a base in the jungle. Then they were transferred here to bring them up to date. Cáceres outdid himself in every interrogation. He made the entire grave you saw almost by himself. Edwin Mayta Carazo was caught in one of his operations. They began to ask him questions and he didn't cave in. Then he began to confess. He confessed to everything they asked but began to contradict himself on the second round of questions. His testimony didn't fit, his facts were impossible . . ."

"Perhaps because he did not know anything."

"Or perhaps because he wanted to confuse us. Do you also think we can't tell a terrorist when we see one?"

The prosecutor drew back in his seat. The commander had turned red with anger but quickly regained his composure.

"I'm sorry," he said. "For whatever reason, Cáceres went too far. As usual. I believe it was respiratory, I don't really remember. I suppose the lieutenant made up a report about his being released and declared him clandestine a few days later. The body was buried in a nearby garbage dump. But that wasn't enough. His mother went every morning to look for her son in the dump. The soldiers tried to keep her away, but at the first careless moment that damn old woman was digging through the garbage. When things became difficult, the bodies were pulled out and piled up in the grave you saw. From then on, whenever they find a grave somewhere, Edwin Mayta Carazo's mother shows up to look for his body. Though it doesn't appear in the press. I don't know how the fuck she finds out, but she's always there, trying to get close, dragged away by soldiers who can't shoot her, pawing through all the bodies. Very often the heads were . . . torn off the bodies to make them difficult to identify . . . but that woman could tell it wasn't her son, even though the body had been decomposing for months."

"What happened to Lieutenant Cáceres . . . when things became difficult?"

"They gave him twenty years in the military prison in Lima. He served two years of his sentence and then was sent to the garrison at Jaén so nobody would see him. They gave him new documents. They ordered him not to exist."

The prosecutor supposed that the orders had been rigorously carried out. Lieutenant Cáceres Salazar no longer existed. The prosecutor completed the sentence:

"Until he disappeared. He ran away from Jaén and came right here. Why?"

"I don't know, Chacaltana." The commander poured himself another *pisco*. "But I can imagine. I've seen it before. People who have killed too much don't get better. Sometimes they have normal, peaceful years. But it's only a question of time before they blow up. Intelligence reported the presence of the lieutenant in Vilcashuamán three days before his death. They said he had established contact with the campesino patrols to organize a 'defense against subversion.' Imagine. Nobody paid attention to him. He had simply gone crazy."

"Perhaps the terrorist groups in Yawarmayo found him and took their revenge."

"Those people are controlled. They don't operate outside their area. But it seems there are others. You were right about the dates. But besides the ones you mentioned, it's the tenth anniversary of the death of Edwin Mayta and the end of the first harvest of the year 2000: 'The blood harvest of the millenarian struggle,' as they call it."

"If they were terrorists, why did they also kill Justino Mayta?"

The commander looked up at one of the flags on the table. Then he looked at the prosecutor.

"I believe the reason for that is you, Señor Prosecutor."

"What?"

"According to your report, you spoke to him, didn't you? The Senderistas usually killed those they suspected of being informers, their own people."

"But he did not tell me anything important!"

"And how would they know that? It's understandable, I would have done the same thing, honestly."

The prosecutor suddenly felt guilty of a death. It never would have occurred to him that one could be responsible for a death just like that, by default, without having done anything to produce it. Perhaps he was not the only one guilty. Perhaps there were more, in fact, perhaps he lived in a world where everyone was guilty of something.

"Why haven't you finished them off, Commander? Why are they still in Yawarmayo? The army could . . ."

"The army has orders not to do anything there. And the police have no resources. Lieutenant Aramayo has spent ten years asking for weapons and equipment. Lima won't give its approval."

"They have to know what is going on . . ."

"Lima knows, Señor Prosecutor. They know everything and are everywhere. If for some reason they have to, they will go into Yawarmayo and massacre them. The operation will be on television. The press will be there."

Everything was becoming tangled in the prosecutor's head. He felt exhausted by thinking. One cannot choose to see or not see, hear or not hear, one sees, one listens, one thinks, the thoughts refuse to leave one's head, they change, they dissolve, they become disturbed.

"Why . . . why are you telling me this, Commander?"

Again the commander showed that turbid smile, a mixture of irony and disillusion. Now he seemed to be in another world, wrapped in a blanket of memories.

"Do you know what Cáceres used to do when he found a terrorist in a village?" he said. "He would call together the entire village that had sheltered the terrorist, lay the accused down in the main square, and cut off an arm or a leg with a two-man saw. He often ordered his *sinchis* to do it, but sometimes he did it himself, with someone helping him. He did it while the terrorist was alive, so nobody in the village could avoid seeing him or hearing his screams. Then they would bury the separate parts of the body. And if the head was still complaining, they would give him the coup de grâce just before putting him in the ground, and then the campesinos were obliged to fill in the hole with dirt. Cáceres would say that with his system, that village would never be disobedient again."

"He died under his law."

"He died under the only law there was, Señor Prosecutor, if there was any."

"Why does it matter so much to you?"

The commander seemed to hesitate over what he would say. He looked at the bottle of *pisco* but did not get up. Then he said:

"At that time I was a captain. I was Cáceres's immediate superior. And according to the signals they're giving, the next victim . . . will be me."

He tried to say the last sentence with self-assurance. A slight break in his voice betrayed his true state of mind. The prosecutor was moved to see this man confess that he was afraid. He felt better about his own fear. He said:

"Why don't you speak to the Intelligence Services?"

"Absolutely no contact with Lima, Chacaltana. Lima shouldn't know anything about this. During Holy Week, twenty thousand tourists will be in this city. It's the symbol of pacification. If they find out there's a recurrence, they'll cut off our balls. I don't want you to talk to anybody. Do you remember Carlos Martín Eléspuru?"

The prosecutor remembered the functionary Eléspuru. His

ubiquity, his almost inaudible voice, his sky-blue tie. His serenity, his superiority.

"He shouldn't hear anything about this," the commander continued. "And if we happen to run into him, you repeat everything I say: that terrorism is finished, that Peru waged a glorious struggle, any fucking stupid thing you can think of."

"I do not understand, Commander. He should not hear anything about this?"

From one of his drawers, the commander took out a leather holster with a pistol inside. He placed it on the table, in front of the prosecutor. He recovered his authoritative tone to say:

"From now on you alone will take care of this investigation, Chacaltana. And fast. You'll deliver your reports directly to me and you'll have all my support, but I want you to find out once and for all what the fuck is going on and where so many terrorists are coming from. Carry this, you'll need it."

"It will not be necessary, Se . . ."

"Carry it, damn it!"

The prosecutor picked up the holster by the barrel of the gun so the weapon would not go off. It was the first time he had held a weapon. It was very heavy for its size.

"Pick it up like a man, Chacaltana. Now leave. I have work to do."

The prosecutor stood. He did not know if his appointment was an honor or a liability. He did not know whether to say thank you or request a transfer. There were many things he did not know. Mayta's was a long act of vengeance. It had taken ten years to arrive. From the door he turned to the commander to ask a final question:

"Commander, I need to know something. Edwin Mayta Carazo . . . was he innocent?"

"I don't know, Chacaltana. I don't think even he knew."

It was afternoon when he left the commander's office and found himself in crowds of tourists waiting for the first processions of the day. He realized it was Friday of Sorrows. No one would be at the Office of the Prosecutor. He hurried to his own office and locked the door.

He put the holster on his desk. He looked at it. He did not want to take it to his house, so close to his mother. He thought about the mother of the Mayta family. Two sons lost at ten-year intervals. The bullets had reached her family from both sides of a battle that this woman surely never understood completely, just like the prosecutor. He opened the holster and took out the pistol with two fingers before putting it down again on the desk. It was black, 9mm, with a box of ammunition on the back of the sheath. The kind of weapon lieutenants use, like Cáceres, who had become intoxicated by the death of other people and in the end had left his job and run directly toward his own. Why?

It was difficult for him to take out the cartridge to verify that the weapon was loaded. It cost him even more effort to think what would happen if Sendero was rearming. He would not be enough to control it, or Commander Carrión, or all the functionaries in Lima. He closed the pistol carefully and put on the safety, or what he thought was the safety. If Sendero was regrouping, the best thing he could do with that pistol was blow his brains out.

But there were some very strange details in the latest deaths. Things he ought to investigate, which did not fit with traditional Senderista methods. His function now was to investigate on his own, to put his head where nobody wanted to put it, not even himself. Perhaps it was a promotion after all. That is what those famous ambitions brought one to.

He returned the pistol to the holster and put it under his jacket, between his armpit and his waist. He made certain it could not be seen. It felt strange and heavy. He took it off again and locked it in his drawer with two turns of the key. Before he closed the drawer, he took out the report and put it in an envelope to take to Carrión personally. When he walked without the weapon, he was filled with a sensation of peace and normality. He left the office at night, when he could begin to hear the procession of the Virgin of Sorrows.

The Magdalena district was packed with Limenians in sports clothes holding beers and cameras in their hands. The younger Ayacuchan girls approached the tourists calling them "amigo, amigo" and smiling at them. The older ones, the ones who had grown up shut in their houses during the war, looked at those brazen girls disapprovingly, though many mothers harbored the hope that some Limenian or, better yet, an American, would fall in love with one of their daughters and take her away from Ayacucho. It became difficult for the prosecutor to move forward. He was trapped by people, by the stands selling drinks, the smell of punch, the din. His mind wandered with the movement of bodies. Each person he bumped into seemed like a blow in his memory.

When he thought he had found a way through the crowd, an even larger surge of people blocked his way. Beside him the platform carrying St. John emerged; it had just left the church. He let himself be carried along, exhausted. The lights of the city and the fireworks gave him the impression of an overpopulated sky filled with souls circulating together toward some destination. At times the explosion of a firecracker startled him, but the sound was muffled by the mass of people. The prosecutor advanced with the procession until the moment he found most interesting: the encounter of the Lord of Agony and the Virgin of Sorrows, which symbolized the suffering of Christ and his Mother. When the platforms began to approach each other, the Associate District Prosecutor felt spurred on by a presentiment. Filled with tension, he tried to get closer, in among the men carrying the platforms, until he felt himself held back by his shirt. Somebody had sewn his sleeve to the sleeve of someone else. It was part of the celebration. The prosecutor freed himself violently, to the surprise of the other man, who laughed. He felt dizzy, perhaps because of the smell of the platforms and the people. He felt a jab. Beside him, several women were jabbing one another with needles and laughing, "to help the Lord in his pain." He managed to move closer to the platform of the Virgin, who now was shining almost above him, like a true apparition of light, like a mother who materializes before her son, the Lord of Agony, the son who is going to die in his final farewell to life. He reached the edges of the platform and at last could see her clearly. The Virgin's black dress, the candles on the platform that illuminated her from below, her immaculate face, and the seven daggers that pierced her chest, as they pierced the chest of Justino Mayta Carazo, the son of the mother who searched mass graves.

The prosecutor tried to kneel before the holy image, but the movement of the people was too dense. He tried to move away, avoiding the jabs like daggers waiting in ambush. With the seven stab wounds piercing his mind, he tried to move away from the center of the procession. He looked up when he calculated he was in front of Edith's restaurant. Shoving his way through the crowd, he reached the door. Edith looked at him from the counter. She smiled, showing her brilliant teeth. Associate District Prosecutor Félix Chacaltana Saldívar got around the last human obstacles to reaching her, went into the restaurant, rushed to her and embraced her, very closely, surrounded by people who for the first time filled the restaurant. Some tourists applauded, others smiled, like the startled Edith herself, but he did not stop embracing her. He clung to that small body, that smell of the kitchen, with his eyes closed, as if it were the last time.

SATURDAY, APRIL 15 / WEDNESDAY, APRIL 19

———————

Associate District Prosecutor Félix Chacaltana Saldívar welcomed in Saturday by dancing. He had not done that for a long time. Since he did not consider it appropriate to his state of mind, he tried to resist. But Edith insisted when she left work and took him to a concert of indigenous groups at a fairground.

In the middle of the field an enormous bonfire was shining, and around it hundreds of bodies were dancing, sometimes embracing, sometimes alone, moving to the rhythm of the folk music and drinking punch and beer. At first, the prosecutor refused to dance. Edith dragged him to the floor, but he felt rigid, incapable of moving a body that was good only for carrying out basic vital functions.

At a certain point, worn out by the crowd and the noise, he went to a food stand and asked for Ayacuchan chorizo and a glass of punch. The woman gave him a piece of fried spiced pork with hot *ají* peppers and vinegar. It was good. As he ate, he saw Edith, who had stayed with the group in the middle to dance. He wondered if what he was doing made sense. Edith was no more than twenty, she had been born at the same time as the war. And he felt old.

He drank a little punch. The taste of the milk and cinnamon with the effect of the *pisco* warmed his body. Now Edith was dancing close to the bonfire, her smile hidden at times by her hair. The prosecutor ordered another punch while the Gaitán Castro brothers came up on stage and people welcomed them with enthusiastic applause. Even in their happiest songs, what predominated was the Andean lament that their public loved. The prosecutor realized he was keeping time with his foot. He took a few steps forward.

Edith saw him approaching and gave him a smile. At times the mass of people hid her, because she was very short. Pushing his way through, and in a good humor after two glasses of punch, the prosecutor reached her side. He began moving his feet, trying to look like all the people around him. It was good to look like everyone else and disappear into the crowd, dissolve in it. Edith directed a smile at him and he did not know if it showed tenderness or mockery for how badly he danced. But he kept on. Now he had to move his arms, as if he were harvesting a crop, now his waist, and again his feet. It was difficult for him to do everything at the same time. As he made the attempt, Edith whirled around him, framed by the fire, moving her head and shoulders, laughing, with a laugh that to the prosecutor seemed as welcoming as a warm room in winter.

The next morning started out gray, but as noon approached, the sky began to clear. Prosecutor Chacaltana got up later than usual and hurried to greet his mother and open the windows in her room. He told her he had danced. He knew she was returning his smile from somewhere. Then he went out.

At the prefecture and at the market they were distributing yellow and green palms brought in from the province of La Mar in Ceja de Selva. The faithful walked through the city carrying their branch for Palm Sunday. At the Church of Pampa San Agustín they were preparing the procession of the Lord of the Vineyard, scheduled to go out that night, holding a cluster of grapes in his hand to guarantee fertility. The entire city was given over to the celebration.

The Associate District Prosecutor appeared at the Church of the Heart of Christ at approximately 11:35. In the priest's office, the stewards of the eight processions of the celebration were arguing with Father Quiroz because they wanted to modify their routes. Quiroz responded without restraining his indignation:

"We've been following the same route for almost five hundred years, and we're not going to change now so that they can stop at the hotels!"

"But that's where the tourists are, Father. The hotels will give more financial support to the processions if we pass in front of them . . ."

The stewards were prosperous merchants and professionals. In earlier years they had tended to be very devout, observant gentlemen, but since the end of the war they had demonstrated more interest in the hospitality industry than in the preservation of traditions. As he listened to their discussion from the waiting room, the prosecutor thought of an impresario from Huanta who had proposed the previous year that the celebration be extended to an entire Holy Month with different processions each day. He had calculated that this would multiply the influx of tourists. And money.

The stewards came out of the office visibly annoyed. The Associate District Prosecutor preferred to wait a moment before going into the office. When he finally did, Father Quiroz was preparing to go out.

"I hope this will be brief, Señor Prosecutor," said the priest, without inviting him to sit down. "This is the most complicated week in the year."

"I understand, Father."

"How are things? Do you have another burned body to investigate?"

"No. Not a burned body. I have Justino Mayta Carazo. Do you remember him?"

The priest seemed to make a slight effort to remember as he looked inside his briefcase. He replied as he closed it:

"Ah, yes. What happened to that little thief? Did they find him?"

"Yes, but dead." The priest froze. The prosecutor wondered if his words had not been too abrupt. "I mean . . . They found him on Acuchimay Hill, eaten by buzzards. It happened early Friday morning."

The priest crossed himself. He seemed to whisper a few rapid words, perhaps some formula for those who rest eternally in peace. Or not. The prosecutor did not know how corpses rest.

"Was it an accident?" the priest asked.

"No."

"Was it the same . . . the same as last time?"

"We think so."

"Come with me."

They went to the eating hall for the poor of the Church of the Heart of Christ, which was half a block away. The Associate District Prosecutor wondered if he would ever succeed in talking to Father Quiroz while they were sitting down. When they reached the eating hall, they found a long line of beggars sitting on the sidewalk in front of the door. The beggars immediately surrounded the priest, who avoided them with an amiable gesture that indicated broad experience of this kind. The prosecutor and the priest went inside, where a short dark nun was waiting anxiously for Quiroz's arrival.

"How are we, Sister?"

"We have a new donation of milk, Father, but it won't be enough. There are too many," she added, pointing outside.

"We'll do what we can. Divide the servings in half, and when that's finished, then it's finished."

"All right, Father."

The nun hurried to give instructions in the kitchen and then returned to the door. She opened it. Dozens of beggars pushed their way in. Some had been disabled during the time of terrorism, others were simply campesinos who had come to the city for Holy Week but could not pay for food. They sat at four enormous tables. The nun, with two other sisters, served pieces of bread, glasses of milk, and a thick soup in deep bowls.

"Your killer seems like a very devout man," the priest remarked, returning to the subject.

"What do you mean?"

"The burning . . . the buzzards. He seems to be trying to destroy the body so it can't be resurrected . . . if you'll permit me a mystic interpretation."

"No . . . that possibility had not occurred to me."

"Hmm. It's curious. We humans, Señor Prosecutor," the priest began to expound, "are the only animals who have an awareness of death. The rest of God's creatures do not have a collective experience of death, or they have one that is extremely fleeting. Perhaps each cat or dog thinks it is immortal because it hasn't died. Do you follow me? But we know we will die and are obsessed with fighting death, which makes it have a disproportionate, often a crushing presence in our lives. Human beings have souls to the exact extent that we are conscious of our own deaths."

Some diners came over to the priest to ask for his blessing. The priest stopped speaking to trace signs of the cross in the air, as if he were tossing them carelessly in every direction. The prosecutor tried to recapitulate what he had just heard. Some words seemed familiar, but taken together their meaning escaped him. Perhaps it was the subject of death that was absent from his thinking. How could he think about death or know what it was? He was not dead, at least he did not think he was. The priest continued:

"We live the experience of death in others but don't assume it in ourselves. We want to live forever. That is why we save bodies for resurrection. Burying them is saving them. Etymologically, 'burial ground' or 'cemetery' are not words that refer to death but to repose, the body's rest until it is rejoined with the soul. It's beautiful, isn't it?"

The prosecutor did understand those words but did not understand what was beautiful about them.

"Yes, very nice."

Quiroz stopped for a second to bless one of the diners, a man without legs who came to him, pushing himself along with his fists. The priest gave him the blessing on his forehead, and the man returned to his table, satisfied. Quiroz continued speaking:

"Some pre-Columbian cultures buried their dead with all their implements so they could use them in the afterlife. Right here, thirty kilometers from what is now Ayacucho, the Wari even buried important people with their slaves. Except that the slaves were buried alive. They were a warrior culture."

They were brought two glasses of warm milk with cinnamon, a nonalcoholic version of punch. The prosecutor did not want to ask if they had *mate*. As he felt the first swallow revivifying his body, the Associate District Prosecutor thought of the meaning of the word "Ayacucho": "Place of the dead." For a moment, he thought of his city as a great sepulcher of slaves buried alive. The grave that he himself had chosen and decorated with old mementos of his mother. He tried to change the subject:

"And the blood? Justino's body was found without any blood. Does that mean anything?"

The priest shrugged.

"If you start looking, everything has a transcendental meaning. Everything is an expression of the mysterious will of the Lord. The blood may have a more pagan significance. It could be the blood of sacrifice. In many religions, the sacrifice of animals is intended to offer to the dead the blood needed to maintain the life ascribed to them. Draining someone's blood is draining the body of life in order to offer all that life to a different soul."

The prosecutor tried to take a drink of milk before answering, but the speckle of cinnamon looked like a bloodstain to him. Without knowing why, he remembered the words: "Ye shall eat the blood of no manner of flesh; for the life of all flesh is the blood thereof: whosoever eateth it shall be cut off." He said them aloud. The priest specified:

"Leviticus 17:10–14. I see you keep up with your Bible reading."

"I don't know where I heard it. I suppose I remember it from some Mass I went to when I was a boy. I used to go with my mother. And the seven daggers in the chest of the Virgin of Sorrows? What do they represent?"

"Seven silver daggers for the seven sorrows that the passion of Christ produces in his mother. Are you investigating a case, Señor Prosecutor, or do you want to take first communion?"

"It is just that the two deaths seem to have something to do with Holy Week: Ash Wednesday, Friday of Sorrows . . . it is . . . too much of a coincidence, isn't it?"

"No. The celebrations are superimposed. Carnival is originally a pagan celebration, the harvest festival. And during Holy Week there are also echoes of the Andean culture that preceded the Spaniards. That's because it doesn't have a fixed date, like Christmas, but depends on the seasons. As I told you last time, the Indians are unfathomable. On the outside, they follow the rituals that religion demands of them. On the inside, only God knows what they are thinking."

The prosecutor observed all the beggars who had gathered on the benches of the eating hall, presided over by an image of the bleeding Christ wearing the crown of thorns. Another beggar approached to ask for a blessing, which the priest gave. The prosecutor remarked:

"They seem very devout to me, Father Quiroz."

"I honestly don't believe that all the campesinos who come to Ayacucho for Holy Week know exactly what the meaning is of what they are doing. Even though this is the Holy Week with the longest tradition in the world. Did you know that? This and the one in Sevilla. Ayacucho keeps the memory of the older Christianity. Friday of Sorrows, for example, is no longer celebrated in most of the world."

The prosecutor wondered in which province of Peru Sevilla

might be. He promised himself to check it on a national political map when he had time. He continued to ask questions:

"Then what significance do the campesinos attribute to Holy Week?"

"I suppose it simply forms part of their cycle. It is the myth of eternal return. Things happen once and then they happen again. Time is cyclical. The earth dies after the harvest and then it is reborn for sowing. Except they disguise the goddess Pachamama with the face of Christ."

The prosecutor was missing a fact. He overcame his embarrassment to ask:

"And what significance do we attribute to it?"

The priest seemed annoyed. He stared into the prosecutor's eyes reprovingly, as he would with a poor student.

"You were doing so well with your biblical quotations . . ." But then he smiled at the corners of his mouth. "Death, Señor Prosecutor. We celebrate the death of Christ and we represent it in order to die with him."

"Oh, I understand that, but . . . I mean . . . Why do we celebrate death? Isn't that a little strange?"

"We celebrate it because we don't really believe in it, because we consider it the transition to eternal life, a life more real. If we don't die, we cannot be resurrected."

That same afternoon, Chacaltana tried to explain to Carrión the little he had understood of his conversation with the priest. But the commander listened to his words with a disappointed grimace.

"Catholic terrorists, Chacaltana? But they're a bunch of damn communists!"

Papers had accumulated in the office, among them the prosecutor's reports, and dishes with the remains of food. The prosecutor guessed that the commander was not taking steps or making visits personally, that he asked for reports on everything, that he did not move from his office even to sleep at home. But he listened to the prosecutor. In fact, Chacaltana had gone through the entrance and the central courtyard of the headquarters building, up to the second floor, with no checkpoints or questions. Captain Pacheco was in the anteroom to the commander's office. The secretary was telling the police officer that Carrión was at a very important meeting but had let the prosecutor go in without a word. Pacheco had looked at him with hatred. The prosecutor knew he would have problems with him. But for now, his problem was how to convince the commander of what he was saying when he himself was not very convinced.

"The two killings are filled with religious references, Señor. They are something like . . . celebrations of death."

"Have you been seeing too many movies, Chacaltana?"

Chacaltana thought about the television set in Edith's restaurant. No. He had not been seeing too many movies.

"It is . . . what I have found out . . . Señor."

Prosecutor Chacaltana felt foolish, slow-witted, like a poor investigator. He thought he would have preferred never to have moved up, to have continued his devotion to his poems and memoranda. He did not like being important, and he specifically did not like being important in this case. If he were just a nobody, at this moment he would be with Edith, thinking about other things. About things that concerned him. About his life and not a pile of dead people. The commander turned and looked at him with suspicion.

"And what did you tell the priest? That we have a serial killer?"

"I did not give him too much information, Señor. Only what was indispensable. He guaranteed his discretion."

"Discretion! A priest! He must have run to the archbishop's to shout about it there. Priests are like gossiping women. That's why they wear skirts."

"I think we can trust him, Señor."

"Trust!" Carrión laughed out loud. "Trust. Do you know why there's a crematorium in the Church of the Heart of Christ?"

"No, Señor."

"To get rid of inconvenient corpses, Chacaltana. It was a good logistical alternative. Fire instead of graves. They offered to implement it themselves. But the solution itself turned out to be inconvenient. It was too visible, all that smoke in the center of the city. Besides, it meant opening a direct window for the priests onto our confidential operations. As it turned out, we hardly ever used the oven, and when we did, we knew that everybody up to the pope knew about it. You can't trust them. If they offered to install it, it was only to spy."

"They offered . . . themselves?"

"It sounded reasonable. We all had the same desire to rid ourselves of the terrorists, didn't we?"

The prosecutor considered it reasonable. But, in any event, he believed in Father Quiroz. He had proven to be very cooperative. Besides, the prosecutor had to believe in somebody. If everything is a lie, he thought, then nothing is. If one lives in a world of falsehoods, those falsehoods are reality. Quiroz spoke of eternal life as a life more real. For a moment, the prosecutor thought he understood what he was referring to. The commander leaned back in his chair. He looked annoyed.

"And you, Chacaltana?" he asked. "Can we trust you?"

Chacaltana wanted to say no, they should not trust him.

"Of course you can, Señor."

The commander was wearing the shirt and trousers of his uniform, but he looked untidy. His shoes and decorations had not been polished. On his lean face the first signs of a thin beard were making their appearance, more like dirt stains than facial hair.

"They're coming for me, Chacaltana. I know it. I can feel it. Every second we spend here is an opportunity for our killers."

"They will not come for you, Señor. That is why we are here: so that will not happen."

The commander flashed a brief smile of thanks. Then his face darkened:

"They'll come in any case," he said sorrowfully. "Death forces its way in. I know that all too well."

At times, Prosecutor Chacaltana realized in a flash that he was carrying out an investigation under orders from a killer. At times he wondered if it was possible to avoid that anywhere in his city or in any other city. But those thoughts always disappeared from his mind by themselves, so he would not be distracted from his duties.

"Perhaps you're right," the commander concluded. "Perhaps this has to do with Holy Week. But not the way you think. You're a strange guy, Chacaltana. You're always about to hit the bull's eye and you always miss."

"Thank you, Señor," said the prosecutor. He wondered if he should have said that.

"They're trying to spoil the celebration. The symbol of Ayacucho, the pacified city. The record tourism of Holy Week. They're trying to show that they're back all over the uplands. And in the middle of the millennium, for fuck's sake. A blow struck for effect. Lucky we managed to hide it from the press. Being in the news would excite them. They don't have many resources yet, but they've become more sophisticated. These kinds of things didn't occur to them before."

"In that case, it is possible to predict that their next blow will be tomorrow. Palm Sunday. The official beginning of Holy Week."

"The triumphal entrance of Christ into Ayacucho."

"Exactly, Señor."

Commander Carrión thought for a few seconds. Then he called his secretary on the intercom and turned toward the prosecutor.

"They're going to think I'm crazy, but what the hell. I'll cancel all leaves for the police and request military reinforcements. I'll have them patrol the entire city, armed but in civilian clothes, so as not to cause any alarm. And I'll invent something to justify it internally. You can go, Chacaltana. And thank you."

The prosecutor stood up. The commander thought of something else:

"Are you carrying your weapon?"

"What? Excuse me?"

"Where's the pistol I gave you? You're not carrying it? Carry it, don't be an asshole! You're a possible victim too. Very possible."

"Yes, Señor."

The prosecutor left headquarters thinking about the commander's final words. He had not been aware that he too was a possible victim. It was difficult for him to get used to the idea of being an official important enough to be annihilated. Annihilated, he repeated to himself. Turned into nothing. He thought it was a horrible word. He went to his office and opened the drawer. He took out the pistol carefully, verifying one more time that the safety was on. He contemplated it on the desk and then he raised it in front of the bathroom mirror. He tried to imagine himself shooting. He could not. He put it in the sheath and placed it in a large manila envelope. It was too big, and the envelope did not conceal it. He placed the envelope inside the typewriter cover. He went out carrying it as if it were a baby. He walked quickly to his house, nervously bumping into groups of tourists and vendors, afraid the gun would go off in spite of the safety because the devil carries weapons. When he was home, he took the package to his mother's room and put it on the bureau.

"Don't worry, Mamacita, I'm not going to open it, don't be afraid. It's just so you'll know I've brought it here. I think . . . I think the best thing is to keep it in the night table, just in case, though nothing's going to happen. Because nothing's going to happen, right? Nothing's going to happen."

He continued repeating those words without taking his eyes off the weapon for at least two hours, until someone rang the doorbell. Before he opened the door, he hid the package in his night table. He was not convinced. He took it out and put it under the bed. Not that either. The doorbell kept ringing. Nervously, he left it behind the barrel of water he used when the water supply was cut. Yes. Nobody would look for it there. Before he opened the door, he took the pistol out again and returned it to the night table. He hurried to the door. It was Edith.

"They gave me the day off because tomorrow I work all day," she said.

They spent the afternoon walking through a city they did not recognize, one filled with blond people with an accent from the capital. A couple of drunk Limenians whistled at Edith when she walked by. The prosecutor shouted at them:

"Beat it, motherfuckers!"

Edith laughed, but when they sat down to eat at a chicken shop, she said:

"You're nervous. What's the matter?"

"Things at work. Nothing important."

"You were at Heart of Christ today, weren't you? They saw you with Father Quiroz."

"Who saw me?" The prosecutor could not repress a touch of distress in his voice.

"I don't know. People. Ayacucho is a very small town, everybody knows everything. Why?" She gave him a mischievous smile. "Was it a secret?"

"No, no. It's just that . . . I'm working on a difficult case."

"That's what happens when they promote you, isn't it? They give you more responsibility."

"Yes, that's true. Did they see me anywhere else?"

"I don't know. I only heard that. Can't you tell me what your case is?"

"It would be better if you didn't know. It would be better for me not to know."

"That priest is a good person. I go to that church a lot. He's very nice."

"Yes. Nice."

"When are you going to take me to Lima?"

For the prosecutor, Lima was merely a memory filled with smoke and sorrow. His work, his ex-wife were disappearing voluntarily from his memory and would never come back. In any event, he replied:

"Soon. When this case is finished."

They watched the twilight from the lookout on Acuchimay, next to the statue of Christ. Edith insisted on going there in spite of his protests. As she drank an Inca Kola and held his hand, the prosecutor began to calm down. He thought that Christ had not protected him very much, but Edith had.

"Last week I talked to a terrorist," he dared to tell her. "And I think this week I'll have to do it again. It frightened me."

Simply by saying that, he understood that he needed to talk. At least, as much as he could. And with someone who would respond. He thought of Justino's body. In the sky, the buzzards seemed to be expecting another meal. She let a few seconds go by before she said:

"Don't be afraid. That's over. The war's over."

He noticed that she called it the "war." No one, except the military, called what had happened there a war. It was terrorism. He grasped her hand even tighter.

"This prairie could catch fire at any moment, Edith. All you need is the right spark."

"The sun's beginning to go down," she indicated. She didn't like talking about that.

Down below, the procession of the Lord of the Vineyard was

setting out. Associate District Prosecutor Félix Chacaltana Saldívar remembered that it was Passion Saturday; and with that in mind, he asked himself if trying to make love to Edith would show a lack of respect for her and Our Lord. To chase away those thoughts, he tried to say something pleasant to her.

"My mother would like you very much."

Edith did not reply.

And she let go of his hand.

On Palm Sunday, after the blessing of the palms and the Mass, Christ entered the city of Ayacucho on the carpets of flowers that decorated its streets. First to appear were hundreds of mules and llamas adorned with broom and wearing trappings of multicolored ribbons and hanging bells. The villagers leading them set off rockets and firecrackers on the way, in the midst of the general uproar. At the front of the procession, sitting on a spirited charger, rode the principal steward, wearing a white and red sash across his chest. The celebration had been announced and was accompanied by a platoon of riders, male and female, on the back of horses adorned according to Huamanguina traditions. The troupe included the prefect, the subprefect, and the muledrivers and campesinos who blew into bulls' horns to celebrate the arrival of the Lord.

The Associate District Prosecutor was in the crowd, beside a carpet of red and yellow flowers that represented the heart of Jesus, alert to any suspicious movement, nervous because of the fireworks at the celebration. He could recognize the agents dressed as civilians because they were the only ones wearing suits, ties, and white sports socks, and because their sentries' attitude needed only a sign saying "secret agent" on each of their foreheads. They were, however, well distributed. There were at least two on each block of the route of the animals, and a net of vigilance covered everything, including the exits from the city. As the celebration approached the center of the city, the prosecutor ran into Captain Pacheco, wearing the dress uniform of the National

Police but in the middle of the crowd, not on the stand of honor. Chacaltana wanted to move away when he saw him, but the captain approached:

"Would you care to explain what's going on, Señor Prosecutor?"

"It is the celebration of Palm Sunday, Captain."

A firecracker went off near them.

"Don't fuck around with me, Chacaltana! Commander Carrión cancels all his appointments except with you. You leave the office and suddenly all the police have to work double shifts. Do you know how my people feel? How do I explain why their leaves have been canceled?"

"I do not know what you are talking about, Captain. I met with the commander only to hand him a report."

At a corner of the square, one of the horses was about to bolt because of the noise and the crowd. The rider managed to control the animal.

"Do you think I was born yesterday, Chacaltana? My horse should have been one of those. I rented the best one and had to give it to my idiot son-in-law because I'm on foot duty. What do you have against us, Señor Prosecutor? Why do you like fucking us up so much?"

"I never wished to disturb your relationship with your son-in-law, Captain. The commander is very concerned with security during these festivities. That is all."

A throng of tourists came between them. The captain pushed against the crowd to say:

"Don't think I'm not aware of things. I know a lot about you. And you should be more careful about the people you go around with. Your friends can make problems for you."

Then he let himself be carried away by the crowd. He disappeared before the prosecutor could respond. What had he meant by those words? Did he know about his real relationship with the commander? Or was he referring to the terrorist? The police exchange information, probably Colonel Olazábal had told the captain about his visit to the prison. He was afraid it could be misinterpreted somehow. He thought it would be a good idea to inform Commander Carrión at the first opportunity that he had gone to the maximum security prison and had done so in strict compliance with his duties.

The beasts of burden began to enter the Plaza Mayor to walk around it. The prosecutor thought that for the llamas, Palm Sunday was the longest route to the slaughterhouse, because afterward the villagers would eat them all. But they kept walking with that imbecilic face that cows have too, that look of not understanding anything. Lucky for them.

A delegation stopped beside the cathedral, in front of the courtyard of the municipal building, to lay down the palm frond that would rest there until it was burned the following Sunday. As they ceremoniously lay down the palm leaves, to flashbulbs and applause, another explosion could be heard. And shouts. These were shouts not of joy but of terror.

The prosecutor and the two police officers on his block hurried toward the shouts. They had to move in the opposite direction from the procession, which was going to the center of the city. Ahead of them, two tourists were on the ground. People had formed a circle around them. Another four police officers in plain clothes arrived at the same time. Two were left to watch over the wounded tourists. The rest ran in the direction indicated by the crowd. The prosecutor saw the backs of several young men running away, pushing their way through throngs of people. They followed them. As they left the square the crowd thinned out, and they could run faster, but this gave an advantage to the men in front. On the way, some uniformed police reinforcements joined the pursuit. Curious onlookers, who at first were in their way, began to let the officers through, but the information they gave only confused them more: "This way, no, that way." When they left the center of town, the young men being pursued separated to escape down the narrowest streets. This was not a makeshift group. They knew what they were doing. The prosecutor chose the ones closest to him and followed them with two of the officers. The fugitives crossed a new construction of similar residential buildings, trying to slip away through the passages between them. The officers divided up to cover the exits and ambush them. One radioed for reinforcements. At the far end of the site, they saw a boy running. The three of them followed. The site ended in a settlement of houses made from rush matting and corrugated tin, on unpaved streets. The perfect hiding place. The three pursuers tried to follow the young man, who had been joined by another boy, around the corners and intersections of the settlement. They separated again. The prosecutor realized he was running alone. He asked himself what he would do if he caught up with one of the young men, how he would stop him, what if his life was at risk, who was pursuing whom. He did not stop. And he did not have time to be surprised at his own courage. As he turned a corner, almost at the edge of the settlement where the slope of a hill began, he found himself face-to-face with one of the officers. They had gotten that far.

"Shit!" said the prosecutor, trying to catch his breath. He had to lean against a wall. The second officer came up a few seconds later.

"They have to be in one of these houses," said the first policeman. "This is as far as they could have gone."

They stood there, not knowing what to do, taking in air in great gulps. One of the officers went in a shop for something to drink. The prosecutor felt frustrated and furious. He followed the officer into the shop, where a girl of about fourteen waited on them. The other policeman remained outside. The girl placed two Inca Kolas on the counter. There was nothing else in the shop but Inca Kola and Field saltines. As they were taking the first swallows, the officer stared at the girl. He seemed to hesitate. He looked toward the back room, hidden behind a curtain. Then he shook his head, as if he had been confused. He smiled at the girl:

"Will you give me some crackers too, Mamacita?"

The girl turned her back to take down the crackers. They were on a high shelf. When she raised her arm, the officer took out his pistol, a 9mm like the one the prosecutor had at home, and jumped over the counter. He grabbed the girl around the neck and pressed the barrel to her head. Then, using her as a shield, he pushed her toward the back room, aiming the weapon and shouting:

"Don't any of you move, damn it, or I'll kill her! Damn it, don't move!"

He went into the back room. The prosecutor did not know what to do. Alerted by the shouts, the other officer came in holding his weapon. In the back room, the shouts of the first officer and two other voices could be heard:

"No, Papacito, we haven't done anything, Papa! Leave us alone!"

The officer pointed at the door. There was the sound of blows, breaking glass, objects falling from shelves, the weeping of a woman, that is, a girl.

"Hands on your head, damn it! Back!"

With hands behind their heads, two young men came out of the back room. The prosecutor recognized the white undershirt of one of the boys he had pursued. The officer waiting for them outside, aiming at their faces, became angry when he saw them:

"You two? Motherfucker . . ."

They put them against the wall, always aiming at their heads, and the prosecutor searched them: he found two clasp knives and a small revolver, a .28. The policemen kicked them a little and had them lie down on the ground, their arms extended, until the patrol wagon came to take them away. They had the girl lie down with them as well.

"You can't be a delinquent in Ayacucho," said the officer who had recognized the girl. "Everybody knows everybody here."

One of the detainees sobbed.

"Shut up, damn it!" said the other officer. He kicked him in the stomach. The other boy held back a sob.

"Who are they?" asked Chacaltana.

"Them? Nothing but trash. When Sendero Luminoso was already dying, it lowered the age of its cadres. It began recruiting kids ten or eleven years old, even nine. They gave them weapons and trained them to handle explosives. Then Sendero was finished, but the kids were still wandering around, nothing but common criminals."

The prosecutor stared at the two boys lying on the ground. One was about eighteen. The other, younger than fifteen.

"And why are they still active?"

"What should we do with them? Until a little while ago they were underage. And there's no reformatory here. But the veterans like this motherfucker," and he kicked the face of the older one, "have been training kids like this one for years," and he stepped on the hand of the younger one. The prosecutor heard him sob from the ground. It was like the whimpering of a child. "The age gets lower and lower and they get worse and worse. And there's nothing we can do."

The prosecutor noticed that the girl had a black eye.

"And what would you do with them?"

The other policeman answered:

"If it was up to me, I'd lock them up and throw away the key. There's no changing them. As the tree grows . . ."

The older boy turned to look at the policeman with hatred. The officer spat at him and said:

"What are you looking at, damn it? You're all grown up, huh? You must be at least twenty, but you play the snot-nose kid, damn undocumented shit. With your record, we can send you to be fucked in maximum security. So don't look at me too much because I'll turn you into a woman, see?"

The prosecutor understood why he did not know anything about them. There were no complaints at the Ministry of Justice, no papers on these boys. As Commander Carrión had said, they did not even have a name.

He went back to the center of town with his head lowered, preoccupied. As he crossed the residential tract he thought someone was walking behind him. When he turned, there was only a woman with some flowers for the procession.

Later, at police headquarters, the officers informed him that the tourists who had been attacked did not have even minor wounds. Pure fright, they said. The one who had taken their complaint remarked:

"Gringos, Señor Prosecutor, they're all faggots. They scream and carry on and nobody's done anything to them. They weren't even robbed because they all started shouting. We ought to export some criminals to them so they'll know what a real robbery is and stop wasting our time with stupid bullshit."

Associate District Prosecutor Félix Chacaltana Saldívar spent the rest of the afternoon watching the festivities. He saw the Lord of Palms leave the Monastery of St. Teresa mounted on a white donkey, accompanied by twelve Ayacuchans dressed as apostles, and the principal civilian authorities of the city. After them came another donkey carrying baskets of fruit. When they reached the cathedral, the sculpture of Christ was taken down and brought into the temple to the sound of hurrahs and applause. The prosecutor recognized the carpet of the Heart of Jesus that he had seen at the beginning of the ceremony. After the passage of people and animals, it had been destroyed. The figure of the heart was torn to pieces, shreds of it still hanging from the hooves of the donkeys.

On Monday afternoon, after having lunch with Edith, the Associate District Prosecutor walked to the maximum security prison of Huamanga. His entrance was easier than the last time. Colonel Olazábal welcomed him with open arms and offered him a *mate* because he knew it was his favorite drink. The prosecutor did not ask how he knew. He imagined the answer: Ayacucho is a small city, everybody knows everything. He assured Olazábal that he had interceded on behalf of his promotion, and then he could see Hernán Durango González, alias Comrade Alonso.

"You're becoming very fond of me, Señor Prosecutor," was the first thing the terrorist said. "I don't have many visitors who are so faithful."

"I have come on a professional matter, Señor Durango."

"Call me Alonso, please."

"Your name is Hernán."

On the previous occasion, the terrorist had been aggressive and self-assured. Now, a certain irony seemed to emanate from his eyes, otherwise as fixed and stony as always. Knowing that Durango always had an answer even before knowing the question, the prosecutor decided to move ahead to what he had to say.

"I want to know what connections . . ."

"Why do you think I'll tell you anything, Señor Prosecutor?"

It was a good question. The prosecutor shuffled through possible responses: because I cannot think of anyone else to talk to, because I have no idea what is going on here, because I am not a policeman and do not know how to investigate, because I have to turn in a report and for the first time do not know how to do it . . .

"Because you like to talk, Señor Durango," he finally said. "You feel superior to all of us and you like to flaunt it."

"It's quite a stretch from that to betrayal, don't you agree?"

"I have already told you there is nothing left to betray. Your people are finished. But I am dealing with a special case, and you might perhaps be helpful."

"Thank you," he said sarcastically. "Can I smoke?"

As on the previous occasion, the terrorist was handcuffed. The prosecutor thought he might relax a little with a cigarette. He opened the office door and asked the guard for one. Chacaltana coughed when he lit it. He went back in and gave the cigarette to the terrorist. Durango inhaled deeply and looked out the window.

"Tell me, it's Holy Week out there, isn't it? I noticed because of the holiday visits."

"Don't tell me you did not know."

"I haven't kept track of time for a long while now."

The prosecutor detected a hint of sadness in the terrorist's voice. He thought it was one of his strategies to confuse him. He tried to confuse him in turn:

"I never would have imagined you were so devout."

The terrorist's eyes were glued to the window. He turned and looked at the prosecutor, and suddenly began to recite:

"And Jesus went into the temple and cast out all them that sold and bought in the temple, and overthrew the tables of the money changers, and the seats of them that sold doves, And said unto them, It is written, My house shall be called the house of prayer; but ye have made it a den of thieves."

He kept staring at the prosecutor with pride. The prosecutor asked:

"Is that in the Bible?"

"In the Gospel of St. Matthew. There are things that are universal, Prosecutor Chacaltana, like indignation at the dens of thieves."

"Interesting. Is there . . . any kind of relationship between your movement and some religious prophecy? The Apocalypse or . . . something like that?"

Now the terrorist burst into laughter. He let the explosion of laughter resonate along the bare walls of the office. Then he said:

"We are materialists. But I suppose you don't even know what that is."

"What do you think will happen after death?"

Comrade Alonso gave a nostalgic smile.

"It will be like the Indian servant's dream. Do you know it? It's a story by Arguedas. Do you read?"

"I like Chocano."

Now the terrorist laughed sarcastically. There was something like cultural petulance in his attitude. He did not consider the prosecutor to be an intellectual.

"I prefer Arguedas. They don't let us read here, but I always think about that story. It's about an Indian, the lowest of the slaves on a plantation, a servant of the servants. One day the Indian tells the master that he's had a dream. In his dream, they both died and went to heaven. There God ordered the angels to cover the Indian with manure until all his skin was hidden by shit. But he ordered the rich man to be completely bathed in honey. The master is happy to hear the Indian's dream. He thinks it reasonable, he thinks that is exactly what God will do. He urges him to go on and asks: 'And then what happens?' The Indian replies: 'Then, when he saw the two men covered in shit and honey respectively, he says: Now lick the other's body until it is completely clean.' That must be divine justice, the place where everything's turned upside down, where the defeated become the victors."

The prosecutor oozed discomfort. He cleared his throat.

"That is a story," he said. "I was referring to whether or not you believe in heaven or the Resurrection . . ."

The prosecutor thought it was a very strange question for an interrogation, but the entire case was more than strange, so he supposed it was an adequate question. The terrorist took his time looking out the window and smoking a little more before he began to speak:

"About four years ago, Comrade Alina was given a radio by one of her visitors, a . . . small battery-operated radio, almost invisible. Sometimes she even managed to get it to us in the men's block. We listened to it for a couple of nights and then sent it back one way or another. Often the police themselves would carry it back and forth in exchange for cigarettes or something to eat. For us it was an event. For years we hadn't seen television or heard the news, no papers, nothing to read. We kept the radio for a couple of months until one of the guards fought for some reason with Comrade Alina, some damn stupid thing, I suppose, and told his superiors that we had it. Colonel Olazábal demanded that the radio be turned in. Comrade Alina and the party members refused. They said we had the right to have a radio according to all the laws and treaties on human rights. The colonel threatened a round of searches, but the comrade didn't give him the radio. She said it would be over her dead body . . ."

The terrorist's voice broke. He threw the cigarette to the floor and stepped on it. He seemed to have collapsed. At first the prosecutor was surprised by his vulnerability but thought again that he was trying to confuse him. Durango continued:

"Olazábal didn't dare to provoke an uprising, and everybody forgot about it. But two days later he had the men and women arrested for terrorism line up in the central courtyard. The rest of the inmates were locked in their cells. We thought it would be a routine inspection. Until the doors opened and in came the Force for Special Operations, accompanied by a prosecutor . . . a prosecutor like you, of course. The prosecutor said he would conduct a search for illegal material and asked if anyone had any object to declare. After a long silence, Alina raised her hand and mentioned the radio but refused to turn it in. The prosecutor asked her for it twice, without result. Then he said he had done what the law required . . . He declared us mutinous . . . and put the officer at the head of the Special Forces in charge. He left. Then . . ."—now his eyes swelled. Threads of spittle formed inside his mouth as he spoke—"when the door closed, the Special Forces attacked us, Señor Prosecutor. There were about two hundred of them armed with clubs, paralyzing gases, and chains, set loose like mad dogs coming toward us across the courtyard. Most of our people were handcuffed or shackled. Some of us, the ones who were free, ran to surround Alina, to defend her . . ."—he stopped for a second.

It seemed as if he would not continue, that he would break down. "About twenty of them came directly toward her. They sprayed chemicals into our faces, and when we couldn't see they clubbed us down to the ground. And didn't stop until they made sure we couldn't get up for a long time . . . They hit me in the head, the testicles, the stomach . . . But they weren't satisfied with that." Now Durango looked at some point on the white wall, some infinite place. "The women, they . . ."—he closed his eyes—"they tore off their clothes, and then, in front of us, they brandished their clubs and laughed, telling them things like 'Come on, Mamita, you'll like it,' they said . . . Do you want . . . do you want to know what they did to them with those clubs, Señor Prosecutor?"

No. The prosecutor did not want to know. He wanted to stand up and leave, he wanted to close his eyes and clench his teeth forever, he wanted to tear out his ears so he would not have to go on listening. The terrorist no longer hid the tears rolling down his cheeks.

"You should know," he continued, staring now at the prosecutor with hatred. "You should know what they did with their clubs to the women, because then they did the same thing to us men . . ."

He tried to control himself, to swallow his tears of shame and rage. The prosecutor tried to do the same. He remained silent. The terrorist, after sobbing for a moment, concluded:

"You asked me if I believed in heaven. I believe in hell, Señor Prosecutor. I live there. Hell is not being able to die."

Félix Chacaltana Saldívar, Associate District Prosecutor, returned to the city at 7:00 in the evening, when the procession of the Lord of the Garden was leaving the Temple of the Good Death on its way to the Plaza Mayor. The platform was decorated with pineapples, fruit, ears of corn, tall candles, and olive branches in memory of Jesus' prayer on the Mount of Olives, when he asked his father to save him from dying. The prosecutor asked himself why no one in the world can choose either not to die or to die later. And his answer was that perhaps no one on high is listening to our pleas, perhaps prayers are only things we tell ourselves because nobody else wants to hear them.

In the procession for Holy Monday no fireworks were set off, since this was a remembrance of an act of sorrow. But that night, as he advanced on Edith's body, trying not to go too far, the prosecutor thought again about blows. Blows that thundered in his ears and on the back of his neck, blows like God's hate, blows that only fire could stop, turn into ash, into silence, into mute supplication. Suddenly, he could not go on.

"What is it?" she asked.

The prosecutor thought of telling her. He remembered Lieutenant Aramayo in Yawarmayo. He remembered his inability to speak.

"I love you," was his only reply.

And then he continued to touch her, to press against his body the first warm body offered to him in years, the only living body he had touched in recent days. He made an effort to remove her underwear, but she resisted. Then he lay on top of Edith and tried to rub his groin against hers, until Edith moved away from his attacks, annoyed.

"That's all you want, isn't it?" she asked.

What concerned the prosecutor most was not the impulse to say yes, at that moment it was the only thing he cared about and he did not feel capable of controlling himself anymore. In reality, what concerned him most was the certainty he could achieve it, so easily, barely stretching out his hand, no longer being as good as he usually was, so amiable, so weak. Almost without realizing it, he tried again. He nibbled at her ears and ran his palms along her back. This time, when she stopped him, she pointed at a photograph hanging on the wall. His mother was observing them and did not seem to approve of what they were doing.

"It's as if she were here," said Edith.

Then, they did not have the courage to continue.

That night, after walking Edith home, he returned to his house, said good night to his mother, made certain he had closed her door carefully, and masturbated in the bathroom, afraid she would hear him.

On Tuesday, the prosecutor had to take part in the procession of the Lord of Judgment, which was the responsibility of the personnel of the Judicial Branch. Normally he would have been proud to be part of the procession, but that day he did not want to. He felt drained and could think only of Edith's bosom. The image of Christ captured by the Jews had its hands tied and displayed evident signs of torture. Out of the corner of his eye he stared at that livid, exhausted body, its welts and scars. He felt he could not look directly at the platform during its passage.

Before the platform went out, Judge Briceño, one of the eight stewards of the procession, came up to him:

"You look tired, Señor Prosecutor," he said with a rat's smile. "Did you have a long night? I hear you're having more of a social life lately . . ."

"It is just . . . I just did not sleep well."

He felt his temples throbbing. Judge Briceño seemed very happy.

"I suppose you've dreamed about Captain Pacheco. Recently, I don't know why, that gentleman has taken an immense dislike to you, if you don't mind my saying so."

"I cannot imagine why, Judge."

"It's inexplicable, isn't it? Well, I want to indicate my pleasure at your sharing this procession with us. It's always a good idea for colleagues to share, isn't it? Keeping things all to oneself isn't very nice."

The prosecutor did not even feel like understanding the subtext of what the judge was saying.

"Of course," was all he replied.

"And now I'll leave you with your thoughts," said the judge as he left.

The prosecutor took part in the procession mechanically, like an automaton, stopping at the fourteen stations required to pray the Via Crucis, intoning from memory the sacred songs in Quechua and Spanish. No one had died that day. He used the prayers to ask for an end to the murders, only two were more than enough for one week, he asked that there not be more, that the prediction of the return of Sendero not be more than that—a prediction. At no moment during the procession, however, could he stop thinking about blows, blows, blows . . .

you heer? its like a pownding.

its time for you to free yourself. its time for you to fly. they had
you too long cownting hours, days, seconds. you had to wate.
you have to wate for important things. but you dont have to no
more.

did you see the proseshun of the meeting today? it was bewti-
ful. all the faithful were upset, yes, sad, yes, they felt deth close by.
today he died. the nazareen. the sisters of saint clare spent too
days dressing him and preparing him, cutting his hair and beerd
that grew since last yeer. he dies every yeer.

come heer, closer, thats it, good. you know something? i bin
lisening to you all this time. yes. i herd your voise. talking with all
those peepel, with the comrades, with the watch dogs of the empire. your voise reeched me. your watch dogs are stupid, they
sleep when you toss them a peese of meet. so today is your day. i
lisened to you all this time, did you lisen to me? you must of herd
me. i talk in your dreems, at the edge of your mind, at the doors
to eden. like this sownd, can you heer it now?

they made him meet his mother. the nazareen. she was in black.
oh what pane she felt. i felt it with her. there were coruses of men.
they sang. yes. they sang for you. veronica was there too, wiping
away the blud and swet of the nazareen so he wood die cleen. you
wood have liked it. what a shame you coodnt go. then veronica
went to saint john to tell him she had bin with jesus. the hoor. she
showed him the hankerchif. and everybody sang.

you like this? shore you like it. you were born for this. dont complane. we all have a cross to bare. it can hurt a little. everything that matters is gotten with a little pane. history is washed only with blud. yes. you tawt me that. im a good student, rite? were all good students because a lot of us are wateing to wake up. youll leed us. i chose you, yes, so youll cross the river of blud.

christ has a tunic of red and gold. they say too angels made it in a nite and then ran away. too angels like us, rite? too angels making christ in their image and likeness, in ours, so that every yeer he can walk the rode to calvary.

no. dont resist. this is your place. you erned it. we fouwt a lot to give it to you. now do you remember me? no? this isnt the first time we seen eech other. and it wont be the last. we saw eech other before, when we were alive. maybe were still alive now. these days i cant reely tell the difrense. you smell good did I tell you? you smell of prarie and the lords day. happy lords day.

my voise was small before, like a little streem. littel by littel its bin growing, like a grate flud. it did that by itself, its bin taking up more room in my memory, it took the place of the others. there are no more voises now. now theres only me and the eckos. yes. eckos of faraway times. but i talk lowder. like now see? your voise isnt herd. only mine is herd and the sownd of the nails, do you heer, going thru wood, going thru flesh, going thru time.

yes. now you heer them.

THURSDAY, APRIL 20

On Wednesday, the nineteenth day of April, 2000, when it was close to midnight, in the act of making the rounds on the night shift in Cell Block E for terrorists in the maximum security prison of Huamanga, police officer Wilder Orozco Pariona verified the absence of the inmate Hernán Durango González, alias Comrade Alonso, from his respective cell. The appropriate guards in the penitentiary having been alerted, Colonel Olazábal summoned the inmates to form in rows in the courtyard of the abovementioned cell block, where the thesis of Officer Orozco was confirmed in practice in the sense that the convicted terrorist had proceeded to escape the prison during the night.

The police garrison at the prison, which affirms that the escape lacked viability and that it has not discovered tunnels or other practical means of escape for the inmate, immediately proceeded to comb the area surrounding the prison to discover some clue regarding the unknown whereabouts of the above-cited inmate, with almost no results during the first hours of the search.

In the early-morning hours of Thursday, the twentieth day of April, as a police patrol was returning to the maximum security prison following a search operation in which the fugitive had not been captured, the duly constituted authorities in this regard declare having seen a bonfire on one of the hills adjacent to the perimeter of the prison, on the slope that faces away from the penal institution, so that in practical terms the fire was not visible from the prison. Considering that the presence of fire was unusual in proximity to the aforesaid penal institution, the patrol resolved to approach for purposes of investigation as well as prevention of sinister possibilities pertaining to the forest.

Having reached the slopes of the aforementioned hill, the police officers state that they were surprised by what appeared to be a human figure of considerable proportions at the foot of the bonfire. However, despite reiterated calls by the patrol, the supposed person did not turn around or give any sign of responding to their calls, appearing instead to have lingered there in thought. Because the darkness did not permit them to distinguish the features or political or criminal affiliation of the abovementioned person, the members of the National Police affirm that they drew their respective weapons in order to proceed to make an approach to the person, who displayed no sign of attempting to flee or of being surprised at their appearance.

Having reached the foot of the bonfire, in the act of requesting the person to stand on his feet with his hands behind his head, which corresponds to procedures employed for reasons of security in searching suspects, the officers declare that they discovered that the object in question, which they had taken for a person, lacked all signs of life and was identified instead as a corpse, whose considerable proportions seem to have been due to the fact that it was resting in a cruciform arrangement on a tree two and a half meters high, to whose branches the upper extremities had been nailed at the wrists.

Similarly, one of the lower extremities had been attached to the lower portion of the trunk by the same method, it having been verified that the other extremity was not found in the same circumstances due to the fact that it was totally missing from the body, from which it had in fact been torn off. The cadaver, by all accounts, displayed a crown tightly encircling its forehead, consisting of approximately a meter and a half of barbed wire, rolled around the head and tightened on it under conditions in which it pierced the skin of the entire cranial perimeter. A cut on the left side, at the height of the heart, was still bleeding.

The officers who effected the discovery have required psychological treatment subsequent to this action. Nevertheless, early the next morning, other police officers, such as Wilder Orozco Pariona and Colonel Olazábal himself, identified the deceased as the fugitive Hernán Durango González, alias Comrade Alonso, and lamented the outcome of his unfortunate escape.

The prosecutor raised his head from the typewriter. This time, he did not even check the syntax of his report. It seemed to him that it was simply a useless piece of paper. The data were not enough. The narrated facts had nothing to do with the murder but with its discovery. It was as if in order to describe a fishing run, one learned how the fish is served at the lunch table. It had nothing to do with what was really important. In reality, none of his reports had anything to do with what was important. He thought the relevant information was precisely what the report did not contain: who did it, why, what was going through his head. A truly useful report ought to be written knowing each detail in the lives of those involved: their pasts, their memories, their habits, even their most irrelevant conversations, the perversions that crossed their minds at the moment of execution, everything that no one could know. A real report, he concluded, could be written only by God, at least by someone with a thousand eyes and a thousand ears who could know everything. But if there were people like that, he thought, reports would not be necessary.

That morning, for the first time, he had been present at the place where the crucified corpse was located. At the top of the tree, like a placard saying INRI, was a note written in the corpse's blood:

KILLED FOR BEING A RAT
Sendero Luminoso

Impossible to know if it was the same writing as on the earlier note. One does not write the same with a pencil as with the tip of a knife. In fact, although being present at the place where the body was discovered had seemed more professional, he did not know more about this body than he had about the previous ones. Nearby were the tracks of a truck, but this was the road to the prison. Almost all the vehicles that drove there were trucks carrying food, inmates, or relief guards.

He returned to the city at six in the morning, when the Masses were over and workers were beginning to decorate the churches with loaves of bread, grapes, and lambs. Ayacucho smelled of the aromatic herbs that the faithful were boiling on braziers.

After writing his report, he went to see the pathologist.

"I can't tell you it's a pleasure to see you more and more frequently," was Dr. Posadas's greeting as he handed him a mask. The prosecutor was going to tell him that the smell of death filled the obstetrics ward, but he decided to say nothing. It was not his problem. He already had enough problems.

The body, which had been taken down from his cross, lay on the usual table, uncovered. The holes in his forearms and only leg permitted a view of the surface of the table underneath. The crown had been fitted tightly to his forehead.

"Spare me the sordid details, Doctor. What's new?"

"More sordid details, Señor Prosecutor. That's the only thing that's ever new here."

The doctor said this with a half smile as he lit a cigarette. He never seemed overwhelmed; on the contrary, he looked almost happy. The prosecutor wondered if the doctor liked his work, if he scrutinized the bodies with real pleasure in what he did.

"Again it looks like the action of a cell. One man on his own couldn't have staged that whole show in so short a time."

"Of course. Then we are talking about a few men."

"It could have been only two. And a woman, usually."

"A woman?"

"A strange thing about the terrorists. They organized into groups of men led by women. I don't know if they're still doing it, one never knows with them. But apparently the women were always the strongest ideologically. And the most bloodthirsty. The men were errand boys, so to speak. They were good for confrontations and technical jobs. But if you had to give a coup de grâce, the woman in charge took care of that."

"A woman couldn't do this."

"No. But she could order it."

The prosecutor collapsed into a chair. He looked exhausted. He said:

"I don't even know if it makes sense to look very hard at the body. Now there are other incomprehensible details. The escape, for example. How did Durango disappear from a maximum security prison without anyone seeing him?"

The doctor took out a chocolate and began eating it. Now he held the chocolate in one hand and the cigarette in the other.

"Is that what's bothering you? If you guarantee your discretion, I'll give you an answer: Colonel Olazábal is a cretin who thinks of nothing but a promotion. They must have bribed him. For a long time he hasn't cared who he works for."

It was the last straw. Now the best allies of the terrorists were the police. But there was still something that did not fit:

"And Durango escaped in order to die?"

"Maybe they're the ones who killed him."

"If you had seen the faces of the police when they found the body, you would not say that."

"That's another problem. I only know what I'm telling you. And remember, I haven't told you anything."

The light flickered. The doctor was right. It really was another problem. But it was the principal problem. All the victims seem to have gone directly, almost willingly, to their murder. With Mayta and Durango it was reasonable. They trusted their comrades, they went along. The first one, Cáceres, also had an explanation: he was hopelessly mad, mad with blood. People who have killed too much never recover. It doesn't matter which side they did it for.

The doctor made a general description of the wounds: hematomas on the shoulders and bruises that indicated a strenuous struggle before being nailed up. Muscular lacerations resulting from long nails in the extremities. Chacaltana did not listen. He barely noticed the mixture of liquids that ran from the wounds. The red of blood and something greenish black: he had no idea what it could be. And he did not ask. He was lost in his own thoughts.

He left the hospital plunged into dark nausea. A crowd had gathered around the bishop of Huamanga, who performed the traditional washing of the twelve beggars. The prosecutor had the report to deliver to Carrión. As he passed through headquarters, he asked himself what in hell he was going to tell him. That he had no idea about anything, that the terrorists were still at large, that he had no more theories, that he had never had any theories. He realized that his eyes were filling with tears. He thought about what his mother would have done in this situation. He decided to leave the report at reception and continue on to the Church of the Heart of Christ. He found Father Quiroz about to leave. Father Quiroz was always about to leave. When the prosecutor appeared, he greeted him with a smile that barely disguised his annoyance.

"Today I really am sorry, Señor Prosecutor, but it's Holy Thursday and, as you can understand, I cannot attend to you. Besides, these aren't working days. Why don't you continue your investigation on Monday?"

"I have not come to investigate, Father."

"Ah, no?"

"I have . . . come to confess."

"Well, perhaps that can wait too. God will understand."

The priest looked toward the door, where two nuns were waiting for him. He looked at his watch. The prosecutor said:

"There's a new corpse."

The priest began to lead him slowly by the arm to the door as he listened to him.

"I'm sorry. How did he die?"

"You don't even want to know. But I know who killed all of them."

"Are you serious?"

The priest did not seem to be listening carefully. He appeared lost in his own thoughts.

"It was me," said the prosecutor.

The priest turned pale. He seemed to stop breathing. As if to recuperate, he sighed deeply and turned toward the nuns at the door. With a gesture he told them to continue on their way. They seemed disappointed but submissive. Then, Quiroz took the prosecutor to a confessional and each of them took his place. The prosecutor kneeled when he heard the confessor's screen move and said:

"I don't know how to do this, Father. I haven't confessed for a long time."

The priest quickly whispered some formulas that Chacaltana could not make out. Then he said:

"Just tell me. We're not going to give you an intensive course on the sacraments now."

The prosecutor swallowed. He looked at the Baroque images in the church, the red candles at each altar, before he said:

"All the people I talk to die, Father. I'm afraid. It's . . . it's as if I were signing their death sentences when I leave them."

"My son," said the priest. Suddenly Chacaltana had stopped being Señor Prosecutor. "Perhaps . . . perhaps you are carrying too much . . . These deaths aren't your fault."

"I'm afraid. I don't sleep well. This . . . all of this is as if I had already seen it. There's something in all this that has already happened, something that speaks of me. Do you understand? You don't understand, do you?"

"My son, the terrorist madness knows nothing of reasons or feelings. If you allow yourself to be morally destroyed by them, you're letting them win. That's what they want. For you to collapse. Then their work will be easier."

Tears escaped again from the prosecutor's eyes:

"I've seen things . . . Things you cannot imagine. They . . ."— he had just noticed how hard it was for him to say it—"they tear off limbs . . . They cut off arms and legs . . ."

"Don't underestimate me, my son. I also fought. I know what you know. I know them."

"Why, Father? Why can't they simply kill? Why does it have to be like this?"

"There is a reason beyond barbarism." The priest's paternal warmth was congealing into a serious, dry tone. "In the Andes there is the myth of Inkarri, the Incan King. It seems to have emerged during colonial times, after the indigenous rebellion of Tupac Amaru. After suppressing the rebellion, the Spanish army tortured Tupac Amaru, they beat him until he was almost dead . . ."—blows, blows, blows, thought the prosecutor—"then they attached his limbs to horses until he was pulled to pieces."

The images of Tupac Amaru quartered followed one another in the mind of the prosecutor as if he had experienced them. His mother had told him the story once, in Cuzco, the city that the chief had besieged and where he had been killed. The prosecutor's mother was Cuzcan. The priest continued:

"The Andean campesinos believe that the parts of Tupac Amaru were buried in different places throughout the empire so that his body would never join together again. According to them, those parts are growing until they can rejoin. And when they find the head, the Inca will rise again and a cycle will be closed. The empire will rise again and crush those who bled it. The earth and the sun will swallow the God the Spaniards brought in from outside. At times, when I see the Indians so submissive, so ready to accept anything, I wonder if on the inside they aren't thinking that the moment will arrive, and that someday our roles will be reversed."

"What does Sendero Luminoso have to do with that?"

"A great deal. Sendero presented itself as the resurgence. And it was always conscious of the value of symbols. They killed a woman and blew up her body with explosives to shatter her into pieces. In this way, her parts will never unite again. Her resurrection was made impossible."

"Against whom are we fighting, Father? They're everywhere and at the same time they're not. They're invisible. It's like fighting ghosts."

"It's like fighting the gods we don't see. Perhaps we're fighting the dead."

They remained in silence for a few minutes. Suddenly, Quiroz seemed to remember something:

"When did they kill the last one?"

"Last night, almost at dawn, after the procession of the Meeting." The prosecutor felt relieved at having spoken with the priest, but exhausted, as if he had lost all his breath in the conversation. He sighed. "There was no special security. We had deployed it for Palm Sunday, and even Monday, but more could not be justified."

The priest thought for a moment and said:

"There's . . . another Andean myth that perhaps you ought to know about. In general, beginning on the night of Holy Wednesday, the Indians abandon themselves to the most . . . sinful celebrations. Torrents of alcohol flow, and a good deal of sex, and usually there are violent incidents. It goes on until Resurrection Sunday."

"Until the Sunday of Glory."

The priest was annoyed:

"It's called Resurrection Sunday. Only the ignorant and the blasphemous call it the Sunday of Glory."

"Forgive me. And why do they do that?"

"It's another Andean superstition. Starting on Holy Wednesday, the day of Christ's Calvary, God is dead. He no longer sees. He no longer condemns. There are three days for sinning."

When he heard this Chacaltana understood he had no time to lose. He would have to reactivate security. It was as if he had recovered consciousness after a long mystic interval. The priest, too, had things to do. When he left the confessional, Chacaltana shook his hand with sincere gratitude:

"Thank you very much, Father. I feel much better. And you have given me many useful clues. I have spo . . ." He stopped himself. Then he decided to say it. "I have spoken with people who do not trust you very much. But there are others who have expressed their appreciation of your person."

The priest smiled as he walked to the door. The prosecutor noticed that he was the only figure who smiled in that church.

"I won't ask you to tell me who has spoken ill of me, but I would like to know who has spoken favorably."

The prosecutor felt he was trustworthy. He thought it would not be a bad thing to tell him. Just the opposite.

"Edith Ayala. The woman in the restaurant on the square."

The priest gave him a big smile.

"Of course I know her! She would come here frequently. Poor girl, she has suffered a great deal on account of her parents."

"Her parents?"

"Don't you know?"

"She does not talk about them very much."

"It's understandable. Her parents were terrorists. They died in an attack on a police barracks. The two of them together."

The prosecutor remembered his conversation with Edith: How did they die? On account of the terrorists. On account of. Not killed by the terrorists but in their name. As he was saying good-bye to the priest, he tried to forget he had heard that. He had more urgent things to think about. He hurried to headquarters, past people visiting churches and enjoying typical food at the stalls in the Plaza Mayor. He thought that any one of them could be a member of the Senderista renascence. He reached headquarters and went in as far as Carrión's waiting room. His secretary looked nervous.

"May I go in?" he asked.

She looked at him in anguish.

"He doesn't want to see anybody. He's been locked in there since Friday. He hasn't even gone out to eat. We bring him food, but he hardly touches it."

"Perhaps I can do something."

"Try, please. Maybe he'll listen to you. If I attempt to announce you, he won't answer the intercom."

Prosecutor Chacaltana opened the door of the office. It was dark inside, and it smelled. The curtains were closed and two full plates of food were rotting beneath the worktable. The commander was sitting at his desk, dark circles under his eyes, gaunt, looking as if he had not bathed in months. He did not greet him.

"Did you hear about Durango?" asked the prosecutor.

The commander seemed to return from a very distant place before responding in a cavernous voice:

"That's no longer my affair."

The commander handed him a sheet of paper he was holding in his hand. The prosecutor managed to read it in spite of the half-light. It was a letter to Carrión from Lima with the letterhead of the Joint Command of the Armed Forces, announcing his retirement.

"It is not time for you yet." The prosecutor was surprised.

"Here it's time for whatever they want. They've modified the chains of command to their liking. It's over."

They sank into a dark silence that the officer broke only minutes later:

"Did you leak information to Eléspuru, in Intelligence? Did you talk to him about this?"

"No, Señor. I do not know how they could have known . . ."

"They know everything, Chacaltana. Everything. But I suppose that doesn't matter anymore. My replacement will arrive when the festivities are over. Perhaps he doesn't even have anything to do with this. There will be new elections, maybe they want to place an officer here who's less irritable than me, or more manageable, or whatever the hell it is."

It was difficult to know if his voice expressed relief or frustration. The prosecutor felt abandoned, betrayed. It seemed to him that for the commander to leave when he was caught in the middle of these problems was the easy way out. He looked carefully at the officer and changed his mind. Nothing seemed easy for that man.

"And what are you going to do?" the prosecutor asked.

"I'll go north, to Piura or Tumbes. I want a quiet place. And most of all, one very far from here."

The prosecutor dropped into a chair. In spite of the size difference between the seats, this time he did not seem smaller than the commander.

"You cannot leave like this," he said with aplomb. "We have not finished yet."

The commander laughed. At first very quietly, then in great bellows. When he managed to control himself, he lit a cigarette between coughs. The prosecutor had never seen him smoke. Carrión said:

"Finished? This is only the beginning, Chacaltana. Our work of two decades has just gone all to hell. We can't even guarantee our own security. We'll never stop them. They'll keep coming back."

"But it is our job . . ."

"To fight the sea? Because that's what we're doing. After all, I've been reading during the days I've been inside. Ayacucho is a strange place. The Wari culture was here, and then the Chancas, who never let themselves be conquered by the Incas. And then the indigenous rebellions, because Ayacucho was the midway point between Cuzco, the Inca capital, and Lima, the capital of the Spaniards. And independence in Quinua. And Sendero. This place is doomed to be bathed in blood and fire forever, Chacaltana. Why? I have no idea. It doesn't matter. We can't do anything. I suggest that you leave too. You must be on the blacklist by now, you'll be next."

"We ought to investigate Olazábal. Durango's escape is very suspicious. Don't you think so? And perhaps it was the colonel who sent a report to Lima about this."

"Are you deaf? Today's a holiday, and on Monday I'm leaving. Do whatever you want, I don't care. And keep the pistol. It's a gift."

Then he made the gesture he always made when he said "Thanks, you can go." But he did not say anything. Again they remained in silence.

"I want to ask you for something . . . ," the prosecutor said at last. "I have reason to believe that the next attempts will take place in the next few days. I want to double security."

The irritation intensified in the already irritated eyes of Carrión.

"Again, Chacaltana? Haven't we already been ridiculous enough?"

"Believe me this time. I am not wrong."

Carrión looked at him as if he were his son, his heir, with more tenderness than pride.

"I was once like you, Chacaltana. I thought we could stop this. But it's stronger than the two of us. This is the history of a country. Spare yourself the disappointment."

Chacaltana was no longer a boy. But perhaps he felt strong in spite of everything. He felt he was coming closer, that his life, after all, would have some meaning, even if that meaning were found in death. It was an idea that no longer seemed contradictory to him. He held Carrión's gaze and said:

"I have to stay. That is also stronger than me. You are still an authority. Sign the security order. I will take care of everything else."

The commander took a blank sheet of letterhead out of his desk and signed it.

"Dictate whatever you want to say to my secretary. It's the last favor I'll do for you, little Chacaltita. I'll ask for one in return: take care of yourself, please."

Chacaltana took his leave of the commander with a military salute. He thought about embracing him but did not dare. In any case, he would have liked to. It would have been like embracing a father. Commander Carrión had been anything but a good man, but at least, perhaps, his final gestures had redeemed him through fear. Perhaps that was the only way to really be redeemed.

Twenty minutes later, he went to police headquarters with the signed order. The usual sergeant was at the door.

"Good afternoon, Señor Prosecutor. Unfortunately, Captain Pacheco has told me to say that for the moment he isn't in, but that if . . . Señor Prosecutor. Señor Prosecutor!"

Chacaltana went directly to Pacheco's office and opened the door. Inside were the captain and Judge Briceño. The sergeant at the door pulled at the prosecutor's arm as he spoke to the captain.

"Excuse me, Señor! I informed the prosecutor that you were absent, but . . ."

"Shut up, you imbecile!" replied Pacheco. "And get out. Come in, Señor Prosecutor. Since you have lost your manners, at least have a seat."

Without sitting down, the prosecutor placed the paper on his desk.

"I have an order from Commander Carrión to double security, effective immediately."

"From whom?" asked the captain, looking as if he did not recognize the name.

"Commander Carrión, who has made clear to me his concern regarding . . ."

"I'm afraid he hasn't heard what happened," intervened Judge Briceño. The captain smiled. "It's understandable. It's clear you're too distracted by your own matters. The commander is no longer in command here."

They seemed pleased by the news. Perhaps they had just been celebrating it. The prosecutor replied:

"His retirement is not yet in effect, Señor Judge."

"When people die," answered the judge, "one doesn't wait for their death to be in effect. They just die, Prosecutor Chacaltana."

Chacaltana looked from one to the other. Then he said:

"The order is in response to the need for extreme security measures . . ."

"In the absence of the commander, I decide what security measures are needed," said Pacheco. "And I'm not going to deprive my men of their time off without a good reason. Unless you have a judicial order. Why don't you ask Judge Briceño for one? Ah, I forgot, it's a holiday, the judge isn't working!" He became serious. "Neither are we."

"You do not understand. There is a killer on the loose!"

"A killer?" asked the judge. "We don't know about any killer. There's no record of any complaint of murder in the judicial district. I don't know if you've been whispering about something with your commander, but we don't know anything. If you want institutions to function, you have to transmit your information to them, Señor Chacaltana. If not, what can we do?"

Chacaltana hesitated. Then he recovered his confidence:

"You two will be complicit if you do not carry out the order."

"Excuse me," a falsely offended Briceño replied. "Are you accusing us of something? If that is so, say it clearly, please. You could be guilty of contempt or insubordination. What are you calling us?"

He made a gesture of taking notes as he waited for Chacaltana's response. The police captain continued smiling, with a smile like that of the president looking at him from his photograph on the wall. The prosecutor thought they were in this office together, law and order. And he understood that it made no sense to continue to insist.

"Nothing, Señor Judge. This . . . must have been a misunderstanding."

"Of course, a misunderstanding," Captain Pacheco confirmed.

The prosecutor noticed that both were looking in his eyes, penetratingly, as if trying to find out something else, something lodged in the interior of his optic nerve, perhaps. Briceño said:

"Now that things are clearer, you ought to sit down. Perhaps we're still in time to chat about the future. The captain and I in fact were coordinating plans with regard to the absence of Commander Carrión. Perhaps you should join our working group."

A month earlier, perhaps, the invitation would have flattered him. He would have visited Edith to celebrate his entrance into the circles of Ayacuchan power. He would have enthusiastically participated in the meetings of the working group, turning in reports and suggesting reforms to streamline administrative processes. But the offer was late, as if it had come to him from another time in his life. He realized that he felt like a mature man now, perhaps for the first time in his life, an adult who would make decisions consulting only with himself. He looked at both functionaries and could not contain a small smile that barely played at the corners of his mouth, a smile of superiority, of self-sufficiency.

"I see that you like the idea," said Briceño. On the other side of the desk, Captain Pacheco seemed to limit his function to smiling and celebrating each of the judge's ingenious, arrogant phrases. The prosecutor first shook his head while continuing to smile. Then he pronounced his decision:

"No, no . . . I think it would be better if I did not."

To the surprise of the other two, he walked to the exit and left the office, slamming the door behind him. He imagined the judge and the captain laughing inside, celebrating death with Holy Week, preparing to drain the city's blood like two vampires. Carrión the cat was out of combat. The mice were beginning to play even before he left the city.

It was already dark outside. There were no processions that day, and the tourists filled the streets in a disorderly way, not going anywhere in particular. Drunks were piling up at the corners of the Plaza Mayor. Chacaltana could not watch over the whole city by himself. He could not have a thousand eyes and a thousand ears; he was not even very good at writing a report. He realized he had not eaten lunch. He needed to sleep. He decided not to look for anyone, not to see anyone, to go directly to his house. He returned home, greeted his mother, fixed some chicken soup, and went to bed. He was sad and tired, tired of not being able to do anything. He thought that tonight there would be another dead body and he was the only one who knew it. Then he became aware that it might be his turn to be the victim. With the tranquility of someone making preparations for supper, he got up and locked the door and the windows of his house. He even put a padlock on his mother's window, begging Señora Saldívar de Chacaltana's pardon for the inconvenience and assuring her it was a temporary measure. He pushed the sofa and an armchair against the door to the house, and the bureau and armoires against the windows. He went back to bed, making certain he had his weapon close by. As he tried to fall asleep, he thought about Edith. Better not to look for her. He would only put her in danger. Everyone I talk to dies, he thought. It occurred to him to masturbate with the memory of her smooth breasts that tasted of trout. He did not have time for that. In spite of his fear, he felt his eyelids closing.

At two in the morning, he was assailed by a new nightmare. It had to do with fire and a church. Blows on a bleeding body in a temple. He saw a white man with a Limenian accent hitting a woman. He saw her blood staining the baptismal font, the white cloths of the altar, the chalice, the chasuble. And then the explosion, the fire devouring both of them. But the man did not stop hitting the woman, kicking her on the ground, shouting at her. He tried to get closer to defend her and went through the flames. The shouts seemed familiar. The man's voice especially, he knew it in some corner of his memory that he had allowed to be consumed by flames. He was closer and closer to the aggressor. In the dream he did not have the weapon but was sure he could bring down the savage with his own hands. Now the blood did not seem to stain the church but to flood it. The pool was growing beneath his feet, it reached his knees, his waist, and interfered with his movement toward the violent man, who had not stopped beating the woman as he began to drown in the red liquid. Once at his side, he took the man by the shoulder and wheeled him around to face him. It was like turning around a mirror. It was his own face held up by the aggressor's shoulders.

He woke with a start, sweating. He went to the bathroom to wash his face. He looked at himself in the mirror. He felt old. He thought about what he had said that morning in the confessional. Everybody I talk to dies. He felt a palpitation. He tried to go back to sleep but could not. He got up, dressed, and moved the furniture away from the door, scratching the floor. He went out. One hundred meters later, he turned and went back to his house. Silently, so his mother would not hear him, he went to his night table. He took out the pistol, hung it under his jacket, and went out again to the Church of the Heart of Christ.

FRIDAY, APRIL 21

you been talking abowt me, fadder?

you been talking abowt me to god?

talk to him about me. tell him to make me a plase. ill make him lissen to you. yes, hell lissen to you. youll be able to put your bald hed on his lap and lick his legs. hell let you touch him, run your hand down his back. youll like it. open your mowth, fadder, like that. let me see your holey tung. let me see your wite teeth. i like wite things, pure things. i have a treet fore you. taste the body of christ.

thats it, much better. now your nice and calm, you know? its better to stay calm. now everythings coming to an end. now its over, now. payshuns. all things have to have an end so they can begin again. you, me, well all have an end. yes. mines close too. but yours is allreddy here. ha. son of the devil.

your dirty, you know? dirty like the beggers in the sity. todays the day to wash you. ill leeve you spotless. oh, youll like it. dont say nothing, fadder, dont talk with your mowth full. its dirty. thats better. do you see how your getting cleen, fadder? your all full of sin. we all remember you here because of that. the bodys you berned remember you for that. did you forget abowt that? did you forget abowt there bodys disapeering into your oven? abowt there ashes?

they didnt forget abowt you. there they are, with god, like youll be, and they think abowt you every day. they cant live again, there bodys arent there anymore. its better. now they have life forever, dont they? true life. now youll meet with them, because your cleen, now you can see them. you and they will talk, yes. world withowt end.

move a little. the holey water has too touch you everywhere. its like a baptisim, unnerstand? a sacramint. a baptisim of fire for you. we lerned that with you. fire cleens. if not, whats the point?

do you heer something? seems like you have a visiter. did you invite another begger to wash him? your charitabel. your good. hoo is it? ah, now i know hoo it is. yes. we seen each other before. he came soon. have you been talking too him about me, fadder? thats good, im not mad at you. well make him one of ours, yes? well love him a lot with our tungs of fire. well wash away his impuritys too, fadder. we have a lot to share.

It was 2:30 in the morning when the prosecutor reached the parish house. There were still some tourists on the street with their Ayacuchan girlfriends, all high but not as noisy now. Some were fighting among themselves or perhaps shouting at the home-town boyfriends, abandoned for the celebration. The faithful had gone to sleep in preparation for the next few nights, the most important ones of the festivities. Prosecutor Chacaltana did not even notice them. He walked resolutely, becoming accustomed with each step to the weight of the pistol at his side, and more and more certain as he approached the door. Before he rang the bell, he wondered how he would justify a visit at this hour. Then he told himself that the priest would understand his concern perfectly, that perhaps he was waiting for him. Without hesitating he rang the bell.

He waited for a moment. He thought he heard something inside, perhaps a voice. He replied by saying who it was.

"I only came to see if everything is all right," he added.

No one answered, and he heard no other sound. The noise of a dull thud attracted his attention. It had come not from inside the house but from beside it. He wondered if he should stay in the doorway or look for its cause. He remembered that just above the basement a narrow window opened onto the alleyway. He wondered if a person could get out of the house that way. He rang the bell again, with the same result as before. The noise died away, and a few seconds later it began again. The prosecutor walked toward the alleyway that separated the house from the church.

He saw no one from the corner, but now a faint groaning came from behind an angle of the church. He caressed the pistol and walked closer. He stopped before he went to the other side of the angle, hugging the wall. Now the echo of a constant scraping and the bang of trash cans joined the groaning, as if someone were pushing the cans against the wall. He realized that his hand was clutching the butt of the pistol though he had not opened the sheath. He did so with his fingers, not moving from where he stood. It seemed to him that what he heard was the agitated respiration of two people, probably agitated because they were dragging a body. He asked himself if they were armed. Considering that these were terrorist assassins, he told himself they were. He was confused. In a gunfight, he was bound to lose. Perhaps the best thing would be only to see who they were without letting himself be seen, and then to pursue them in the light of day. Or perhaps he should drop the case and visit Judge Briceño to take part in his working group and buy a Datsun someday. He thought it was too late for that. After all, the killer was following him and almost seemed to be playing hide-and-seek with him. He thought, this is a case I cannot drop. Perhaps I will not be able to drop it even if I solve it. Solve it. Until a month ago, his function was simply to submit reports, not to solve things. He inhaled deeply, trying not to make noise. Holding his breath, he looked on the other side of the angle. In a corner, behind the trash cans, two shadows were moving in an agitated way. Their backs were to him. The prosecutor thought he could take advantage of the opportunity to apprehend them officially in the name of the law. He was aware that he did not have the legal authority to arrest anyone. As he was making his decision, he took a step forward and kicked a beer can, which noisily hit the stone wall. The two shadows stopped panting and moving. They whispered a few words. The prosecutor discovered that in fact only one figure had his back to him, a tall blonde who murmured in a foreign accent and held the other one, a woman, against the wall as she wrapped her legs around him. The prosecutor moved his hand away from the weapon. He could not suppress a choked sigh of relief as he leaned against the wall. His eyes met those of the other two. The man had remained motionless, not knowing what to do. It was the girl who said:

"Are you a cop?"

The prosecutor replied:

"What? Oh, no. Of course not."

"Then get the hell out of here, damn it!"

She certainly had a Peruvian accent. Chacaltana thought about making them leave. They showed a lack of respect for Father Quiroz and for the church. But he felt ridiculous. He went back to the door of the parish house. He wondered if someone might have opened it while he had been distracted. There were still no lights on inside, but that did not mean anything. He rang the bell again. Perhaps the priest was not even inside. His encounter with the couple made him think that perhaps his nerves were getting the better of him. Perhaps the priest had left Ayacucho and stayed in some village to sleep. Impossible. Not during Holy Week. He thought about going in through the window, but it had wrought iron bars. He rejected the idea of going in through the little basement window. The couple would not allow him to. Besides, he would have to break it. It occurred to him to look for a telephone, but he did not even know if there was one in the parish house. The priest had used the phone in his office. Then too, if he did not answer the door, he would not pick up the phone either. Guided by an irritated, frustrated impulse, he put his hand on the doorknob. To his surprise, the door responded to his push. Inside everything was dark. He stood for a few minutes in the doorway. Now he would have to go in. He supposed he wanted to but did not know if he really wanted to. He wanted only to sleep quietly. He called to Father Quiroz. There was no answer. He looked around. The street was empty. He took two steps inside without closing the door, to take advantage of the streetlamps. The shadows produced in the house by the lights on the street seemed to move, shaken by the night breeze. As he looked for the light switch, he called again:

"Father Quiroz?"

Now he heard it clearly. It was the sound of something dragging along the floor, like a deep hissing.

"Father? It's Félix Chacaltana."

He found the switch and turned on the light. He was startled by the image of a man, but it was really a crucifix a meter high. The room was in the same disorder he had seen the last time. The heavy door to the basement was open. He went through the living room to the priest's bedroom. He opened the door, standing to one side. Since nothing came out, he turned on the light.

Here, by contrast, everything was in the most scrupulous order. There was only a worktable, a bureau, and a meticulously made bed with no wrinkles on the sheets. On the wall hung another crucifix, a very small one, which seemed to watch over the peace of the bedroom. He heard the hissing again outside, in the living room. Almost by instinct, he unsnapped the holster and took out the weapon. He returned to the living room pointing straight ahead, at the chests, and cocked the gun so the bullet would come out faster in case of an emergency. He realized his hand was trembling. He leaned his back against the wall and began to move that way around the perimeter of the room, edging past the chests where they stood, then taking out his handkerchief to wipe away perspiration. He was soaked. He reached the door to the basement and began to go down the stairs, still hugging the wall. He did not know where to aim the weapon. He opted to point down, where the darkness was most dense. He recognized the smell of incense and dampness, mixed with a chemical odor he could not identify.

When he reached the bottom of the stairs, he tried to remember where the switch was located. Since he had the weapon in his right hand, he felt up and down along the wall on the left with his free hand. All he found was the cold, mildewed wall. He moved the weapon into his other hand and repeated the operation on the right. There it was, fairly low on the wall. He turned it on. The flickering light suggested there was someone else in the room. He raised the weapon in his direction and shouted:

"Freeze, damn it! I'm armed!"

There was no reply. When the light stopped trembling, he could see more clearly. The body, in reality the half body coming out of the oven, was Father Quiroz. He was still wearing the vestments for Mass, his arms in gathered sleeves opened in a cross. Overcoming his revulsion, the prosecutor moved closer. Something emerged from the priest's mouth, like a rigid, very long tongue. When he was beside him, the prosecutor discovered that it was the hilt of a knife. The rest was inside, piercing the priest's throat to the nape of his neck. The blood flowing out of his mouth had not yet coagulated. It was still dripping on the damp floor of the basement and staining the edges of the oven. The death was very recent. Blood was not the only thing dripping. Before or after the execution, the killer had poured acid on the face and arms of the priest. The open bottles were still to one side. The body parts that had touched the liquid looked eaten away and liquefied, the skin creased and torn, transformed into a sticky gum of flesh. Inside the oven, the prosecutor saw that one leg had been separated from the trunk. He shuddered and moved back. The priest's face looked blindly at the basement ceiling, perhaps trying to see heaven, but for him heaven was underground.

The prosecutor heard a sound on the stairs. Despite the horror of what he had found, or perhaps precisely because of it, he reacted in time. He turned and fired. It was the first time in his life he had fired a gun. The shot sounded much louder than he expected and pushed him backward until he tripped over the body. The bullet rebounded against the walls, thundering through the house with sharp echoes as it crashed against stone. In a corner he saw the little window. He estimated that the couple outside were only a few meters away. They must have heard it. Perhaps they would call the police. He hoped to God they had. Now he clearly heard a metallic clink coming from the stairs. The sound was moving away. He supposed the killer did not have a firearm and was fleeing. He ran after him. He threw himself onto the stairs just in time to see the basement door close. Before he reached the top of the stairs he heard the key turning in the lock. He shouted. He banged on the door with all his strength. He kicked it. But the door did not move a millimeter.

Slowly he went downstairs again. Father Quiroz seemed to be waiting for him. His face gave the impression of a disillusioned grimace. The prosecutor decided to wait. The authorities would come, alerted by the gunshot. He could explain to them what had happened. Perhaps they would come in time to pursue the killer. Then he reconsidered: What could he explain to the authorities? What could he say to them? They would find him locked in with a corpse, carrying an unlicensed firearm, near all the instruments of the crime. Then he thought too that each of the last three victims had spoken to him shortly before dying. He tried to clear his head. No. He was innocent. That same afternoon he had requested protection for the city streets. His request had been denied. Protection for the streets. He had not mentioned the parish house. It might seem that he had requested protection precisely to provide himself with an alibi. Pacheco would be delighted to sign that investigation, and Judge Briceño would sentence him with the same pleasure. Perhaps not even Commander Carrión would feel sure about him.

His heart began to pound. He imagined himself before the judges, who probably would transfer him to military jurisdiction. Or perhaps civil jurisdiction. He would face a prosecutor, a prosecutor "like you," the terrorist had said, referring to the one who had cleared the way for Special Forces in the maximum security prison. If he were his own prosecutor, he could write thousands of probative briefs against himself. He imagined the documents:

"Friday, the twenty-first day of April, 2000, with regard to the discovery of Félix Chacaltana Saldívar in possession of a firearm . . ." He could not even get rid of the weapon in that place. He tried out a defense: "I was attempting to pursue the murderer." He saw Judge Briceño clearly: "Why didn't you request the intervention of the police? Prosecutors don't go around pursuing thieves. I mean, after all." Attempted usurpation of functions would be added to his charges. Perhaps withholding information as well. None of the accusations had reached the Judicial Branch. Carrión would prefer to deny everything rather than find himself involved with a serial killer.

He tried to expel from his mind the entire judicial process, which seemed to unfold before his eyes. He did not entirely succeed. As he saw Captain Pacheco making his statement, it occurred to him to pile up all the chests until he could reach the window and get out through there. He crossed the room and began to move them. They weighed too much to carry. He would have to drag them. When he moved the first one, he accidentally knocked over one of the bottles of acid. The liquid spread along the floor until it reached Quiroz's hands and head. The prosecutor retreated to the stairs. If he moved forward, he would leave prints all around the room. Now the liquid ran everywhere, all the way to the bottom of the window. He climbed up two steps.

Then he remembered that he had the pistol. He would have to use it again. He went up to the door and calculated the most distant angle from which he could hit the lock. He fired when he was halfway up the stairs. The first shot went through the wood but did not hit the lock. The second was almost a direct hit. The prosecutor went to open the door. He had to kick it, and when he shoved it with his hand, he got a splinter. As he pulled out the splinter and sucked the blood, he understood he was leaving his fingerprints and even his blood all over the wooden door. He took out his handkerchief to wipe it down. From outside he heard the sound of people returning to their houses and hotels in the small hours. Men and women laughing. Strange accents. He thought he should hurry. Leaning against the door, he kicked the lock with the sole of his shoe until he broke it and opened the door. He went into the dark living room, then out to the street. When he was on the sidewalk, he looked around. The couple he had surprised in the alleyway were a few meters from the door. They were petrified when they saw him. He realized he was still holding the weapon. He gestured to them to calm them down as he tried to put it away. They put their hands up. They looked rigid.

"Listen, this is not what it seems . . . please . . ."

"Easy, easy," said the man, "nothing's going on . . . We didn't see anything . . ."

They took a few steps backward as he came closer.

"Don't go, listen to me . . . We have to call the police . . ."

When they reached the first corner, they stopped moving. The prosecutor thought that at last they would listen to him. He moved faster, but they turned and started to run. He tried to follow, but they quickly disappeared down one of the streets.

Now they had seen him clearly. Chacaltana thought that each of his advances was a step backward. He tried to think calmly. He closed the holster to avoid any more trouble. No neighbor had looked out. Perhaps they thought the shots were fireworks. Yes. Perhaps the best thing after all was to wait for the authorities and explain everything properly in order to open an investigation. Then he recalled the faces of the judge and the officer in the captain's office. Unable to control himself, he broke into a run.

After running for a few minutes he tried to think where he was going. Not to his house. The killer or the police would probably be waiting for him there if they were not already following him. And not to the Office of the Prosecutor or headquarters. He passed the Arch and continued toward the far end of the city, heading for the San Juan district. Fifteen minutes later, he arrived at Edith's house, which was almost at the edge of the city. He placed his finger on the doorbell and decided to leave it there until the young woman gave a sign of life. He realized he was crying. He kicked at the door. He shouted Edith's name. Then he thought that this would attract the attention of the entire neighborhood. He tried to regain his composure. He was a prosecutor. He knew how to accuse, he had to know how to evade accusations. He took a deep breath. An old woman, her head covered in rollers, looked out a second-story window.

"What's going on? What do you want?"

"I'm looking for Edith."

"And do you think this is a decent hour? And do you think that's any way to ring a doorbell?"

"I'm sorry . . . I . . ."

I what? What could he say? He thought about saying the police were after him, or that he was with the police and chasing someone. The woman continued to watch him as he asked himself if it would not be better to run away from there too. Then the door opened. There was Edith, half asleep, wearing an undershirt, flannel bottoms, and flip-flops. Her hair was loose and shiny. Behind her was a staircase. Félix Chacaltana had never seen the interior of Edith's house when he had walked her home. It was an old, subdivided, three-story house where the same doorbell apparently was heard in all the apartments. He realized the old woman did not live with Edith when the young woman let him in and apologized to her. He heard her say he was her cousin who had just come from Andahuaylas for Holy Week. She promised it would not happen again. The woman did not reply. She simply pulled her head in from the window and back into her own life.

Félix and Edith went up to the third floor, to a tiny room with an electric hot plate in a corner. There was no bathroom and no refrigerator. Chacaltana supposed she shared those facilities with some neighbors, perhaps with the same old woman who had reprimanded him. He thought no more about it. As soon as she closed the door, still half asleep, he put his arms around the girl and held her very tight, as if he wanted to fuse with her. As they embraced, she felt the shape of the pistol against her body. She tried to pull away.

"What's happened to you? What's going on?"

Félix did not let Edith go. He clung to her for a long time before he realized that tears were falling from his eyes.

"Do you want a *mate*?"

He nodded. She heated the water on the hot plate while he kept holding her. She served the *mate* and sat down. She caressed his hair gently while he, on his knees, rested his head on her lap and clasped her around the waist, trembling.

"Don't you want to tell me what happened? Does it have to do with your work?"

Now not even images of fire and blows passed through the mind of Prosecutor Chacaltana. There was only a great void, a hungry darkness, the maw of nothingness closing over his head. He needed to talk. He needed to tell everything that had happened to him in the past month and a half. He needed to cry like a baby. He began to tell it all, urged on by the young woman's caresses. When the first light of dawn sifted through the small window in the room, he had finished his story. Edith's lap was warm and dry. Seconds later, as if a great weight had been lifted from him, he was asleep.

He woke at eight in the morning. He had not slept very long. And he could not sleep any more. He did not even think he could move. After the initial shock of not knowing where he was, he looked around Edith's small apartment. He was in the bed. His jacket and the holster were hanging from the only chair, and under that were his shoes, one beside the other, as orderly and unwrinkled as the other things Edith had touched. She was there too, standing across from him, taking off her undershirt and bottoms. She had gotten a dishpan of water from somewhere and was carefully washing her underarms and crotch, her neck and feet, in the still tenuous morning light.

"Good morning," said the prosecutor.

When she heard him, she did her best to cover her body. Her right arm crossed her chest and her left hand covered her sex.

"Turn around," she replied. "I have no place else to go in here."

The prosecutor did not turn around. He smiled at her. She returned the smile. She had turned red.

"Turn around," she insisted.

Sluggishly, the prosecutor turned around. He remained in that position for a few seconds until he turned back to her, not so sluggishly now. She covered herself again.

"If you don't behave, you won't come back. Remember you're my cousin."

The prosecutor thought of the previous night. His head was teeming with fragments of his encounter with Father Quiroz in the basement, his arrival at Edith's house, the young woman's tender lap. He wanted to touch her. Take refuge in her.

"Come here," he said. It sounded like an order.

"I have to go to work and I'm already late. My boss will be there because we're expecting a crowd. Don't move from here. Doña Dora is furious. She scolded me for twenty minutes when I went down for water."

"Come here," he repeated.

She wrapped a towel around her body and approached him. She touched his forehead and let him bring her hand slowly to his lips. He kissed her palm and the back of her hand. He put her hand gently into his mouth and sucked each one of her fingers.

"What are you doing?" she asked.

"Thank you for helping me," he said. "I'll never forget it."

She leaned over to kiss him. He took her by the waist and pulled her to the bed. She refused, first with her body and then with her voice, but then she let herself sink down.

"I have to go," she reminded him, laughing.

He lay on top of her body and put his tongue in her mouth. He no longer felt like a little boy needing protection. On the contrary, he wanted to recover his adulthood. Show her that he could also be a protective man, a man. He kissed her neck, her shoulders, the back of her neck, where a few short black hairs escaped, like long down. She responded with kisses on his forehead and cheeks. She tried to move him to one side. He resisted.

"Don't go to work," he said.

She laughed.

"Don't go."

He wondered if they had discovered the body yet. Then he removed the thought from his mind. He needed something else, something besides so much death. He needed something with life. He was breathing heavily. Her mouth was partially open. He bit her lips.

"Ow!" Edith groaned. "Does your mama know you do those things?"

"She doesn't see us here."

"She's always with you. That's the problem."

The prosecutor became perturbed. He did not think this was the right context for talking about his mother. He replied:

"She likes you very much." It seemed to him a delicate moment, one of those moments when important things are said. "She would not object if . . . if I married you."

The color rose in Edith's cheeks. She seemed surprised.

"She?"

He smiled but did not receive a smile in return. This disconcerted him, it disconcerted him not to receive from people what he had planned. Smiles are repaid with smiles, that must be written down somewhere as a norm. She caressed his forehead and said words he did not expect.

"Listen, Félix . . . I love you very much but . . . the truth is . . . to marry you . . . I'd need for her not to be here."

"What?"

"I understand your feelings. But I couldn't go to live in a house that belongs to another woman. Least of all one . . . who isn't really there."

"She is there," said the prosecutor. "Do you believe that only things you can see are there?"

She lowered her eyes.

"No, of course not. I'm going to get dressed."

She stood. He tried to hold her back but failed. Something in the air had broken, and the prosecutor tried to put the pieces back together.

"Listen . . . You have to understand . . . I love you but . . . my mother . . . just now . . ."

He knew there were words caught in his throat, trying to get out, but it was not clear to him how to pull them free, he would have liked to scoop them out with a spoon. He had always been good with words, but he seemed incapable of summoning the exact ones to talk about what mattered to him most. And the worst thing was that right now he did not have the time of a functionary at his desk or a poet facing a sheet of paper. The words he needed should have burst directly from his heart, but his heart was dry.

She picked up her clothes from the chair. The prosecutor felt he would never again see her undressed.

"It's not a problem," she said. "I understand."

It was as if she had spoken from the other side of the world. From the tip of a glacier. He went over to her. He tried to embrace her but she eluded him. He held her tight and kissed her shoulders. He felt a great need to control her, to not let her go, and he felt that no words could restrain her. He removed the towel from her body with a single movement and lowered his head to her chest and belly, kissing her constantly. She tried to push him away by the shoulders.

"That's enough . . . ," she whispered.

But he did not let her go. He held her around the legs and lowered his mouth to her sex until he felt her pubic hairs brushing his tongue. Her vulva tasted of soap and of her. He felt a tug on his hair. He raised his head. She was looking at him in a fury.

"Let me go," she said dryly. "I'm going to . . ."

Normally the prosecutor would have let her go and apologized for his behavior. He would have said he had not intended any disrespect. But without knowing why, his reaction surprised even him. He lowered his head again and held her more tightly around the legs. He sucked. This time she shouted:

"Let me alone!"

And she shook him by his hair. He pulled Edith's hands away from his head. They came away filled with black hairs that jutted out between her fingers. He brought her hands down to the bed and climbed on her again to trap her between his body and the mattress. The bed creaked and rocked back and forth. Now Edith's eyes reflected fear. Inexplicably, that excited him even more. Trembling, Edith tried to free herself from his embrace. He squeezed her neck with one hand while he unzipped his fly with the other. He saw the red marks his paws had left on the young woman's wrists before she scratched his face and put her finger in his eye. Then he became violent. He slapped her on the bed and lowered his trousers as he got into position. He saw his own aged penis contrasting with Edith's fresh, clean flesh. His round stomach fell on her flat belly. He thrust forward. She closed her eyes and clenched her teeth. He thrust again, over and over again, shaking her as the bed creaked, feeling how her small body grew more and more diminutive as it trembled beneath his body, wrinkled but strong, still strong, stronger than ever.

When he finished, he rolled off her and lay to one side. He was perspiring. His head was spinning with memories of the previous night and what he had just done. She did not move. It was difficult to tell if the drops rolling down her face were perspiration or tears. He felt a strange pleasure when he asked himself the question in silence. She trembled. She felt raw, torn apart.

"Yesterday I shot a man," he said. "I don't know who he was

or if I hit him. But I might have killed someone. I felt it was a kind of test, a kind of training for something. I felt that something was changing in me."

All the people I talk to die.

"Get out," she responded, first in a whisper, then in a howl. "Get out! Son of the devil!"

It sounded innocent as an insult. But Prosecutor Chacaltana knew what it meant. *Supaypawawa*. Son of the devil. It was a direct translation of the worst thing you can say to a person in Quechua. He knew he really would have to get out. His crotch was wet but she would not let him wash. She was wet too, and a thin line of blood trickled between her legs. The prosecutor did not want to ask her if she was a virgin. He wanted to think she was.

As he was closing Edith's door, he saw her sobbing on the bed. He began to walk down the stairs as he put on his jacket and made certain the holster for the pistol was carefully closed. At the door he passed the neighbor from the previous night. He greeted her by name, Doña Dora. When he walked out to the street, it seemed to him the city was filled with light, much more than had come into Edith's small room. He walked toward police headquarters. He had decided to turn himself in.

He moved forward slowly, as if he had cement in his shoes, along the streets where the town was preparing for the procession of the Holy Sepulcher. He felt dizzy. He thought he would go into the captain's office, hand over his weapon, and recount step by step everything that had happened last night. It would almost be a relief if they did not believe him. It would almost be a relief to be arrested and be able to forget. If the captain insisted, he would even tell him what he had done to Edith. He felt too tired to try to run away or even to think where he could run to.

Before he reached police headquarters, he passed by his house. There were no guards at the door. He thought perhaps they had entered to search it during the night. He opened the door and walked in. Everything was just as he had left it: his room, his mother's room. He picked up the smiling photograph of his mother in Sacsayhuamán. He kissed it.

"You can see, Mamacita, I haven't managed to do anything to make you proud of me. I hope I won't disappoint you too much."

He continued talking to her as he cleaned himself up. He thought he might be allowed some of her photos in a cell. He cleaned his private parts with special care. They smelled of Edith. He tried not to cry. He tried not to cry any more. He went out again. As he approached the Plaza Mayor, he passed more and more police rushing past him, carrying their orders from one side of the city to the other. He was waiting for the moment when one of them would aim at his chest and order him to drop his weapon. He was hoping they would save him the trouble of confessing to something he had not done, that they had already connected him to the crime scene, and that the couple from last night had identified him beyond any doubt. He lamented that there had not been more light on the street. He regretted not having continued firing the gun until the police had arrived. He passed some soldiers too. He felt as if he had impunity. He knew what it meant to walk among his pursuers without anyone turning around to look at him, like a ghost. He wanted to shout that he was a murderer, that he had already killed four people, that perhaps he had just committed rape, of that he could not be sure because of legal regulations. Legal regulations. He could not control his laughter. He began to laugh right in the middle of the square. He wanted to dance but thought of his mother. She would not have liked seeing him like this. He controlled himself but continued to laugh as he approached police headquarters. He thought about Pacheco. He would be happy to see him. Certainly he would give himself all the credit, he would say he had captured him after a long pursuit filled with bullets and patrol cars. He laughed again, louder and louder.

At the door to headquarters, the guard seemed to be asleep as he leaned on his rifle. The prosecutor stopped to admire the flag with the national seal hanging over the entrance. He turned to see the city bustling with preparations for the procession. It seemed that centuries passed before he took the last step to reception.

The usual sergeant was at his desk. It amused the prosecutor to think he would have to wait hours to turn himself in, that they would keep their murderer sitting beside the door for a good long time before allowing him to confess. The sergeant stood when he saw him walk in. The prosecutor waited for his words. He knew what they would be. He smiled again. He felt the weight of the weapon at his side. He had become used to the pistol. The sergeant saluted, his hand at his cap:

"Captain Pacheco is expecting you, Señor Prosecutor."

They knew. They knew everything. He felt as if he were floating to Pacheco's office. He wondered if he should hold out his hands for the cuffs. Pacheco was sitting with papers in front of him, and he too stood when he saw him come in.

"Chacaltana! Where the hell have you been? I've been looking for you all morning."

Chacaltana tried to impose some order in his mind before explaining where the hell he had been. But the captain continued:

"They killed Father Quiroz. Damn, Chacaltana, you have to see him. They really fucked him up."

"They" killed? Not "you" killed? Chacaltana had been so ready to confess that now he did not know what to say. He had even begun to convince himself that he was guilty.

"How . . . ?"

"They found him at dawn. The neighbors reported shots. But he wasn't shot to death. It seems the killer wanted to announce what he had done. The only thing the motherfucker didn't do was set off fireworks."

And the couple? And people who saw him leaving the house?

"Are there . . . witnesses . . . statements from neighbors?"

"Witnesses? You know how it is, Chacaltana. Nobody talks,

nobody makes a statement, nobody wants any problems. Even the call that reported it was anonymous. This is a fucking mess. I'm sorry about what happened yesterday. You . . . you were right."

He noticed that it was enormously difficult for the captain to apologize. It caused him pain. Chacaltana could not believe what he was saying when he said:

"Don't worry, Captain. I understand. We all have too much to worry about, don't we?"

The captain thanked him for his understanding with a gesture.

"The fact that people don't talk isn't so serious. By some miracle we've managed to keep the matter out of the press. Even though we're crowded with tourists and reporters. Sometimes I ask myself if all these people aren't blind."

Prosecutor Chacaltana was asking himself exactly the same question. But the captain gave a military pitch to his voice and said:

"I want you to tell me everything you know about this case."

Prosecutor Chacaltana told him slowly and in detail, as if he were reciting all his reports. He did not mention the detail that all the people who knew about his investigation had been killed. He thought the captain would discover that for himself. The police official was thinking about taking charge of the investigation. He seemed very interested. Perhaps they had called him from Lima, they always knew everything, if they had retired the commander it would be precisely because they were up to date on everything. In reality, the prosecutor was not concerned about any of that. When he finished his account, the captain said:

"Go see the pathologist and prepare a report to open the case."

For a moment, Chacaltana wanted to say that he could not become involved in this matter quickly. That what they faced had been going on for centuries and would last for many more centuries. That they were fighting against ghosts, against the dead, against the spirit of the Andes. That he had just sexually violated the person who was probably the best woman he had ever known in his life. That according to the law he ought to marry her now. That he no longer wanted to deal with this case, that he preferred to get away with Carrión to some pretty beach on the northern coast. He opened his mouth and finally said, with all the conviction of which he was capable:

"Yes, Señor."

On the twenty-first day of April, 2000, the priest of the Church of the Heart of Christ, Sebastián Quiroz Mendoza, was discovered dead in the environs of his basement, when neighbors requested the intervention of the police force to guarantee order and safety while the perpetrator fired his weapon in the streets adjacent to the parish house.

According to the reconstruction effected by the forensic pathologist, the aforementioned priest was first tied by the hands and feet and gagged, which is suggested by hematomas at his joints and the corners of his mouth, then subsequently subjected to the amputation of his lower left extremity while alive. Likewise serious wounds were inflicted with acid, and the trachea and larynx were perforated with a sharp cutting instrument through to the nape of his neck, until he was left in the interior of the crematory chamber located in his basement.

According to verification effected by police authorities, the perpetrator subsequently proceeded to open fire at the walls and doors of the property, after which he fled, carrying the amputated lower extremity and his instruments of mutilation in a clear demonstration of a lack of the mental faculties required for sanity. The shells discovered at the scene correspond to a regulation weapon, which suggests that the perpetrator could have been a terrorist with access to military arsenals, or had stolen a pistol, with premeditated treachery and a clear advantage over his victim, from a member of the nation's security forces.

It is important to note as well that the wounds inflicted on the aforementioned priest Sebastián Quiroz Mendoza could not have been perpetrated by a person older than forty, due to the fact that they required considerable physical strength, or by a functionary or person who works or carries out his assigned duties in an office, for example, the need having been demonstrated for training in either police or subversive operations, which the perpetrator displayed in his actions.

Further, the signatory, who at the time of the outrage was asleep in his own residence, suggests, based on his criminological experience, that the crime would have to have been committed by vandalistic elements or groups especially dedicated to the perpetration of homicides with the intent to commit larceny or robbery.

Associate District Prosecutor Félix Chacaltana Saldívar looked again at the page he had just written, thinking about another way to cover his presence at the site. No. It was sufficient. He erased the word "police" to avoid arguments with Pacheco and considered the report concluded. He would not have to face the couple from the previous night, who were probably more terrified than he was, in a confrontation with witnesses, but he knew that sooner or later the authorities would get around to him. On the previous night he had not even been careful to avoid leaving prints in the basement. On that basis they would have sufficient cause to accuse him. The prints would have to go to the laboratory in Lima, they would take a while, perhaps enough time to find the real killer. A matter of days. God willing.

In spite of having to find a quick solution, he could not get the incident with Edith out of his head. He did not understand why he had done what he had done. He tried to remember and at the same time forget the episode that morning. He had not been looking for sex but for a kind of power, a kind of domination, the feeling that something was weaker than he was, that in the midst of this world that seemed to want to swallow him whole, he too could have strength, potency, victims.

Or perhaps he had simply wanted sex. In either case, he felt like a perfect imbecile. It would be very difficult to convince himself otherwise. Above all, it would be very difficult to convince Edith.

He decided to concentrate on his investigation in order not to think about her, although moments he had been beside her returned like flashes to flog his memory. Her closed eyes, squeezed tight like her clenched teeth, her legs trying to resist his attack. He would return to the archives of the Office of the Prosecutor. He wanted to know if Father Quiroz had been threatened or undergone earlier attempts on his life during the years of terrorism. Perhaps that would give him a clue. This time there had been no note from Sendero, but that must have been due to lack of time. Chacaltana had interrupted the killers in the middle of their work, who knows how they had proposed to end it.

For lunch he ate a chicken sandwich at a street stand and then went to the Office of the Prosecutor. The faithful were forming lines at the Church of Santo Domingo, holding pieces of cotton in their hands to clean the wounds on the image of the Lord of the Holy Sepulcher. The prosecutor imagined all those hands, one after another, touching the wounds of Christ. Without knowing why, that made him think of his mother and of Edith.

Again he walked down the deserted corridors of the Office of the Prosecutor on a holiday, until he reached the file room. He began the search. Quiroz did not appear among the papers. Or perhaps he was there in a place beyond the images of Edith glued to the prosecutor's eyes: her body wrapped in the towel silhouetted against the first light of day. Her small feet, two soft packets. The taste of her pubis. The shining path that joined her neck to her navel, a road the prosecutor would never travel again. Perhaps she would accept an apology, he thought, as he opened boxes of abandoned cases. After all, he was not a bad sort. He had behaved well with her . . . at least until that morning. Perhaps she would be able to forget about it quickly. He would bring her flowers that night. Ask her to dinner. Take her dancing. She would like that. Soon, the morning's disgraceful incident would be only a bad memory, easy to erase.

Without realizing it, in a reflexive way, he was looking for Edith's name in the files. He tried to recover from his not very professional deviation from his subject. Then, out of curiosity, he looked for it deliberately. Her parents, at least, had to be there somewhere. He wanted to know more about her. He felt like looking for her everywhere, learning how he could make a good impression on her, finding her at every moment of her life. He was afraid he would not see her again in person, that she would not want to see him. But at least there, among the accusations, the victims, the perpetrators on both sides, Edith Ayala, at least a little of her, would be present.

He spent the afternoon looking through the old papers and enduring the allergic reaction produced by the dust. Edith's parents, Ronaldo Ayala and Clara Mungía, did not appear among the abandoned accusations. He continued looking until he found them in the reports of battle casualties. The attack they had led on the police post had been a desperate maneuver. Six poorly armed terrorists against a station with ten police. They had attacked at dawn on a day in July in the mid-eighties. Apparently, they miscalculated the number of men waiting for them. The police had been warned of the attack. The assault was a massacre. One policeman died, two were wounded, and all the terrorists were annihilated. The legal reports indicated shots in the back of Ronaldo Ayala's neck. They had finished him off after the assault. His wife showed wounds in the stomach and a final shot in the chest. When she was already wounded, she had continued to advance. In the photograph she looked a little like Edith: the hair, the neck the prosecutor remembered so well, were a maternal inheritance. But Clara Mungía did not have her daughter's sweetness. The identification-size photograph, taken in a previous arrest, showed the inexpressive, resolute gaze the prosecutor had seen so often beneath the eyebrows of Senderistas.

The file included an attachment that spoke of Edith. In the mid-nineties, a repentant Senderista had accused her of being a member of the logistical apparatus of the party. She was not yet sixteen, but according to the witness she passed weaponry and messages among the cells that survived in Ceja de Selva. She had been interrogated, but nothing of interest had been learned. She showed no lesions when she left the interrogations. After that, she had been left in peace. A report from Intelligence added that for two years she had dedicated herself to bringing medicine and food to those imprisoned for terrorism at the maximum security prison in Ayacucho, while she worked as an assistant in a butcher shop in the central market.

Butcher shop. Prison. Inevitably, he thought of Hernán Durango, Comrade Alonso, and his tale of the Indian servant's dream, and his stories. He remembered the first time he had seen him. The party has a thousand eyes and a thousand ears, he had said. The eyes of the people. Or perhaps only two eyes like two nuts in their shells, above two clenched jaws sweating with rage, two eyes vacant in their sockets. Almost in spite of himself, the prosecutor made some deductions and came to a conclusion. Perhaps he had the killer. At that moment, his blood turned to ice in his veins.

He thought it was an unfounded suspicion and returned to his office. He wanted to reject it. He wanted to remove that possibility. He telephoned Colonel Olazábal:

"Good afternoon, Colonel. How are you?"

"Well, I'm fucked, Chacaltana. Just like you, I suppose, working on a holiday."

"I spoke about your promotion to Commander Carrión," the prosecutor lied. "He seemed very well disposed, but he has been retired."

"Yes. Well, news flies."

"We will have to begin that task again with his successor. Do not be concerned, I will help you."

"Thank you very much, Señor Prosecutor. You know that if there's anything I can do for you . . ."

"Well, to tell you the truth, yes, now that you mention it. I need a list of visitors to Hernán Durango González."

"Right now?"

"If that might be possible, yes, Colonel."

The colonel promised to call him back in five minutes. The prosecutor sat waiting by the phone. It had to be a coincidence, a miscalculation, a dead end. This whole story was filled with them. He spent an hour and a half next to the phone, caressing his pistol, until the colonel called.

"Let me see . . . Here it is: to begin with, the inmate's parents: Román Durango and Brígida González . . ."

"Ah ha . . ."

"A sister named Agripina . . ."

"Yes . . ."

"And just one other person. Not a relative. Maybe a girlfriend, though in that case, she was very patient, don't you think? Though you know, there are girlfriends who wait twenty years, let me tell you . . ."

He gave a short speech on girlfriends and inmates until he said a woman's name, and then the prosecutor moved his lips and felt a huge pain in his chest. Without saying good-bye he hung up the phone and hurried out of the building.

Outside, night had just fallen. The Lord of the Holy Sepulcher, lying in a transparent case on a bed of white roses, had taken over the streets. Blood dripped from his forehead, his side, his hands and feet. Only the candles of the town's notable and wealthy citizens who surrounded him illuminated his figure in the darkness. The faithful were dressed in black. Streetlights had been turned off. At that moment, the silence was absolute.

Chacaltana pushed his way through the solemn crowd, advancing directly to the restaurant on the square. Some people pushed him back, but no one dared to break the silence of the Sepulcher. Even among the tourists inside El Huamanguino restaurant, the atmosphere was one of reserve and silence. Edith was at her counter when he came in. She looked at him with an expression of surprise that quickly turned into fear and then hatred. She stepped back reflexively but did not move from the counter. It was he who approached her and took her by the arm.

"What are you doing?" she protested.

"I have to talk to you."

"Don't touch me!"

Her eyes. The hatred of those eyes he had seen in the files that afternoon.

"Ssshhhhh!"

The clients demanded silence. The owner of the restaurant approached and said, in a quiet but firm voice:

"I'd like to know who the hell you are."

"Office of the Prosecutor," Chacaltana said authoritatively. "I have to speak with Edith Ayala. This is an official investigation."

The owner looked at him and then looked at Edith, at both of them, with a censure that the mention of the Office of the Prosecutor attenuated and transformed, perhaps into fear. Prosecutors are not police, but the restaurant owner knew very well that anything official could be a constant source of problems. Edith was red with rage and embarrassment. She wanted to avoid a scene. She said:

"Can I go out for a moment?"

The owner agreed with a look of annoyance, more to get rid of them than out of courtesy.

"Five minutes, that's all," he warned as they were leaving.

They moved away from the crowd, walking with long strides toward the district of Carmen Alto. The prosecutor remembered having gone to the cathedral when he was little, on another Good Friday. He had heard a long lament and then the church, covered in purple mourning cloths, had darkened. One after another, the canons had gone up to the altar, dressed in black robes whose trains dragged as they walked forward. They carried immense black flags and waved them in the air, like wings of sinister birds. Without knowing why, it seemed to him that the ancient ceremony had something to do with all this. As soon as they reached a quieter street, the prosecutor looked for a place where they could talk calmly. He held Edith's arm tightly, perhaps as he had that morning. She shook him off:

"You're hurting me!"

"I'm hurting you?"

The prosecutor was furious. If he had been brutal that morning, now his fury seemed like something just and honorable.

"I don't want to talk to you," she went on. "I don't want to see you again!"

She turned and began to go back to the center of town. Several people passed them. Some children were playing with a plastic ball. He caught hold of her again and pushed her against a wall.

"You knew Hernán Durango, Edith. You are the only person who could have talked to him about me, about my mother."

She looked surprised. Then she started to weep without saying a word. The prosecutor grabbed her hair:

"You knew him!"

"So what?" she shouted. "Tell me! What difference does it make?"

"Why did you talk to him about me?"

"Why couldn't I? I didn't know you knew him until last night."

"Don't lie to me!" He raised his hand but stopped it in midair and did not hit her. He did not understand why he wanted to hit her so much. "Why did you talk to him about me? Tell me the truth!"

She tried to break free but he pushed her back against the wall, this time more violently. When Edith looked up again, it was difficult to know if the gleam in her eyes was due to terror or hatred.

"Because I liked you!" she said in a faint voice. Then she began to cry again. The children, who had not moved, ran away. Several couples passed close to them, walking faster. No one approached. "I thought you were different . . . ," she continued. She sobbed and gasped for breath, like a small animal. "I thought you were a good man, not the wretch you are . . ."

The prosecutor let her go. His body became rigid. His voice hardened:

"I know dirty terrorists like you, Edith. I know your lies. You won't deceive me anymore."

"Then let me alone."

"Be quiet!" The shout came out louder than he intended, but it worked. She was quiet and trembling, like a chick in a raffle at a fair.

She began to swallow snot and saliva.

"Are you . . . are you accusing m . . . ?"

"There are sufficient indications of your connections to Sendero. And your parents, obviously. The savages who brought you up. Look what they did with you."

"You wash your mouth when you talk about my . . ."

He did not let her finish. He covered her mouth and pushed her head against the wall.

"The murderer I am looking for knew the victims. He could go in the parish house, and had the trust of Durango, and certainly of Justino as well. And he knew I had talked to them. As you did. But you did not act alone. Where is the rest of your cell? Talk!"

"What the hell are you talking about?"

"You could never forgive him, could you? You waited fifteen years to take your revenge. You kept that hatred your whole life. What did you do? Did you deceive him into coming to Ayacucho? Or did you simply find out he had come and then could not control yourself? Durango helped you from prison?"

"What are you talking about? Who am I going to take revenge on?"

"Lieutenant Alfredo Cáceres Salazar! The man in charge of the station where your parents were killed. Or do you think I am an idiot? Did you think it would never be traced back to you if you killed everybody involved? When were you going to kill me?"

Now she could no longer speak. Her body was sliding down the wall to the ground. She looked like a half-empty sack of rice, almost shapeless. The street was deserted and silent now, except for what gushed out of her mouth, the mouth he had kissed.

"If I wanted to kill you," she said suddenly, "I would have done it last night. I should have done it . . ."

The prosecutor thought about Cáceres Salazar brandishing the pistol that had pierced the back of her father's neck. He thought about the scene that morning as he had penetrated her body. He did not feel repentance anymore, he felt pleasure. The pleasure of a job well done. He took out the pistol and aimed at the small head trembling near the ground. He recalled all the dead he had seen. He realized his hand no longer trembled.

"You don't deserve a trial either," he spat at her.

Edith did not move and did not look up. He thought she had not even realized he was pointing the gun at her. She had become a weeping, crouching thing sliding down along the wall. Perhaps she had seen the weapon and did not care about dying as her family had. Prosecutor Chacaltana cocked the gun. He pointed it right at her forehead. He thought she ought to die looking at what she had searched for. She raised her head and fixed her eyes on him, as if her gaze were going through the weapon to lodge directly in the prosecutor's eyes.

"I won't be the first who dies like this," she said. "And I won't be the last."

That was a confession. Now the prosecutor felt certain. He moved the barrel slightly to the right to place the bullet just between her eyes. He adjusted his finger on the trigger. He gave her a final look, a look of disappointment, pity, and hatred. Perhaps he also felt disgust for having touched that body stained with blood, submerged in death, like the sinister birds of the Sepulcher. Now he would never touch it again. In his mind he said good-bye to her. After all, he would miss her. At least he would miss the warmth of her hands, the smell of her neck, the almonds of her eyes, the balm of her smile. He gripped the weapon more firmly and took a few steps forward. But as soon as he had taken aim at the target, the blows, the fire, the rain of blood returned to his mind, as if all the things that had appeared in his dreams were really inside Edith's head. The black flags. He wanted to fire immediately, without waiting anymore, he wanted to wipe away once and for all the life that had been hers, he wanted to do away with the nights of love he would never have now and the ones he had never had, all in one stroke, all in one shot, with all his might he wanted not to have to hear her lies ever again, not to have her face remind him of how stupid he had been. And his eyes blazed with a red fire, he heard shouting in his ears, he felt punches, kicks in his stomach. He wanted to be able to end everything with a single, final, fatal movement of his finger.

He could not.

He moved a few steps away from her and then came closer again. Now her gaze that had not wavered turned into a shield. He thought of himself at the edge of the mass grave, a weapon pointing at his head. At his back. He wanted to ask her not to look at him, he wanted to slap her, he wanted to tear off her clothes and rape her. But that gaze paralyzed him. He still had the weapon raised when he spoke, his voice breaking with grief:

"Why like this? Why did those people die so cruelly? Why the awful brutality?"

She was no longer sobbing. She seemed like a statue of black ice. When she responded, her voice sounded strong and resolute:

"Is there any other way to die?"

No. No there is not. The prosecutor tried to rally. He felt inexplicably defeated, vanquished, as if the pistol were pointing at his head, not hers. His arm was slowly lowering. As if an invisible hand were calming it and stopping it. When his arm had lowered completely, Edith was on her feet, facing him, defiant. She actually seemed taller. He could not even hold her gaze. With his eyes fixed on the sidewalk, the prosecutor said:

"Tomorrow morning I am going to file a complaint against you with the Ayacucho police. Before I do, you have time to escape.

If they capture you, I suggest you betray your accomplices. In exchange for your statement, they will reduce your sentence."

She gestured as if she were going to speak. He stopped her with a hand in the air. It was not an aggressive hand or an armed one. It was only an open hand.

She moved along the wall, walking sideways, never turning her back to him. When she reached a corner, she began to run. The prosecutor dropped to his knees, as if praying for protection. He hid his face in his hands. He fell to the ground. After a while he discovered that people were walking along the street again. Matrons looked at him disapprovingly and murmured complaints to one another about the drunkards who were destroying the city. He did not move. At one point he felt observed from a place beyond the street but did not see anything strange. He thought that perhaps it was time to get up and go home. He could continue to cry there. He looked at the time. It was midnight.

SATURDAY, APRIL 22 / SUNDAY, APRIL 23

we reeched the end. oh, ends are so sad. no. this is a happy end. its reely a new start, rite? you unnerstand. i can see it. i can see the choris of the ded greeting me, patting me on the back with there hands sweting with blood. itll be soon. we can play together, for eternity, in a new world, in a world of peepel who live ferever.

it wasnt always like this, you know? there was a time i thowt you cood live another way. but thats a lie. i was inosent. if historys going to come for us anyway, the best thing is to speed it up, forse it forward, control it. like we did to you. well be mirrers of the universe, sacrifises of flesh that skech the wake of time. itll be nise.

i like your sholders. there soft. the others will like you too. your the senter of everything, did you know that? all the parts will go to you, youll have a grate responsibility. i hope your up to it. did you ever do what im doing? its like cutting up a chicken, allways full of bones and things. but what you eat is the mussel. you dont eat the blood. thats a sin.

but dont let your mind wander. yesteday was the day of the sepulcher and today will be the day of glory. they stoped waving the black flags in the cathedrul. its a good day for you. tomorrow god will begin to resurrect. and sunday the sun will shine on a new world. all thanks to us. the world will know what we did. i made shure of that. itll be sad, because theyll come for me too because of that.

oh i dont like it eether. but grate changes are like that, there born of pane. i dont want you to think this is a punishment, no.

its penitense. an act of convershun. we take our flesh and purify it until we turn it into lite, into eternal life, into something devine. well be angels, angels with sords of fire, the ones who watch the entrense to paradise. gardians of eden. do you like that? i like it. gardians of eden. ha. nobody will get in unless we test him first with our sharp, burning blades. well all be there, and well all be one and the same, multiplyd by the mirrers we are for each other. itll all end in our hands and itll all begin there. maybe some day we can overthrow god. and then nobodyll be able to stop us. forever and ever.

but for that, im telling you, theyll have to come for me first.

On Saturday, April 22, at nine in the morning, the prosecutor was awakened by the bells of the city's thirty-three churches announcing the resurrection and glory of Christ. At the same time, the police were pounding loudly, almost angrily, on his door. Before he opened it, he imagined what he would hear them say.

"We have orders from Captain Pacheco to take you to the examination of a body."

As he washed quickly, he regretted having allowed Edith to escape. It had not occurred to him that her homicidal rage would continue unrestrained even after his warning. He reproached himself for his own weakness and stupidity. Above all, he reproached himself for having chosen that woman in particular. And still, the news had not surprised him. Perhaps he was growing accustomed to death. Before he went out, he had time to be surprised at not having been the last victim. He discovered he was almost wishing for that.

Outside, preparations were beginning for the end of Holy Week. On Acuchimay Hill, celebrants from Andahuaylas, Cangallo, and even Bolivia were gathering around the stands that sold handicrafts, *chicha*, fresh cheeses, gourds of pumpkin soup. Some drunks, bottles of cheap cane liquor still in their hands, were lying in the streets. Here and there were the globs of green spittle of those who chewed coca. There was also elegance. Notable citizens were going to the blessing of new fire and Easter candles in the cathedral. Some would spend the entire day at vigil masses. Others were beginning the celebratory transfer of the bulls to the old-age home and the prison. The guards had mentioned to the prosecutor that Olazábal had tried to prohibit the transfer of the bull for reasons of security, but his own men had wanted some kind of celebration in that dismal place.

The prosecutor was still drowsy. He was thinking how to formulate the charge against Edith in his report. In spite of everything, he would regret having to do it. It would be sad but necessary. But as they moved forward, he suddenly recognized the road they were taking. The progressive aging of the houses, the painfully modernized neighborhood, the edges of the city on the hill, the three-story building, the neighbor Dora, shattered, looking at him suspiciously from her window. After a few seconds of paralysis, he ran up the stairs to the third floor. The stairs creaked at each step as if they were going to collapse. Captain Pacheco stopped him at the door.

"I don't know if you should come in here," he said.

He had to go in. He shoved the captain aside and crossed the threshold. The small room was almost entirely spattered with blood. The floor was covered with sheets of transparent plastic so that people could walk without leaving footprints, and go out with no blood on the soles of their shoes. On the only wall not completely covered in blood were scrawls of Senderista slogans, written with a pencil that the killer had dipped into the body lying on the bed. Body. It was not really a body. When the prosecutor approached the sheets—the sheets he had already stained with blood and sweat—he discovered that this time everything was reversed: two legs, two arms, a head. Piled on the bed, leaving the space for the trunk free. And nothing else. He still had a hope before he recognized, in the absolute red of the limbs, Edith's gleaming tooth and the luster, now vermilion, of her hair. He could not repress a long howl. He had to stop himself from stomping all over the room, destroying it, as if in this way he could destroy memory too. He had to go out to the staircase to vomit, to cry, to stomp his feet.

Half an hour later, he had recovered somewhat. At least he could see now without a red mist blurring his vision. A police officer showed him a faucet where he could wash his face. He did not know what to feel: rage, sorrow, frustration, self-pity . . . All these feelings were accumulating in his chest undefined.

When he went down, Captain Pacheco was waiting for him. Judge Briceño was there as well. His gaze was strange, distant. The prosecutor thought he must look pitiful. There had been no mirror at the faucet. He did not care. At this point he cared about very few things. Instinctively he tried to smooth back his hair, but without conviction. He tried to say something, but not a word came out of his mouth. The judge spoke:

"A slaughter, right?"

He nodded. He tried to get back to work. It made no sense, but perhaps it was one of those useless gestures that one makes, like smoothing back one's hair, like being horrified, like being afraid or crying, useless things we cannot avoid.

"Give me . . . give me the certificate of examination of the body. I'll sign it and be present at the autopsy if . . . if the pathologist can do anything with this."

Pacheco and Briceño exchanged glances. The judge said:

"I'll take over the investigation. I don't know if you . . . are in any condition."

"I'm in condition," said the prosecutor, looking down at the ground. He tried to hold back his tears. "Edith was . . . a member of a terrorist cell. They killed her to keep her quiet. You just have to find her accomplices. There's . . . a very clear line of investigation to follow."

Pacheco shook his head. He took off his kepi and turned it in his hands as he said:

"We already have a very clear line of investigation, Señor Prosecutor."

The prosecutor stood there, waiting for the rest of the sentence. Since it did not come, he looked up. The looks of the other two were icy. Pacheco took out a notebook and read in the tone of an official report:

"Last night you were seen leaving El Huamanguino restaurant in the company of the victim. According to our information, you were visibly agitated. There are witnesses who affirm that the two of you were arguing. A good number of witnesses. Several of them state that you threatened her with a firearm in a public street. After that, she did not return to the restaurant. No one saw her alive again. What do you have to say?"

Nothing. He had nothing to say. Not even the sickly giggle that had afflicted him the day before at police headquarters came out now in his defense. The police coming toward him seemed surprised that he offered no resistance, that he let himself be dragged off like a toy in the wind, like a paper doll. They put him in a patrol car and took him out at police headquarters. They threw him in a cell the size of a closet. In a corner was a hole to be used as a toilet. He knew by the stink that he was far from the first one to occupy the cell. Scratched on the walls with pieces of stone there were still *"vivas"* to the people's war. He spent several hours there, trying to think of a solution, but it seemed there was nothing left to think about, that everything he needed to know was now beyond his thoughts. That afternoon, Pacheco himself interrogated him. It was not necessary to employ violence:

"Why don't you confess once and for all?" the captain asked. He seemed serene, protective, paternal. "We've sent the prints we found next to Quiroz's body to Lima. The results will be here on Tuesday, but they're not even necessary. There are more witnesses who saw you come out of the parish house carrying a weapon. And Edith Ayala's neighbor saw you crazed when you went into the girl's house the night before, immediately after the bloody acts you perpetrated at Heart of Christ. You're on the list of visitors to Hernán Durango, and Colonel Olazábal states that you offered to negotiate a promotion for him following the escape of the terrorist. We have obtained a report signed by you in which you declare that you made contact with Justino Mayta Carazo in clandestinity. That makes you the last person who claims to have seen him alive. From what we have observed, you carried out the investigation without informing us and wrote reports intended only to cover your back . . ."

Prosecutor Chacaltana responded to everything with vague movements of his head, like a senseless lump. For the first time, the captain lost patience.

"You've killed as if you were in your own home! Even the terrorists left fewer clues when they placed bombs!"

The prosecutor did not even look up. The captain recovered his serenity and continued:

"It's understandable, Chacaltana. It isn't justifiable, but it is understandable. Death floats in the air of this city. I've seen others like you lose their heads. But no one in the way you did. For now, you can be certain of life imprisonment, and thankful the death penalty was never enacted. Still, your regimen in prison can be made easier to the extent that you cooperate. Do me a favor, do yourself a favor . . ."

The prosecutor did not react. He seemed stupefied, beaten. The captain showed him some papers. They were the Senderista notes left on the bodies of Durango and Mayta.

"Let's go one step at a time," he said. "Did you write these notes? You can tell me in confidence. Just tell me that. Did you write them?"

The prosecutor looked at the papers. He remembered the notes. He remembered the scrawls in Edith's room. The signature: Sendero Luminoso.

"You did it badly," said the captain. "Very badly. Sendero never signed like that. They signed PCP, Peruvian Communist Party. Or they simply left their slogans: Long Live the People's War, Long Live President Gonzalo, that kind of thing. Hmm? How obvious it is that you didn't live here in the time of terrorism. Your efforts to throw us off wouldn't have convinced an eight-year-old. These papers don't help you. On the contrary, they work against you. And your methods. The Senderistas were savages, but they made a certain political sense. Do you understand? But what you did is slaughter plain and simple, Señor Prosecutor."

For the first time, the prosecutor showed signs of responding. He moved his mouth, as if he had to get rid of the numbness in order to speak. Then he said, in an inaudible whisper:

"It wasn't Sendero?"

Pacheco, who'd had a moment of animation, seemed disappointed again.

"Señor Prosecutor, show us a little respect and stop acting like an imbecile. Confess everything once and for all and get it off your conscience. We'll bring you a statement, you'll sign it, and you'll be able to rest easy. After all, you're one of our own, Chacaltana. That will be taken into consideration, no one will hurt you."

"It wasn't Sendero . . . ," the prosecutor repeated.

Now he did feel incompetent. All this time he had been following a dead end, pursuing ghosts, pursuing his own memories rather than a reality that was laughing at him. Then, only then, the light began to shine in his mind. Perhaps the light of the fire, perhaps the light of the burning torches on the hills, but a bright, intense light beginning to make its way through the darkness of his reason. He remembered Pacheco warning him about evil companions. This is a small town, everybody knows everything. They had been following him, they had always known where he was going, they had always known to whom he spoke. His eyes lit up. With recovered self-assurance, he asked:

"Did you say you have my reports? How is it that on Thursday you did not have the reports and now you do?"

"Excuse me?" said Pacheco. He still wore a peaceable smile.

"Why did you obstruct the entire investigation and suddenly take it over now?"

Pacheco's smile of superiority was disappearing from his face.

"Well, the departure of Carrión has left a gap in the city's security that . . ."

"Why was I free if witnesses incriminated me on Thursday and again on Friday night? Why didn't you come for me right away?"

Pacheco began to stammer. He had suddenly turned pale.

"The witnesses . . . well . . . the fact is . . ."

"You want to incriminate me. You want to incriminate me in this! You want to lock me away!"

"Chacaltana, calm down . . ."

Chacaltana did not calm down. He got up from the table and lunged at the captain. He grabbed him by the neck. Everything was so clear and so late. Now that he was lost, perhaps he would at least be able to take Pacheco to hell with him. He threw him to the floor and began to squeeze his neck, the way he remembered Mayta squeezing his. In the end, the killers are exchanging faces, he thought, they become confused with one another, they all turn into the same one, they multiply, like images in distorted mirrors. Pacheco tried to throw him off, but the prosecutor was too enraged. The captain was turning purple when the prosecutor felt the blow to his head. He tried to squeeze a little more as he felt himself losing consciousness, sinking into sleep, while everything around him turned into the same, single darkness.

The last dream Associate District Prosecutor Félix Chacaltana Saldívar had before what subsequently occurred was very different from all his previous ones: there was no fire or blood or blows. There was only an enormous, peaceful field, an Andean landscape, perhaps. And a body lying in the middle of it. Little by little, slowly at first, then with increasing agility, the body was getting up until it stood on its feet. Then it could be seen clearly. A body made of different parts, a Frankenstein sewn with steel threads that did not close the seams very well, for clots and scabs were dripping from them. It had two different legs, and the arms did not correspond either. It had a woman's trunk. The sight of the body was macabre, but it did not seem to have a violent attitude. It limited itself to standing and recognizing itself gradually as it became aware of itself. What really startled the prosecutor came only at the end of the vision, when the monster finished standing, and on its shoulders the prosecutor saw his own head, trapped on that body he had not chosen, before the light became more and more intense until it blinded him completely in a luminous white darkness.

Then he awoke. Beside him, the bars of the cubicle were open. Two police officers extended their hands toward him and dragged him out. They shoved him into the captain's office and threw him at Pacheco's feet. The prosecutor thought that everything was over, that he would not even deserve a trial, that they would simply take him to one of the graves and that would be the end. Case closed, no terrorists here, and nothing ever happened. He thought about the grave almost with relief as he raised his head toward his captor.

"You have powerful friends, Señor Prosecutor," said Pacheco. "Who's in this with you?"

The prosecutor did not understand the question. The captain looked furious.

"I shouldn't ask, right? Sometimes there are so many things you shouldn't ask that you no longer know which ones you can ask. Sometimes, Señor Prosecutor, I wonder who we're working for. Especially when I see you."

The prosecutor began to stand. It seemed, in fact, that the body he inhabited was not his, that it was made of other people's parts, that someone had lent it to him to use like a marionette.

"Is it an Intelligence matter?" the captain asked again. "That's it, isn't it?"

The prosecutor did not respond. The captain seemed satisfied by his silence.

"Get out," he said.

"What?"

He was certain he had misheard.

"Get out, I said! There's no record of your being here, Señor Prosecutor. You never came here. But know I won't be responsible for this, Chacaltana. And at the first opportunity, I'll cut you down. Take him away."

Chacaltana tried to protest but did not know what to protest about. Then it occurred to him to ask something. Again, he did not know what. He let himself be dragged by the same officers to the door. The noise on the street seemed like a distant, vague memory. When they let him go on the corner of the square, his own legs felt strange, as if he had to grow accustomed to them. He wondered if the odor of punch and the sound of bands on the square were the sound of heaven. Or of hell.

He walked to his house. His whole body ached. When he arrived, he hurried to his mother's bedroom. He gathered all the photographs and placed them on the bed. Then he lit candles in the four corners of the room, as if he were performing a ceremony for his mother. He knelt beside the bed and kissed the sheets. He caressed the wood of the canopy. He wept.

"I know what has happened, Mamacita. I know what they have done to me. A body is missing, you know? Tomorrow is Easter Sunday. And the head is missing. I am the head, Mamacita. Tonight they are going to kill me."

He stayed there for several hours, wondering what death was like. Perhaps it was not all that terrible. Perhaps it was a soft bed with a wooden canopy. Perhaps it was simply nothing. Living in no one's memory, because everybody you knew was dead. He wondered when his killers would come for him. It was after midnight. He wondered if he would be safer in the cell at police headquarters. He laughed weakly at his own idea. He waited for them impatiently. He imagined the saw that would cut his neck. He thought of it passing with difficulty through his vertebrae, his veins. At a certain moment he grew annoyed, he wanted them to come and be done with it. He spent some time meditating, remembering isolated, chaotic images of his mother smiling at him, advising him, embracing him, waiting for him there where she was, where she had always been, in the fire. When he evoked the image of his mother emerging from the flames, an idea took shape in his mind. Perhaps all was not lost. Perhaps there was a place where he could be safe. Only one, the last one. He made a decision. Before acting on it, he kissed all the photographs of his mother one by one, in a kind of long, affectionate farewell on the sheets. Affectionately, he put out each of her candles. Then, with new energy, he returned to his room, took out the weapon, loaded it, placed it in the holster under his arm, and went out. He felt that perhaps he would not die that night.

He walked through the street festivities like a zombie, brushing against people who were dancing and singing. Sometimes those who saw him approach moved aside to let him pass. He understood that he did not look clean and decent. He did not think about it anymore. After walking for about ten minutes, he reached military headquarters. Perhaps because of the celebration, there were no guards at the door. And he did not see anyone inside. He pressed the intercom and the commander opened the door for him from his office. He sounded pleased to hear him. The prosecutor crossed the gloomy courtyard and climbed the wooden stairs that creaked beneath his feet. When he reached Commander Carrión's office, he went in without knocking. The commander was inside, packing a suitcase. When he saw the prosecutor, his face contracted into an expression of shock:

"Chacaltana. What the hell happened to you?"

"Don't you know?"

"Nobody tells me anything anymore, Chacaltana. My retirement has broken speed records."

He said it sadly. He felt nostalgia in advance for the Ayacuchan horror. Chacaltana took a few steps forward and caught a glimpse of his reflection in a mirror in the office. He really did look awful. As if he had come out of a sewer. Or a mass grave.

"They accused me of the murders," the prosecutor explained, "and then they let me go again. Strange, isn't it? These weeks have been very strange."

"I know. They haven't been easy for me."

The prosecutor noticed the things the commander was putting in the suitcase. Photographs, papers, old albums of his military promotions. Memories. Only memories. Outside was the sound of fireworks and voices and singing, but dim, as if it came from another world. The commander went to the window and looked at the festivities. He closed the curtain.

"Sendero did not do the killings," said the prosecutor. He had not sat down. "Did you know that? It seemed . . . but no."

The commander smiled faintly.

"I was afraid of that. Sometimes I think it's better that I've been retired. I won't be the one bearing the weight of all this. Is there some new line of investigation?"

The commander lit a cigarette. He offered one to the prosecutor, who declined.

"There is something, yes," he replied.

The commander exhaled smoke while he waited for the prosecutor to explain. The prosecutor had an absent gaze, as if he were seeing fireworks through the blinds.

"And?" asked the commander. "Don't leave me like this. Whom do you suspect?"

The prosecutor seemed to return to himself. Then he said:

"You, Commander."

The commander laughed, as if he appreciated the joke. Then he realized that the prosecutor was not joking.

"I think . . . I don't understand," he said.

"Neither do I, Commander. I thought you would explain it to me."

The commander took some papers from his desk without los-

ing his composure. Chacaltana had seen that they were all written in lower-case letters and filled with spelling errors. The commander closed the suitcase and said:

"I'm afraid you're making a mistake . . ."

"You were the only one who could have sent my reports to the
police, because you were the only one who had them, Commander." The prosecutor's voice had risen in volume and authority. "You were also the only one aware of all my movements.
And the only one interested in wiping out your own past, the
1980s. Pacheco was posted to Ayacucho much later, and the only
thing he wanted was to get out. Just like Briceño, just like everybody."

Commander Carrión took a long drag on his cigarette. His eyes
pierced the prosecutor. Now they were like the eyes of Edith's parents in the photographs. The prosecutor continued:

"You sent me to Yawarmayo so that Justino could get me out
of the way. But Justino failed. He was so terrorized he could not
even kill an unarmed, cowardly man like me. Besides, he talked
too much. What he really wanted was to accuse you. Then you
killed him too and decided to hand over the investigation to me
in secret to keep me quiet and, in the process, get rid of everyone
who could ever incriminate you: Quiroz, Durango . . . In the end
you would incriminate me . . . or to make certain of my silence
you would kill me too, as you planned to do tonight. That is
why you ordered the police to let me go. Here no one says no to
a top military officer, even if he is retiring. Lima knows everything, the Intelligence Service is aware of what you have done.
But it's an old story, isn't it? When the pus spurts out, they retire
you or transfer you. Nobody touches a military officer. It's what
they did with Lieutenant Cáceres."

"Cáceres was an animal!" said Carrión, suddenly losing his
patience. "Everything was fine, everything was quiet until that
shit came back from Jaén. He said they kept him behind a desk.
He said he was a war hero, that he had risked his life for this

country. He wanted to be recognized. He's the biggest killer we've had. And he wanted us to build him a monument, the son of a bitch! He assumed the right to organize civilian defense militias. Defense against what?"

"Maybe against all of you."

The commander seemed larger now and was breathing hard, like a wounded animal. He ignored the interruption:

"He left us no alternative. He was reviving old phantoms. The population realized that. The Senderistas in Yawarmayo were more agitated than ever. It wouldn't take long for some opposition shit to let the press know that the lieutenant had returned to Ayacucho. Or even worse, there would be a terrorist attempt during the elections and Holy Week. If that happened, we'd be done for. I tried talking to Cáceres, I tried explaining things to him, I tried calming him down. Cáceres was my friend, Chacaltana, we had fought together. Do you know what it means to hurt a friend? I understood what he was feeling. I felt the same way! We shed blood for this country!"

"But that blood was not yours, Commander."

"Don't interrupt me, damn it!" he shouted. Then he paused to calm down. It was a sad pause, dedicated perhaps to his old dead friend. "It was easy to convince Justino Mayta to get rid of the lieutenant for us. No soldier would have killed another soldier."

The prosecutor thought: No soldier except you.

"Justino, on the other hand," the commander continued, "remembered very well the police coming into his house. And he wanted to avenge his brother. He believed . . . he believed his brother was acting through him, that he was like the hand of God. Some religious shit. That stupid man was very devout. It occurred to him to use Quiroz's oven to disappear the body. And Quiroz agreed, because he also had a great deal to lose if Cáceres talked. It was all a disaster from the outset. The oven was so old that it fucking broke down halfway through the burning. Quiroz and Justino didn't stop shouting at each other. We had to pull out the scorched body, take it to Quinua, and leave it there. Even after that we thought everything would stay calm and nothing would happen. Everything was going to be fine. It would end there. But you showed up and everybody got nervous. Quiroz wanted to throw suspicion on Justino. Justino didn't even know what he wanted. They had to be silenced. Just like Durango . . . There was no way to know what you talked about with Durango . . . Or with your girlfriend, that lousy terrorist."

His last words cut Chacaltana like a knife.

"Edith Ayala wasn't a terrorist, you son of a bitch."

"It doesn't matter now, Chacaltana. She isn't anything now. You handed her over to us. After the scene you made last night, it was very easy for me to finish her off. I even thought I was doing you a favor because you didn't have the courage."

The commander's gaze was not repentant but defiant, like a sudden blaze or a gust of wind. The prosecutor thought about him, Durango, Justino, Cáceres, Quiroz. Murderers killing murderers. Killers exterminating one another, a spiral of fire that would not stop until we were all one, one single giant of blood. But not Edith. Not her at all. He thought of her remains scattered on the bed. He thought of her entire body surrendered in that same bed, forced, broken in advance.

"You are a monster, Carrión. Even if what you say is true. Why like this? Wasn't a bullet in the back of the neck enough for you? Wasn't that the usual method?"

The commander darkened his gaze. He showed him the papers he held in his hand.

"I've written down everything. I've explained everything."

Chacaltana took the papers and tried to read. But there was nothing to understand in them. Only incoherence. Barbarity. Not simply spelling errors, it was everything. There is no error in chaos, and in those papers not even the syntax made sense. Chacaltana had spent his entire life among ordered words, Chocano's poems, legal codes, sentences numbered or organized into verses.

Now he did not know what to do with a heap of words thrown haphazardly at reality. The world could not follow the logic of those words. Or perhaps it was just the opposite, perhaps reality was simply like that and all the rest was pretty stories, like colored beads designed to distract and pretend that things have some meaning.

The commander lowered his voice. He had a new gaze, one the prosecutor had never seen. He said:

"It's clear, isn't it? Now do you understand? Do you need more explanations?"

The prosecutor wondered if he could be the one who read in twisted lines. If his reports were the ones that lacked meaning. If perhaps Carrión's papers were the truly legible ones but he no longer was capable of understanding them. Then he thought of Edith and realized that in reality it no longer mattered.

"There is no explanation for what you have done," he said.

As Carrión walked slowly to his desk, the prosecutor moved his hand toward his weapon. The commander said:

"I didn't want it, little Chacaltita. I didn't want it to be this way. They forced me."

"Who?"

Now the commander twisted beside the desk, fell to the floor, and his eyes filled with tears. He was trembling.

"Don't you see them, Chacaltita? Is it possible you don't see them? They're everywhere. They're always here."

Then Chacaltana saw them. In fact, he had been seeing them for a year. All the time. And now the blindfold fell from his eyes. Their mutilated bodies crowded together around him, their chests, split open from top to bottom, reeked of the grave and death. There were thousands and thousands of corpses, not only there in the commander's office but throughout the city. He understood then that they were the dead who sold him newspapers, drove the buses, made handicrafts, served him food. There were no other inhabitants in Ayacucho; even those who came from elsewhere died.

But there were so many dead that by now no one could acknowledge it. He knew a year too late that he had come to hell and would never leave. The commander continued speaking in a cavernous, guttural voice:

"They asked me not to spill blood in vain, Chacaltana, and I didn't: a terrorist, a soldier, a peasant, a woman, a priest. Now they're all together. They form part of the body demanded by all those who died before. Do you understand? They'll help to construct the history, recover the greatness, so that even the mountains tremble when they see our work. At the beginning of the eighties we promised to resist the bloodbath. Those who have been sacrificed recently have not died. They live and feel in us. Only one more is needed to make the earth shudder, the prairie burn, the world turn upside down. Only the head is missing . . ."

He disappeared behind his desk. The prosecutor took out the pistol. He aimed in his direction. At that moment no image made his hand shake. It was as if all his bad dreams had come to an end.

"Get away from the desk, damn it!"

The commander peered out and suddenly smiled, as if he thought everything was amusing and original.

"I see you're using my weapon. Are you getting used to it?"

"Raise your hands and move back. If I don't blow your head off right now it's only because you didn't act alone. I want you to tell me who your accomplice is—or who they are. And I want you to tell me before I lose my patience, because after that you won't be able to say anything."

The commander remained motionless beside the window. His hands were raised, more in an ironic gesture than in surrender. The smile had not left his face.

"To tell the truth," he replied, "my best accomplice was you."

At that moment, the lights in the office went out. The prosecutor tried to look through the half-open door. He did not even know where the door was. The blackout affected the entire building. The blinds were closed.

"Who's out there? Who turned out the light?"

In the dark he heard the voice of the commander.

"You must feel a little guilty, Chacaltana. All the people you talk to die. That's very bad."

He heard a drawer open and close. He fired toward the place the sound came from. For a moment, the darkness of the empty building returned only the echo of the bullet. Then he heard Carrión's voice again:

"After all, it isn't the first time you've killed, is it? Perhaps that's why I've enjoyed all of this so much. It's a game between equals."

He moved the weapon toward the voice, but the commander moved constantly. He wanted to follow him. He wanted to speak to him in order to track his voice, though that would also reveal his own position:

"What the hell are you talking about?"

When he bumped into a lintel he realized he was going through a door. The voice seemed to be very close, but it rebounded all around him in the open space of the building.

"Why don't you ever talk about your father, Señor Prosecutor?"

He leaned against a wall. He was afraid. Suddenly, the memory of his dreams was projected on the darkness. He heard the commander again:

"I knew your father."

"I never had a father."

The prosecutor felt a tremor coming from his stomach.

"We all had one, Señor Prosecutor. Often they turn out to be motherfuckers, but that's no obstacle to paternity. Yours was almost better than mine."

The prosecutor fired. He heard a board creak. He supposed

they were out of the office, near the stairs. The commander continued:

"Yours was a soldier too. A handsome young man, a white man. He married a very sweet girl from Cuzco. I know she's always present for you."

"That's enough, Carrión. Shut up!"

"Why? Do stories of the dead frighten you? Because he's dead. The living ought to frighten you more. And you also must have known that he was dead. You must have known that very well."

The prosecutor stumbled on a step and fell. Four steps down he managed to grab the banister. He got up aiming in front of him, not knowing what was before him or behind. Now he was trembling. The blows from the staircase did not hurt as much as those from his memory.

"Now do you remember?"

"Be quiet, Carrión! That's enough!"

"He was something of an animal, that young man. A good kid, except when he drank. Then he became difficult. You weren't so little that you've forgotten . . ."

The prosecutor fired again. Now he heard a piece of plaster fall off the wall.

"Your mother suffered a good deal when he got like that . . . Especially because he was a . . . let's say . . . a violent drunk. You didn't like it either. But in those days one didn't object to a husband, and you weren't old enough to return the blows. Isn't that right? There were too many blows. Whole rainstorms of bruises. He broke your mother's arm twice. You almost lost an eye. Remember?"

Now the images came one after the other in the prosecutor's mind. As if he were rebelling after decades of being forgotten, his father appeared before him. His twisted smile, his alcohol breath, the blows, the blows, his belt, his fist, the blows.

"He doesn't exist . . . He no longer exists . . ."

"You were a smart kid. And there were kerosene lamps in your house. Or maybe oil. One of those flammable things that always has a flame burning. Let's be frank, the supply of electricity in Ayacucho was always pretty unreliable."

"That isn't so . . . It's not true!"

The prosecutor did not know if the commander's voice came from one floor or another. Now it came from everywhere, from inside himself, from the dark.

"Did you enjoy it as I've enjoyed it, Chacaltana? Did you like it? He was too busy kicking her to see what the boy was doing, the boy he thought was retarded. Were those his words?"

"Leave me in peace!"

But the whirlwind of memories was not going to leave him in peace. It would never leave him in peace.

"Do you realize what you did, Chacaltana? And how you ran away? You didn't even go back to hear your mother's screams, you didn't take a risk even for her. You only ran, you ran wherever your legs took you, and you got to Lima, far away, very far away, where the cries of Señora Saldívar de Chacaltana wouldn't reach you. But the dead don't die, little Chacaltita. They keep screaming forever, demanding a change. And now when we're about to change everything, you don't like it. Now when only one more life has to be given, you find it repugnant. You'll give a life, Chacaltana. And after you give it, you can be at peace. It will all have ended. You won't have to worry anymore."

"Noooooo!"

The rest was a matter of a second. Perhaps a thread of air, the slight vibration a body produces when it moves through space. Perhaps for Chacaltana it was an intuition. He turned, still shouting, and emptied the magazine of the pistol into the body he felt close by. Again and again and again he pulled the trigger, as if his entire life were devoted to that, as if he alone waged war against the killers, as if the pistol were a machine gun in a helicopter, or a two-man saw, until he sensed he was no longer shooting, because he was out of bullets or simply because nothing was breathing on the other side.

He spent another hour crouched on the staircase, afraid to re-load the weapon or move, afraid he would hear Carrión's voice again.

But that did not happen.

The prosecutor breathed heavily and heard no other breathing in the air. Outside, he could hear the songs of Easter Sunday that he had heard so often. He felt along the wall until he reached one of the windows and opened it. In the light that filtered in from the street and the fireworks, he saw Carrión lying on the landing. The shots had pierced a lung, his forehead, a kidney, and a leg. When he approached to inspect the body, he discovered that the commander was not carrying a weapon. Commander Carrión had not been trying to kill him in this final duel. He had merely walked to his death, just like the others, just like all of us. The head of the monster was his. Now his work was done.

Wiping away his tears, the prosecutor walked out to the street. At each corner of the crowded square, the previous Sunday's branches were burning. In the cathedral, the imposing white pyramid of the Resurrection was about to appear at the door, to the accompaniment of fireworks. It carried lighted candles on each of its steps. The prosecutor was lost in the crowd. Slowly, from the interior of the pyramid, the resurrected Christ emerged to the applause of the people. More than three hundred of them began to pass the platform from shoulder to shoulder around the square. When the platform reached his shoulders, Chacaltana crossed himself and said a silent prayer. In the background, between the dry hills, the sun intimated the first light of a new time.

WEDNESDAY, MAY 3

The bullets found in the body of Commander Carrión came from the same weapon that had been fired in the parish house. Based on this evidence and on statements attributing recklessly violent attitudes to Prosecutor Chacaltana, as well as the presence of motive and opportunity for the crimes, the Fourth Criminal Court of the Judicial Branch has initiated proceedings against him for multiple aggravated homicides, a procedure which for the moment is pending until the accused appears in person for the oral hearing.

The officials who are supposed to testify as witnesses in this case, however, have been transferred following the bloody deeds recorded during Holy Week: Colonel Olazábal, promoted to the rank of general, is currently responsible for logistical supply in the Second Police Region. Captain Pacheco, although he did not receive a promotion, was transferred to the district of Máncora, on the northern coast of Piura, to guarantee the security of the area. Judge Briceño, for his part, is a regular member assigned to the Family Court of Iquitos. As for the accused, the whereabouts of Félix Chacaltana Saldívar are unknown.

It must be emphasized in this extensive report that the armed forces, in conjunction with the institutions responsible for maintaining public order and the Army Intelligence Services, have been able to keep the facts out of the press, thus avoiding the spread of panic throughout the region. Similarly, it is a noteworthy achievement to have removed all the files related to the case, which have been transferred to the National Intelligence Service so that it may act in accordance with its judgment and at its own discretion. It should be noted that the opening of proceedings in criminal court lacks binding power with relation to the aforementioned Intelligence Service, and by the same token, civil institutions lack competence in cases that may be related to national security, such cases being automatically transferred to the jurisdiction of the Supreme Court of Military Justice.

Remitted to the Intelligence Service, along with these files, is the totality of documents referring to disappearances, torture, and mistreatment engaged in during the period of the state of emergency by the following members of the military and police, to wit: Alejandro Carrión Villanueva, commander in the Army of Peru; Alfredo Cáceres Salazar, lieutenant in the Army of Peru; Gustavo Olazábal Goicoechea, general in the National Police. For the moment, it is not expected that these cases will be brought to civil justice or to the attention of the press, lest they be manipulated by unscrupulous elements with the intention of damaging the image of our nation abroad or obscuring the significant achievements of the government with regard to the countersubversive struggle.

The documents missing from the records, that is to say, the reports signed by Associate District Prosecutor Félix Chacaltana Saldívar and the lower-case notes written by Commander Alejandro Carrión Villanueva, are attached to this report, along with a detailed and exhaustive narration of the facts known firsthand by the undersigned, due to his having carried out his duties close to the suspects during the interval of time corresponding to the first six-month period of the year 2000.

Recently, new reports from the Army Intelligence Service indicate that the accused, Félix Chacaltana Saldívar, Associate District Prosecutor, has been seen in the environs of the Ayacuchan localities of Vischongo and Vilcashuamán, on the occasion of his attempting to organize "defense militias" with intentions that remain unclear. Our informants state that the abovementioned prosecutor displayed evident signs of psychological and moral deterioration, and that he still retains the murder weapon, which he flourishes constantly and nervously at the least provocation, although it lacks the appropriate ammunition.

Neither the patrols in the area nor the outposts of the forces of law and order have attributed excessive importance to the bellicose attitude of the abovementioned prosecutor, whom they do not consider to constitute a serious danger for the moment. Although members of the police have requested instructions in this regard, the command staff has issued orders not to carry out the detention and capture of the accused, at least while the nation is still engaged in the electoral process, since under these circumstances the case could come to light, with lamentable consequences for our institutional structures.

Having taken these steps, the undersigned official considers his work in the district concluded and takes the liberty of recommending that, for reasons of security, he be transferred to a new post. My sky-blue tie has been destroyed and my connections to the military forces, in expectation of a replacement for Commander Carrión, have been weakened. Furthermore, the intervention of the Intelligence Service in this case has fulfilled its mission of safeguarding the peace and security of the region, at the same time that it has directed information to the channels most suited to the interests of law and order, thus collaborating in the future development of a nation like ours.

In witness whereof the above is hereby signed, on May 3, 2000, by

Carlos Martín Eléspuru
Agent of the National Intelligence Service

Author's Note

The Senderista methods of attack described in this book, as well as the countersubversive strategies of investigation, torture, and disappearance, are real. Many of the dialogues of the characters are in fact citations taken from Senderista documents or the statements of terrorists, officials, and members of the armed forces of Peru who participated in the conflict. The dates of Holy Week, 2000, and the description of its celebration, are also factual. However, all the characters, as well as most of the situations and places mentioned here, are fictitious, and even factual details have been taken out of the context of their place, time, and meaning. Like all novels, this book recounts a story that could have happened, but its author does not confirm that it did happen this way.

My thanks for their reading the original manuscript, and for their suggestions, to Pablo Lohmann, Diego Salazar, Juan Ossio, and Jorge Villarán.

Meet with Interesting People
Enjoy Stimulating Conversation
Discover Wonderful Books